786

A M E R I C A

RSVP...Baby

PAMELA BROWNING

CELEBRATING FIVE DECADES OF ROMANCE

The Wedding Party

HARLEQUIN®
*M*akes any time special ™

ISBN 0-373-16786-5

AVAILABLE
THIS MONTH:

"Can we go somewhere? Just the two of us?"

Neill spoke the words with quiet intensity and was looking at Bianca so earnestly that she didn't want him to stop. She wanted him to go on looking at her that way forever. It was the openness of his expression that was so disarming, and it made her feel as if she could keep no secrets from him. And that was ridiculous; she had one big secret that she must hold in her heart forever. She pushed the thought into a separate part of herself, isolating it from what was happening here and now.

"I need to pick up the baby at the sitter's."

"You know, you're hiding behind that baby," Neill said.

Bianca attempted a laugh, but didn't carry it off very well. "Don't be silly," she said.

"Maybe...but why don't you indulge me?"

Bianca didn't think that being alone with Neill was the wisest thing to do. A sick feeling stole into the pit of her stomach, and she turned away in an attempt to hide her anxiety. If Neill asked her who her baby's father was, she wasn't sure she could put him off again.

ABOUT THE AUTHOR

Pamela Browning is the award-winning author of thirty romance novels—many of which appeared on numerous bestseller lists. Her books consistently win high ratings from reviewers and readers alike. She makes her home in North Carolina.

Books by Pamela Browning

HARLEQUIN AMERICAN ROMANCE

RSVP...Baby
PAMELA BROWNING

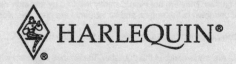

HARLEQUIN®

TORONTO • NEW YORK • LONDON
AMSTERDAM • PARIS • SYDNEY • HAMBURG
STOCKHOLM • ATHENS • TOKYO • MILAN • MADRID
PRAGUE • WARSAW • BUDAPEST • AUCKLAND

ISBN 0-373-16786-5

RSVP...BABY

Copyright © 1999 by Pamela Browning.

This edition published by arrangement with Harlequin Books S.A.

® and TM are trademarks of the publisher. Trademarks indicated with ® are registered in the United States Patent and Trademark Office, the Canadian Trade Marks Office and in other countries.

Visit us at www.romance.net

Printed in U.S.A.

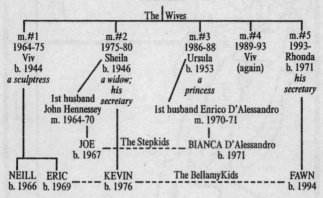

WILLIAM "BUDGE" BELLAMY aka The Pretzel King b. 1939

MARRIED

The Wives

m.#1
1964-75
Viv
b. 1944
a sculptress

m.#2
1975-80
Sheila
b. 1946
*a widow;
his
secretary*

1st husband
John Hennessey
m. 1964-70

m.#3
1986-88
Ursula
b. 1953
*a
princess*

1st husband Enrico D'Alessandro
m. 1970-71

m.#4
1989-93
Viv
(again)

m.#5
1993-
Rhonda
b. 1971
*his
secretary*

JOE
b. 1967 — The Stepkids — BIANCA D'Alessandro
b. 1971

NEILL
b. 1966

ERIC
b. 1969

KEVIN
b. 1976

The Bellamy Kids

FAWN
b. 1994

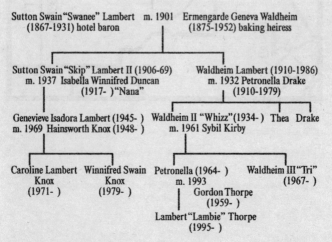

Lambert Family Tree

Sutton Swain "Swanee" Lambert m. 1901 Ermengarde Geneva Waldheim
(1867-1931) hotel baron (1875-1952) baking heiress

Sutton Swain "Skip" Lambert II (1906-69)
m. 1937 Isabella Winnifred Duncan
(1917-) "Nana"

Waldheim Lambert (1910-1986)
m. 1932 Petronella Drake
(1910-1979)

Genevieve Isadora Lambert (1945-)
m. 1969 Hainsworth Knox (1948-)

Waldheim II "Whizz" (1934-) Thea Drake
m. 1961 Sybil Kirby

Caroline Lambert
Knox
(1971-)

Winnifred Swain
Knox
(1979-)

Petronella (1964-)
m. 1993

Waldheim III "Tri"
(1967-)

Gordon Thorpe
(1959-)

Lambert "Lambie" Thorpe
(1995-)

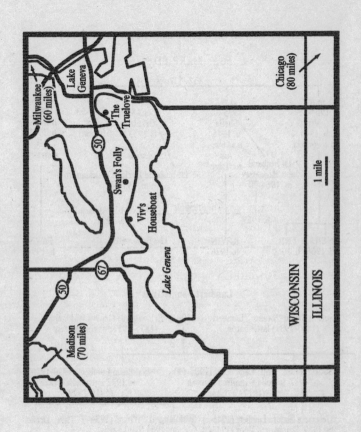

Chapter One

Lake Geneva, Wisconsin

The best sex I've ever had.

That was the way Neill Bellamy thought of the elegant blonde who stood with her straight shoulder-length hair wafting languidly in the breeze off the pond. Every other woman at the garden party was decked out in voile or dotted swiss, tucked linen or lace for this event on the gently sloping lawn of Swan's Folly, an exclusive hotel in the small Wisconsin resort town of Lake Geneva. Bianca, standing apart from a swarm of guests chattering and trilling their excitement, wore black.

She had always been different. In the years since her mother had divorced his father, she'd acquired the patina of sophistication and glamour befitting a fantastically successful designer of fine jewelry. Her company, D'Alessandro, was well-known in Paris and Rome. And she was beautiful enough to stir up all kinds of problems.

Nana Lambert, grandmother of the bride, clutched Neill's arm, digging lavender-tinted acrylic nails into the sleeve of his blazer. Neill was supposed to keep

her out of trouble at this event, the first of many during
the next four days. Fifteen minutes ago when the
eighty-something-year-old Nana had pranced out of her
suite trailing a purple print scarf and wearing jeweled
lavender fetish shoes with ankle straps, he knew he had
problems.

Neill wished he were still in South America. He
wished he'd never heard of the Knoxes or the Lam-
berts. And he wished he didn't have to see Beans again.

Not Beans. *Bianca.* She was all grown up now. But
back in the days when her mother Ursula had been
married to his father Budge, Neill had called her Beans.

Bianca. She'd been named for her Italian grandmother, a contessa, and it was an exotic name, like her.
It put Neill in mind of pale swaying flowers amid cool
Roman ruins. It made him think of windswept pines on
a rocky coast. It was the whisper of the wind, the rush
of the sea to shore.

Hell, it reminded him of that night in the gazebo
when they hadn't been able to get enough of each
other, when she'd torn at his clothes and he at hers,
when she'd gasped his name against the hollow of his
throat and he'd cried out hers for all the world to hear.

Bianca. He'd thought of her too much ever since.

Nana pushed him inexorably across the sprawl of
velvety green grass toward the creek and in Bianca's
direction. He tried, not so subtly, to nudge Nana toward
a far corner of the garden where his brother, Eric, the
groom, was holding forth with Caroline, his bride, under an arbor clotted thick with climbing roses. But
Nana, lurching along on those impossibly high heels,
wasn't having any of it. She pressed on, sinking into
the bouncy turf as if intent upon wrenching her ankle.

One by one, Neill considered his options. He could

feign a sudden attack of appendicitis. He could forcibly pick up Nana and deposit her in a chair, all one hundred pounds of her, and then figure out some way to keep her there, like sitting on her. He could yell "Fire!"

Of course he couldn't. His former stepbrother Joe, a Chicago fireman, would heartily disapprove.

As they drew closer, the crowd parted. The guests' pastel kaleidoscope shapes drifted away toward the Folly to reveal Bianca in her stark black silk knit. Her figure was more voluptuous than Neill remembered—high round breasts, narrow waist, impossibly slim hips. And long, long legs. Limousine legs, Eric called them.

One of Bianca's impeccably manicured hands rested lightly on the handle of a baby carriage. A big gray English pram. The baby's mother was nowhere in sight.

Nana stopped stock-still. "Who's the blonde with the baby?" she said loudly into a sudden silence. "Who *is* that girl?"

Nana was hard of hearing. And getting worse, from the sound of things.

"It's Bianca D'Alessandro," Neill said, leaning closer. "You met her a year ago at Caroline and Eric's engagement party." He couldn't imagine how Nana could have forgotten. Bianca had caused no end of trouble that day.

Everyone else resumed talking, their words rising and falling in genteel murmurs. There was nothing genteel about Nana's tone of voice, however.

"I want to talk to that girl. She looks interesting. More than I can say about these other folks." Bianca's style had always charmed people, and Nana was no exception. She released Neill's arm and plunged through the narrow path between guests.

No time to think about how much Bianca had hurt him by disappearing the morning after that memorable night. No time to figure out what to say to her.

Bianca was staring straight at him, through him, an enigmatic smile playing across her lips. The crowd disappeared for Neill, their chatter muted; the sky seemed wider and bluer than before, and colors more brilliant. He wanted to say something clever, something memorable.

But all he said was, "Bianca."

A GUST OF PANIC shook Bianca when she first saw Neill Bellamy; she fought it down, contained it deep in the pit of her stomach where it nestled like a litter of horned lizards. The moment she had dreaded for months was finally here, and all she could do was brazen it out.

She forced herself to smile as if she were only taking time out from a cheerful conversation with fascinating friends, which was anything but the case in this gathering. Neill advanced across the lawn, a shaft of sunlight blazing a shimmering path across his dark wavy hair. He was the kind of man whose easy masculinity called out to be tamed, but not just by any woman; she'd have to be a match for him. Last year, when she'd seen him again after years of no contact, Bianca had decided she was the woman for the job.

Not any more. A year ago, Bianca had scuttled her chances with Neill Bellamy once and for all at Eric and Caroline's engagement party.

As Bianca's smile stiffened and she briefly wished for a moving train under which she could fling herself,

Neill continued to move easily through the crowd, bigger than life, handsomer than any man had a right to be, and tempting as the devil. Just for a moment she remembered the thrill she'd felt glancing at the dark outline of his profile as he led her by the hand into the blue dusky shadows of the gazebo on that night exactly a year ago, and her breath caught in her throat.

It wouldn't do. She couldn't think about things like that, about the comfort he'd offered after that dreadful day, about her compliance when he first kissed her and even her eagerness and then her passion and then—*no*. She wouldn't think about it.

But how could she *not* think about it when faced with the commanding presence of this man she'd known half her life and with whom she had briefly dreamed of spending all the rest of it?

Nana Lambert peered up at her. "Do I know you, honey?" she blurted in a voice so loud that Bianca, pulled back from a precipice too dangerous, cringed.

Neill cleared his throat. "Nana, this is Bianca. Bianca, you remember Caroline's grandmother, don't you?"

Who wouldn't? The woman insisted she had long been inhabited by the spirit of Isadora Duncan.

"Of course," Bianca said smoothly, marveling that she sounded so remarkably ordinary. "How are you, Mrs. Lambert?"

"Blissfully light-spirited. And please call me Nana."

Bianca saw Neill looking at her, looking at the baby. She moved slightly forward to position her body strategically between the pram and Neill.

Nana batted lavender-lidded eyes and fluttered her scarf in the direction of the swans skimming the surface of the pond. "There's something so hopeful about a wedding, don't you think? Music! Poetry! Dancing! Such enthusiasm and joy. I do believe my heart will break of it.''

Caroline's grandmother, Bianca thought, didn't know anything about heartbreak if she thought it had something to do with joy. On the other hand, Nana might find out about heartbreak soon enough if the looks on the bride's and the groom's faces were any clue to the way they felt toward each other. Caroline was storming across the lawn in the direction of the gazebo with Eric in full pursuit. Bianca resolutely turned away. If they were having prewedding jitters, she wanted no part of them.

Neill, wearing a navy blazer and pearl-gray pants, stood too close. He was invading her space. And a blazer didn't fit his personality; Bianca always pictured him wearing khakis as he grubbed around in that mine of his in Colombia where he had something to do with producing emeralds. And money.

Eric had told her that Neill's net worth was even greater than Budge Bellamy's. Which was really something considering that Neill was only thirty-three. Budge, his father, was the famous Pretzel King. Worth millions. And so were his three ex-wives, including Bianca's mother, Ursula, whose motto for divorcing a mate was, "Don't get even. Get rich."

Another of the groomsmen—Kevin, who was Neill and Eric's half brother, and Joe, their ex-stepbrother—swooped in from the sidelines.

"Mrs. Lambert, here's a plate of strawberries in Devonshire cream," said Joe.

"Nana, you're looking as elegant as ever," said Kevin.

"Why, you charming young men," she gushed, accepting the plate and thus distracted from Bianca and the baby. "You must both promise to dance with me at the reception. Joe, I hope you've been practicing. One, two, cha cha cha!" With her free hand, Nana latched onto Joe's arm, launching fully into her free-spirit act. The three of them moved slightly away into the dappled shade of an oak tree, leaving Neill and Bianca to stare blankly at each other.

Neill said, "You're looking well, Bianca."

"So are you," she replied evenly, staring straight at him. He hadn't called her Beans. Her heart sped up a little, wondering what that meant. That he considered her a grown-up at last? He should; she was twenty-eight. But with Neill she always felt like the awkward fourteen-year-old she'd been when they first met.

Bianca lifted her chin ever so slightly. It made her feel taller, more in charge. But Neill's height was well over six feet, so the unnatural angle put a crick in her neck.

"Did your mother come with you?" he asked.

"No. She's on her honeymoon. With my new step-father, Claudio Zepponi. He owns wineries."

"I didn't know. How nice for her." Neill looked surprised at the news of the marriage, but Bianca couldn't fathom why. His own father had been married five times including twice to Neill and Eric's mother.

"Nice for her? Well, maybe. Right now I'm steeling myself to make nice to Caroline and Winnie and what's the name of Caroline's cousin? The one who always looks as if she has a slight head cold?"

"Petronella Lambert Thorpe. Petsy. Your fellow bridesmaid," informed Neill.

"Oh yes, how could I forget dear Petsy? Tell me,

Neill, how'd we get into this? And why couldn't we get out of it?''

He grinned in the lopsided way that had always intrigued her. "We're Bellamys."

"Not me," she retorted.

"You're a Bellamy by association, Bianca. Your mother was married to Budge for a year and a half."

"Fifteen months. It only seemed longer."

"It was long enough for you and Eric to teach each other to raise hell."

"We had more fun than our elders, no doubt about it," Bianca said wryly. "And Eric and I ended up being friends, which is more than we can say for our parents." She paused for an awkward beat. She and Eric had barely spoken since shortly after the engagement party.

"When did you get back from Colombia?" she asked, not knowing what else to say. She couldn't very well tell Neill what she was thinking: that if it had been remotely possible, she'd have stayed in Europe, where, although she was an American citizen by birth, she lived and worked most of the time.

"I arrived here last week, and it's a good thing. The waistcoat they rented for me was almost two inches too short. We had to place an order for another one."

"At least you don't have to wear a dress of putrid pink taffeta with a butt bow as big as Rhode Island," Bianca said. Rhode Island was where Bianca wished she were at this very moment. Anywhere would be better than here.

Neill laughed, a long deep-throated chuckle. "They're not calling the shade of the bridesmaids' dresses putrid pink. The dresses are pink-on-pink, cyclamen-on-carnation. Caroline said so."

"Putrid-on-Pepto-Bismol is more like it. Anyway, the combination makes my stomach heave, never mind those horrible little embroidered swans. Sorry, Neill. Maybe I'd see it differently if I weren't jet-lagged and exhausted." Bianca couldn't help letting her weariness creep into her tone.

She was also tense; she kept expecting Neill to ask about Tia. No one else, in the few minutes since she'd arrived at the garden party, had mentioned the baby either. Besides Caroline and Nana, only Lizzie, a college acquaintance, had greeted her at all. Perhaps their consternation over the continuing battle of bride and groom made them wary of talking to Bianca, especially since some might think she had something to do with it. Which she did not. But try telling that to Caroline's mother, the redoubtable Genevieve.

Bianca hadn't expected Caroline and Eric to be having a tiff; she'd thought they'd worked through all their differences during a lengthy courtship. What she *had* expected was that after a year of conferring and planning and anticipating the big Knox-Bellamy society wedding, this reunion of the wedding party would be punctuated by Caroline's friends' squealing and laughing and exchanging the usual banalities.

And it was, in a limited way, which assured that they'd get to Bianca eventually, and then someone would catch on that last year she hadn't had a baby; this year she did. She'd fluff it off, evade explanation, think of something to say. Word would get around that she didn't want to talk about it. She'd be mysterious, European, oblique. They'd all assume that Tia was the product of some unspecified love affair, consummated far away.

Or at least that had been the plan. But Neill had found her first.

Okay. So if Neill *did* ask about her baby, what then? Many sleepless nights hadn't provided an answer to that question. The only thing Bianca knew for sure was that Neill Bellamy was a confirmed bachelor and had never wanted children.

Sudden tears weighted her lower eyelids. In confusion, she bent over the pram under the guise of fussing with the baby's blanket, and one crystalline tear fell on the sleeping baby's cheek. Bianca hastily brushed it away, but Tia was startled awake and began to wail.

In the face of Tia's discomfort, Bianca couldn't worry about whether or not Neill got a good look. She picked up the baby and cradled her close. She stroked the flaxen hair, nuzzled the rosy dimpled cheek. Tia only cried louder. In desperation, Bianca offered the pacifier, which Tia promptly spit into the petunia bed. "Hush, *cara*," she whispered, hoping that her eyeliner hadn't left a telltale smear on her cheek.

"Why is that baby crying?" demanded Nana, heading toward the pram.

Bianca kept shushing, and Nana kept wobbling in her direction.

"That baby's crying sounds like hornets buzzing inside my hearing aid," Nana said fitfully. "Kevin, let's go into the hotel. I'm going to teach you the rhumba," she said as she improvised a few hip-twitching steps. Kevin tried unsuccessfully to hide his dismay as Nana dragged him toward the French doors opening onto the terrace.

Neill poked around in the flower bed before retrieving the pacifier. "Here," he said, holding it out to Bianca.

Bianca squinted. "I can't see a thing," she said.

"Contact lens problem." In one fell scoop, she yanked the baby's bag out of the pram and headed across the tiny creek bridge toward the gazebo, inconveniently banging her ankle on the curving leg of a white wrought-iron settee as she went. She ignored the pain, desperate to get away.

Hysteria rose in her throat when Neill followed her. *How appropriate,* she said to herself. *The two of us on our way to the gazebo again, a year later. With Tia.*

She stumbled into the gazebo hoping she wouldn't find Caro and Eric. Her ankle hurt where she'd hit it, but inside were inviting shadows and a surrounding fragrance of nearby lilac bushes blooming in profusion. Bianca sank down on the wide chintz-covered seat with Tia balanced on her lap. The baby kicked away the blanket as Neill sat down beside them. Tia's bootee had come off. Bianca found the bootee and shoved it back on the tiny foot. Then she wrapped the blanket tightly again, but not before shooting a panic-stricken look at Neill out of the corners of her eyes.

He couldn't have seen Tia's foot, Bianca told herself. *He'd been looking the other way. Hadn't he?* To hide her confusion and rising panic, Bianca lowered her head so that her hair fell forward to screen her face.

Tia was still screaming at the top of her lungs, and Bianca pleaded, "Hush, oh please hush." Her eyelids grated and her eyeballs felt gritty from lack of sleep, or maybe there was a speck of dust on her contact lens, or maybe she was going to cry again.

"Give me the kid," Neill said, raising his voice to be heard over Tia's cries.

Bianca's first horrified reaction was *No!* But Neill reached out for the baby, and her eye was flooding, and before she knew it he was holding Tia. The baby immediately stopped screaming and gazed up at him, clearly puzzled.

With tears streaming down her cheeks and her stomach clenching, Bianca groped in the baby's bag and wrapped her fingers around the bottle.

"Here," she said in desperation. "I think she's hungry."

Neill, rocking the baby uncertainly against his broad chest, stared first at the baby, then at the bottle. "You want me to feed her?" he said.

"Well, I can't. I have to figure out what's doing with my contact lens. Can't see a thing." She wanted Tia safely back in her arms, and soon.

Neill tentatively offered the bottle to the baby. Tia stopped crying, latched onto the nipple, and didn't make another peep.

Bianca hauled out a lens case and saline solution and a small mirror. "Maybe my lens has floated up under my eyelid," Bianca said. Not that she thought Neill cared. He held the baby awkwardly, looking all elbows and thumbs, or maybe it only appeared that way because she couldn't really see. But Tia remained quiet, thank goodness.

"She likes it," Neill said in surprise.

"She must be hungry. Oh, I do wish Franny would show up."

"Who's—"

"I think I've found it. The lens, I mean. It's way over in the corner." Bianca tilted her head back and lifted her eyelid with a cautious finger.

"Franny shouldn't have gone off and left you to mind her baby," Neill said.

Bianca froze, which wasn't the most comfortable reaction considering that the tip of her finger was wedged in the corner of her eye socket.

"She didn't," Bianca said cautiously. She held her breath, waiting to see where this conversational avenue would lead.

"You volunteered? Well, Bianca, what's the deal? Are you trying to redeem yourself after last year's debacle? Doing a little public relations work to prove you're not as bad as they think you are?" He spoke teasingly, but his words stung. She *was* responsible for the ruckus at the engagement party. She'd even tried to get out of this bridesmaid stint, but Caroline, playing the guilt card, had insisted that Bianca show up.

"I'm *not* as bad as they think I am," Bianca said indignantly. A little indignance was a good idea; it impressed people with one's sincerity as long as it wasn't overdone. And in this case, it was her natural reaction.

"I know that. But does the bride's mother? Listen, Bianca, if you need help with Gen, let me know."

"Mmm," she muttered in a tone that didn't exactly convey assent.

"Why don't we do this—when Franny reclaims her baby, we'll go back out into the garden and we'll make a point of greeting Gen." Neill shifted Tia against his chest.

Without comment, Bianca continued to work at the lens, which had not only lodged itself at the outer limits of her eyeball but seemed to have arranged itself in accordion folds. She knew that she should stop right here and tell Neill who Franny really was—the babysitter.

But even though Bianca couldn't see well at the moment, one possibility stood out with twenty-twenty clarity: She *could* let Neill think Franny was the baby's mother. Tia would be out of sight most of the weekend anyway, and there would be so much going on that maybe, just maybe, it might work. Everybody at this wedding would be better off if no one found out that Tia was her own child, born three months before.

Only Eric knew. But he'd keep his mouth shut.

Except did she want to deny her own child? The baby she loved so much and of whom she was so proud?

No. *No.* How could she? Tia was part of her, part of her life.

"This baby's cute. She's like a real little human, isn't she?" Neill said in a conversational tone.

"Of course she's a human," Bianca snapped irritably, caught up in the disloyalty of her deception. Well, it wasn't exactly deception yet. But it could be.

"I meant that she's apparently got all her fingers and toes and everything, only in miniature." He sounded amazed, then abashed. "I don't think I've ever held a baby before."

Fingers and toes. With a foreshadowing of doom, Bianca prayed that he wouldn't demand to see the toes. They were webbed, like the toes of every natural-born Bellamy she'd ever met.

Bianca believed in bold strokes, both in life and in design, and in this case she had an opportunity to design her life. In that moment, Bianca knew she had to try to pull it off. She wouldn't like it. It seemed unnatural to pretend that she wasn't a mother. She enjoyed being a mother. Loved it, really. Tia had added an unexpected joyful dimension to her life that she could never have imagined beforehand.

But it would make these four days so much easier if no one knew that this was her baby. Or could speculate who the father might be.

If I can pull this off, I'm the world's best actress, she thought. Forget Helen Hunt, forget Meryl Streep, forget Holly Hunter. Next year's Academy Award could go to—ta-dah!—Bianca D'Alessandro! *In your dreams,* she told herself. This performance would have to be secret.

"Uh-oh, she's pushing the bottle away," Neill said in alarm.

Bianca, having made a momentous decision, said, "You need to burp her." Her eye felt as if it were being stabbed with daggers. Her heart, too.

"Burp?" Neill said.

"Hold her over your shoulder and pat."

Neill flopped Tia onto the front of his blazer. "Pat what?"

"Her back." She now saw two Neills and two Tias. Tia started to fuss.

Bianca stopped concentrating on unpleating her contact lens. "For heaven's sake, Neill, just pat her gently."

"I am," he said in a voice that told her he was losing patience.

"Not on her bottom. On her *back.*" The lens unglued itself and floated jellyfishlike to the middle of her eyeball. She could see.

What she saw when things swam into focus was a wriggly baby draped haphazardly over Neill's sleeve.

"I'd better take her," Bianca said unsteadily, holding out her arms. As uncomfortable as Neill looked at this moment, he was one magnificent specimen. She'd been better off when she couldn't see him. At least then she'd been immune to his dark smoldering gaze, which was focused on her. Or maybe on the baby. Whatever and whoever, it unnerved her.

Bianca held Tia close for a moment, loving her and wishing beyond hope that she was able to provide the kind of close-knit family life that she had never had herself. Then she arranged Tia tenderly on her lap and slowly massaged the little back. Tia promptly spit up on her skirt.

"Do they all do that?" Neill asked.

Bianca, operating on emotional overload, blotted wearily at the spot with a tissue. "I think so," she said as Tia began to cry, this time in earnest.

Tia wouldn't be comforted, and knowing that she had to do something, anything, Bianca tossed everything into the baby bag and charged out of the gazebo and into the midst of the party.

"Bianca, wait," Neill called after her. Bianca didn't know what he wanted to say to her, and she didn't care. She was determined to find Franny, the manager's daughter, who had assured her over the phone that she needed money for college and would be available to baby-sit whenever. But somehow they'd gotten their wires crossed, and when Bianca had arrived earlier with the baby, Franny was away from the hotel at some post-high-school-graduation bash.

Well, Franny'd had more than enough time to get back by now. Which meant that Bianca could hand Tia over. Quickly. *Vite,* as they said in Italy. Which was where Bianca, who was half-Italian, wished she were at this moment. Faraway Italy sounded a heap better than Rhode Island by this time.

Because if she and Tia were in Italy, Neill Bellamy wouldn't have the slightest chance to figure out that Tia was her baby. And his.

Chapter Two

"Punch anyone?" inquired a white-coated waiter as he advanced a tray full of cups in her direction.

"I'd certainly like to, but I really wouldn't know where to start," said Bianca through gritted teeth, leaving the waiter staring after her in perplexity.

Neill accepted a cup of punch as the waiter swept by. He tried to fathom what Bianca was up to. She had deposited the baby in the pram and was pushing through the crowd with stolid determination. Everyone was munching on little sandwiches; Neill snapped one up from a tray and grimaced when it turned out to be watercress. He pitched the sandwich into the nasturtiums and decided he needed some decent food. He hadn't eaten a real meal all day.

The baby was crying louder than ever. Somehow the wails galvanized him into action.

"Why don't you give her this?" Neill said, catching up to them. He pulled the pacifier out of his blazer pocket.

Bianca regarded it disdainfully. "It's dirty and smushed and might give her some awful earthworm disease."

"Maybe there's a spare in her bag," Neill said hopefully.

"Hello, Neill," said a voice at his rear. It was Winnie, Caroline's flaky younger sister. Winsome Winnie, as Eric called her. He and his brother had a difference of opinion on that subject. Winnie, in Neill's opinion, was a prime candidate for the Dingbat of the Year award. If she had a brain, it consisted of canned vanilla pudding. Still, he was mindful of a sexual aspect to her bold-breasted strut, which thrust her most significant attributes toward him like a tray of fruit.

"Hi, Winnie," he said, keeping his eye on Bianca and the pram, still plowing toward the front of the hotel.

"Been out on Black Jack lately?" Winnie fluttered her eyelashes at him.

"Yesterday," Neill said. In the week since he'd arrived, Winnie had insisted that he exercise her horse, a recent birthday gift from her father even though the stallion was way too much horse for her. Neill, an excellent rider, had been only too happy to oblige. It had given him something to do while everyone else was going ga-ga over the wedding.

Winnie sidled closer. "Would you mind getting me some punch?"

"Here. You can have mine." Neill pressed his cup into Winnie's hands and left her gaping after him as he ran hell-bent-for-leather after Bianca.

He was desperate to get out of the blazer and tie. In full revolt, he ripped the tie off and stuck it in his pocket. He never wore ties except for family functions, where they were considered de rigueur. He hated family get-togethers; he didn't like families. Which was why, when considering possible career options after graduating from Harvard Business School, he had put a whole continent between him and the Bellamys.

And even that wasn't enough space. Once this wedding was over, he was going to climb Mount Everest, which you could do if you were reasonably fit and had $75,000 to spare. Neill was and did. He was pretty sure he wouldn't find any Bellamys or Knoxes or Lamberts on the top of Everest. Then again, you never could tell. They tended to pop up in unlikely places.

Bianca, he'd already decided, wasn't any more enamored of this family than he was. Which was why he thought it might be pleasant to invite her to his room for a drink.

Well, to be honest, that wasn't it. He'd like to get her in the sack again. Or in the sack, period. Last time—well, the only time—he and Bianca had made love, they hadn't even been near a bed. Except for afterward, when he'd scooped her up into his arms and carried her up the twisted little flight of stairs to her hotel room and tucked her in. She'd said something funny, like "Isn't bed the best invention ever?" She'd looked adorably cute in that moment, and it was all he could do not to stay.

But he didn't think it would look right if someone saw him sneaking out of her room the next morning. And so he'd administered a chaste kiss to her forehead and left. He thought they'd see each other in the morning, at which time he'd suggest that she pay him a lengthy visit in South America. But when he went to Bianca's room the next day, she had already gone. He hadn't heard from her since.

Which seemed, now, like a shame. Last year, he'd halfway fallen in love with her, which was about as much as he thought he could fall in love with anyone.

He wasn't the kind of guy to have long relationships; he was a chip off the old block. Well, maybe not quite. He'd never committed to a woman in his life. He'd never said the words, *I love you* to anyone.

Any Bellamy wedding was bound to be stressful. Things happened at Bellamy weddings. Crazy things. Off-the-wall things, like the time when Budge married Rhonda and a sudden storm had ripped the roof off the yacht-club dining room in the interval between the vichyssoise and the salmon course. Or the second wedding of his mother to his father when Budge had shown up in tennis shoes with his wedding finery and his mother wouldn't marry him until he went home and changed shoes. He'd come back wearing bedroom slippers just for spite. The *Chicago Tribune* had printed his picture in those slippers, too.

Yes, Bianca to warm his bed during this ordeal, and, briefly, his heart—now that had possibilities. She was the only other person here who knew he'd rather be somewhere else. And so would she.

He caught up with Bianca near where he'd parked his rented car on the drive in front of the lobby. She'd been talking with the bellman, and her shoulders slumped dejectedly. The baby was still crying. Bianca's eyes, he noticed, were smudged with exhaustion, and she looked at her wit's end.

"Franny's not back," Bianca muttered.

Who the hell is Franny? Neill wanted to ask, not for the first time, but then he recalled that reddish-brunette with the long thick hair who had accompanied one of the other bridesmaids, Lizzie, uninvited. *That* must be Franny.

"And Tia won't go to sleep without her Binky."

"Excuse me?" Neill was feeling confused. Confusion wasn't unusual, considering that this was a Bellamy wedding. One of the *many* Bellamy weddings he'd attended in his life.

"That's what Tia's pacifier is called. A Binky."

Binky rhymed with *slinky,* a word that accurately described Bianca in her clingy black knit. Which smelled, he noticed with a twitch of his nostrils, like baby puke.

Suddenly he'd had enough. Bianca was ridiculously involved with this baby that wasn't even hers, and who knew what she was up to? Who ever knew what Bianca would do next? Here he'd actually been thinking that maybe they could console each other during this ordeal when she'd already shot him down by greeting him so nonchalantly and without even the slightest flicker of pleasure.

So maybe sex with him hadn't been the big thrill for her that it had for him. *That* was humiliating. Did he want to let himself in for more of the same? A few wild nights, then goodbye again, so long, nice to see you, and so what? Did he, Neill Bellamy, *need* this?

Absolutely not. What Neill really needed was a Burger King Whopper. You couldn't get those in the part of Colombia where he lived most of the year; rice and beans and wild boar meat was what he lived on much of the time.

"Look, I'm leaving. See you around," he said gruffly, wheeling and heading in the direction of his rented convertible. He shrugged out of his blazer as he went.

"I was just going to ask you if you had a car I could borrow," Bianca called after him when he was half in and half out of the convertible. A note of desperation in her voice stopped him in his tracks. She looked absolutely gorgeous and as if she might drop where she stood in front of the hotel. The black dress made those shadows under her eyes seem darker than they probably were; while he watched, she skimmed her hair back with one hand, and he thought he detected that her hand was trembling. Why it was trembling he wasn't sure, except that it might have something to do with hunger.

"Come with me and we'll get something to eat," Neill said much too impulsively, regretting the invitation almost as he spoke. He contemplated rescinding it but couldn't think of a way to phrase it so that she wouldn't be offended. Bianca looked dubious anyway.

"The baby..." she said, almost to herself.

"We'll get her a new Dinky," he said.

"Binky."

"Whatever. Suit yourself." He got the rest of the way into the car, but before he could turn the key in the ignition, he saw the ramrod-straight Genevieve Knox, mother of the bride and resident barracuda, heading toward them from the doors on the other side of the lobby. She was followed by that mousy social secretary of hers, Anne somebody. Bianca saw them, too. While Genevieve paused at the desk, Bianca produced a baby safety seat from behind the bellman's stand, and before Neill could say "Mrs. Robinson," she'd secured Tia in it in the convertible's back seat. She slid into the front beside him and slammed the door.

"Let's get out of here," she said tersely. She looked ruffled beyond words and smelled really awful.

Neill hit the accelerator, spewing a tail of dust to their rear. "Should we put the top up?" Neill asked.

Privately, he thought it was a bad idea. The sour-milk smell would be even worse if confined to a small space.

"Not on my account. I love the wind in my hair. And the baby will probably quiet down as soon as we get rolling," Bianca said. The gate to the hotel, featuring two swans beak-to-beak forming a heart, swung open automatically in front of them. Bianca cast a worried look over the back of the seat as they barreled through. The hotel, modeled after an English country house, looked undeniably charming. A former mansion which once served as a weekend retreat for Sutton Swain "Swanee" Lambert, Caroline's great-grandfather, it was now the most exclusive hotel in the Swan's Inn hotel chain.

A couple of men lounging outside the gate leapt to attention when the convertible passed. A camera flash went off in Neill's face.

"What's that?" Bianca said, craning her neck backward to see who had taken their picture.

"Oh, just the paparazzi. They're hanging around hoping to get pictures of the Society Wedding of the Year."

"Good heavens, is it that big a deal?"

"Well, Hotel Chain Heiress marries Pretzel King's son, and Pretzel King's son is an up-and-coming magazine publisher who's amassing a fortune of his own. Genevieve's prominent in the society pages, and to a lesser extent so are Caroline and Eric. Genevieve has ruled that no reporters from publications other than Eric's will come to the wedding, and the premises of Swan's Folly are off-limits to anyone not on a special list. The weekend is private, Gen says. Thus we have reporters up the wazoo and increased security because Genevieve is paranoid." He'd never liked Genevieve, who popped tranquilizers like breath mints and washed them down with Scotch in a teacup.

"I see," Bianca said thoughtfully, but he didn't think she did. *He* understood. With all the wealthy people who had been invited, you couldn't be too careful.

Tia's sobs tapered off into a few token whimpers and then silence after only a mile or so. Neill glanced at Bianca. She appeared as if she regretted her decision to come with him, and when she saw him looking at her, she swiveled her head away and gazed at the rolling Wisconsin countryside. He cleared his throat.

"Where do we get this—this Binky?" he asked.

"I'll watch for a drugstore," she said.

At least Bianca seemed calmer now. Well, the baby's crying had even made him feel jittery.

It was on the tip of his tongue again to ask how Bianca happened to be in charge of this baby when she exclaimed as they approached the outskirts of town, "There—a drugstore! On that corner! Park in front and I'll run in. I'll only be a minute."

Neill swerved the car over to the curb and Bianca jumped out, running into the store on light feet. He suppressed a smile. In that moment, he remembered how, when she was a teenager, Bianca had reminded him of a young filly, awkward and ungainly but holding a promise of eventual grace.

Not that he'd ever told her or anyone else what he thought about her. She was five years younger than his lofty nineteen years when his father married Ursula, and he'd been away at college for most of the marriage. Bianca had soon become co-conspirator with Eric, only two years her senior and still living at home. They'd teamed up to make life difficult for the rest of the Bellamys. Hellraisers, the two of them. Who would have ever believed in those days that Eric would become the successful publisher of a Chicago society magazine, *The Loop,* and that Bianca would gain a growing reputation as a jewelry designer in Europe?

The baby in the back seat was awfully quiet. He cast a skeptical glance at it. At *her.* It was a girl, he reminded himself.

The baby, held firmly in the egglike shell of her safety seat, gazed back, clearly interested. Neill wondered what one said to babies. They couldn't exactly converse.

"Great weather we're having," he offered experimentally.

The baby frowned. He hoped she wasn't planning to start wailing again. He thought maybe he should joggle her just to let her know that everything was fine, the Binky was on its way, and soon the car would be soothingly in motion again. He decided against any of that when the baby blew a bubble. Who knew what that meant?

"Good baby, nice baby. We'll have your new Pinky in no time. No, make that a Binky. Or whatever," he amended on a note of desperation.

The baby—what had Bianca called her? Tia? Well, Tia looked distinctly unsettled. In fact, she looked downright disgruntled. He didn't know what he was supposed to do if she began to cry again.

Fortunately, Bianca dashed out of the drugstore in the nick of time and waved a pacifier in Neill's face. "This will put Tia right to sleep," she proclaimed. She leaned over the back of the front seat and popped the pacifier in the baby's mouth.

Neill breathed a sigh of relief as he started the engine and pulled out of the parking space. He had to admire how competent Bianca was with the baby; was she that way about everything? She'd certainly been competent last year in the gazebo. Thinking about it made it difficult to concentrate on his driving.

Bianca seemed buoyed by a kind of nervous energy that Neill attributed to her jetting across time zones. "I bought some other things, too," she said, pulling a small box of baking soda out of the drugstore bag. "To mix with water. It'll get rid of the spit-up smell."

Or maybe it wasn't nervous energy. Maybe she was talking only to keep talking. In a way, he wished she'd shut up and give him a chance to explore what was really going on here.

"I misted myself with perfume while I was inside," she said sheepishly. "Something vanilla-y. I don't know which smells worse, the perfume or the sour milk."

He liked the vanilla smell, but it didn't fit Bianca. "Don't you, um, usually wear a more sophisticated scent?"

"Joy. By Patou," she said. "They don't sell it in drugstores."

If Neill remembered correctly, her mother had always worn Joy. It was his favorite scent. He remembered a time when—

"Remember the time—" Bianca began, voicing his thought exactly, but she stopped talking and looked away.

Neill knew without a doubt what she was thinking. "The time when you and Eric were smoking cigarettes in the game room and I came home and caught you?" He'd been home from college for a couple of months in the summer; the teenaged Bianca and Eric had driven him and everyone else slightly crazy.

"Mother and Budge drove in right after you did, and I galloped upstairs and sprayed myself with Mother's Joy so she wouldn't smell the smoke on me." Bianca smiled, remembering.

Neill smiled, too. Bianca had reeked of perfume, but neither parent had noticed. Or if they had, they hadn't connected perfume overkill with any misdoings. "It was a gambit that worked. Ursula never said a word."

"I haven't touched tobacco since. At the time, Eric and I were sure you'd tell on us."

"Not me. Not then or even when Eric kidnapped you for a wild ride through downtown Chicago in Dad's new Rolls-Royce on your sixteenth birthday."

She turned, her eyes grown wide with astonishment. "Eric told me he had permission!"

"He didn't," Neill assured her as they approached the Burger King.

He quickly hung a left turn into the drive-through lane figuring she wouldn't want to get out of the car with the baby.

"What do you want?" he asked as he focused his attention on the menu with its squawk box.

"A Whopper with everything but onions, large fries and a chocolate shake," Bianca said promptly. "Oh, and a glass of water."

"Welcometroburgerkingmayitakeyourorder?" The tinny voice, running all the words together, startled them.

"Twowhopperswitheverythingbutonionslargefries-andtwochocolateshakes," Neill fired back. "And a glass of water." Bianca stifled a giggle.

"Two whats?" said the dubious voice of the order taker.

"Yeah. With everything but onions. And don't forget the water."

Bianca did giggle then while he straightened out the order. Neill couldn't remember ever hearing Bianca giggle before. With him, she'd always been so solemn. It was Eric with whom she'd shared all those good times. Neill had felt kind of left out, to tell the truth.

When they'd picked up their order and were headed down the main street of the town, he said, "I thought we could park near the lake and eat there. Would that be okay?" He glanced briefly over his shoulder. The baby was sleeping, her fists curled under her plump cheeks.

Bianca had mixed some of the baking soda with water and was energetically swabbing the solution into the spot on her skirt. "I know a place," she said. She directed him to a park, and he pulled the convertible under a spreading maple before switching off the engine. Out on Geneva Lake, a boat's multicolored sail billowed in the breeze.

Bianca opened the bag and handed him a burger and a container of fries. "I get hungry for a real American hamburger sometimes," she said wistfully. "In Europe, they just don't taste the same."

"I know. Have you ever wanted to move back here?"

"I'm thinking about it," she admitted. "This hamburger has just about made up my mind for me."

"*Could* you move back?"

"My business is doing so well that it's not out of the question to open an office in the States. In fact, Eric and I talked about it last year."

This was news to Neill. "I thought Eric told me he hadn't seen you since the engagement party."

"That's when we discussed it."

"Did he think it was a good idea? To open an office here?" Since Eric had become successful in the publishing business, Neill had developed a great deal of respect for his younger brother's business acumen.

Bianca swallowed and shrugged. "We were in the middle of our discussion when all hell broke loose and we never had a chance to talk about it again." She looked down at the packet of French fries in her lap, and he saw that she was embarrassed.

He tried to put her at ease. "As I mentioned last year, I thought Gen was way out of line when she lit into you in front of everyone else."

"We didn't mean to be late and cause a problem. We lost track of the time, and it *was* my fault. But when else were we going to talk about things?"

"Bianca, neither you nor Eric could have known that the photographer moved his appointment to an earlier time because of a conflict."

"Conflict? Believe me, by the time Gen got done putting me through the wringer, I could have told that photographer something about conflict," she said.

Neill had helped look for Eric that afternoon, even phoning the styling salon where he supposedly had gone for a haircut. "We were on the verge of calling the police to check if Eric had been in an accident when the two of you turned up together. You understand how that could raise eyebrows, don't you?"

"Eric and I are close friends and have been since we were kids," Bianca said firmly. She didn't say anything about being on the outs with him.

Privately Neill wondered if friendship was all there was to the relationship between Eric and Bianca. Neill really didn't understand why, if they were such good friends, they were hardly speaking. If indeed Eric and Bianca had indulged in a little fling, Eric certainly wasn't talking. Nor was Bianca, apparently.

Bianca sighed. "Anyway, most of the people here seem determined to ignore me this year. That's good, I suppose."

"Don't let them get to you, Bianca," Neill said.

"I've got other things to think about. Like the new gemstone line and our New York show of popular-priced jewelry in October." Bianca licked ketchup off the corner of her mouth; the tip of her tongue was pink and moist. It made Neill think of things erotic, the same kind of thoughts he'd been entertaining about her for the past year. The very long past year, it now seemed to him.

"What's the new gemstone line?" His mine produced emeralds; he couldn't help but be interested.

"So far, I've only used gold, silver and platinum in my jewelry designs. I've been experimenting with some interesting amber from Russia that we plan to include in our holiday show. My business manager wants me to incorporate rubies, emeralds and even diamonds, but I don't know. I'm thinking about it."

"Why do you let him call the shots?"

"Oh, he knows the business, and he came out of retirement to help me. With him in charge, I can concentrate on the creative end of things. He worked for my father for years, and he's one of the reasons D'Alessandro is such a success."

"And what does your father say about a new direction for D'Alessandro?" Neill knew that Bianca's father, a wealthy Italian industrialist, had bankrolled her first design shop in Rome; because of that, she'd been able to expand to Paris in short order. Now she divided her time between the two cities.

Bianca shrugged. "My father is in favor of the gemstone line and wants me to go full speed ahead. As for the office on this side of the Atlantic, he's willing to finance any new venture I want to try. He's recouped his initial investment in my business many times over."

"It sounds like he's confident in your ability."

"I don't know if it's that as much as that he wasn't around much when I was growing up. He wants to be there for me now."

"I think it's great that you're so successful."

Bianca looked uncomfortable at this compliment. "I only wish someone would tell me why I feel like a little kid again when I'm with this group."

She *looked* like a little kid again, and his heart went out to her. "Because it brings back all the feelings of inadequacy you felt when you were growing up. I know. I've been there, done that."

She focused her eyes on him, long-lashed blue eyes, eyes as blue as the depths of the ocean, as blue as a mountain pool, as blue as priceless sapphires. Unbelieving eyes.

"You, Neill?"

"Yeah, me. It has to do with the way everyone here sees me. In Colombia, I'm the take-charge guy, the one who manages the business end of the Viceroy-Bellamy Mines. Here—well, I'm the Pretzel King's kid. Not a lot of prestige in that, is there?"

She looked away, then back. "You always seem so self-assured," she said in a low tone.

"I am. But I'm also the same person who had to put on a brave front every time Dad got another divorce.

I'd barely get to know the latest stepmother, and then she'd be gone. Oh, and don't forget—Dad married Mom again after he divorced Sheila even though he left her for Sheila in the first place. Later he and Mom divorced for good.''

"Your mother's here, isn't she? I thought I saw Vivian breeze through the lobby when I registered, only this year she has red hair.''

"You know Mom—outrageous as ever. Red hair suits her.''

"So you took it hard when your father and mother divorced for the second time?''

"I hoped when they remarried that it would work out. But then I was always getting my hopes up, thinking that we Bellamys could somehow manage to be normal, and then things would fall apart and I'd be trying to be the responsible son, the older brother consoling the younger brother when my own world was being torn apart. Bellamys normal! Now that's a futile wish if ever there was one.'' He managed a bitter laugh.

"It was like that for me, too, Neill. Mother married my father, then divorced him, and I spent my childhood unsure if I was American because I was born in New York or Italian because I was shunted off to Rome for every school holiday. And I was always feeling neglected when Mother remarried—to your father, then to my last stepfather, and now her new husband. I wanted a home, a real home. I remember thinking that living in the same house all year, every year, would be heaven.''

Neill watched the sailboat out on the lake as it headed toward shore. His had been a difficult childhood. He hardly ever talked about it.

"The Bellamy curse," he said. "It's why I've decided to remain single. I doubt that I'm capable of a good marriage. Or that Eric is."

"Oh, Neill," Bianca said. "Surely Caro and Eric will be happy." She sounded upset.

"They've been fighting ever since we all arrived here. From the looks of things, I don't think they'll make it to their first anniversary." He said it bitterly, cynically, perhaps more so than he'd intended.

Bianca recoiled in shock. "Maybe their disagreement is only temporary. Anyway, I have to think that Caro and Eric will do better than our parents did."

"Maybe. Maybe not. I've decided that I can't fix what's wrong between him and Caroline, but I *can* humor him. As usual."

"What do you mean?"

Neill shrugged. "We both had a hard time growing up. I always tried to make our family life better for him. If getting married makes him happy, that's good. I've gone along with it. But so far, he and his chosen bride seem miserable. As far as I'm concerned, that makes this whole whoop-de-doo a travesty, Beans. Remember, Eric's a Bellamy. We're not good marriage material. We don't even come close."

Bianca's features went blank; it was as if she had wiped them clean of all feeling. She withdrew to the corner of the seat and refused to look at him.

They sat staring out at the lake, at the clouds in the distance. Over to their right, a man, woman and small child were romping with a Labrador retriever. The woman kept throwing a chartreuse tennis ball up in the air and batting it for the dog to chase. The child chortled with laughter every time the dog returned with the ball in its mouth. They looked like such a happy family.

A bleak feeling swept over him, and he turned his head so he wouldn't have to see them.

"I'm not hungry anymore," Bianca said in a muffled tone. "Could you please take me back to the hotel?"

When he looked at her, Neill thought he detected a note of resentment in her eyes. But then he wouldn't be surprised if she resented all Bellamy males—his father for failing to be a good husband to her mother, Eric for being unable to get along with Caroline, and himself for—well, for just being a Bellamy. And maybe for that night a year ago when he had been overwhelmed with her beauty and his feelings for her. Maybe she thought he'd taken advantage of her.

Neill gulped the rest of his Whopper and crumpled up the bag. Brusquely and without speaking, he started the engine and pulled out of the parking place.

He hadn't meant to drive a wedge between himself and the one person he saw as an ally at this wedding. All he'd wanted was validation of his own feelings and to share them with someone who might understand. He knew now that he should have guarded against revealing too much. It wasn't good for anyone, much less Bianca D'Alessandro, to know what he really thought of himself and this family.

Oh, and mistake number two: her name was Bianca, and he shouldn't have called her Beans. It was a nickname she'd always hated.

Chapter Three

Neill drove. Bianca thought.

What she thought was, *Never mind that what happened last year in the gazebo changed my life. Never mind that it blew my chances with Neill Bellamy. Never mind, never mind, never mind.*

But she did mind. She minded terribly. Her anguish was made even worse because despite everything, she felt comfortable with Neill. Just now, for instance. She'd allowed herself to think that possibly things could work out, that perhaps someone who seemed so sensitive to her feelings could care about her in a meaningful way. But he'd made it clear—again—that he wasn't interested in permanence, and there wasn't a thing she could do about it.

Neill drove through the gates and looped around the semicircular drive up to the main entrance of the hotel. From the moment when she'd first seen it, Bianca had loved Swan's Folly with its eccentric mazelike hallways and its oddly placed staircases. Under different circumstances Bianca would be delighted to be staying here again. But not now.

She was out of the car before it rolled to a full stop.

"I'll help you with the baby," Neill said, but Bianca

was already loosening the straps and lifting Tia out of the back seat.

"No need," she said curtly. "If you want to be useful you could stash the car seat behind the bellman's stand. He'll know where to put it."

"Bianca," Neill said, but she didn't dare look back. If she did, she might show her weakness for him.

She raced past the jardinieres full of flowers on the front steps and through the lobby, hair flying, heels clicking on the wide plank flooring. The garden party was over; everyone had dispersed. Bianca kept on going right through the lobby toward the pond and its bordering path that led to the manager's house.

Tia, held close, was satisfied to suck on her Binky and gaze wide-eyed at their surroundings.

"I am going to find Franny, no matter what," Bianca said to her. "And then I'm going to shower and dress for the rehearsal later. And I'm not going to waste one more minute thinking about Neill Bellamy and what might have been." Tia sighed and snuggled deeper into Bianca's arms.

At any other time, Bianca might have enjoyed strolling beside the pond, which was bordered by water lilies and, at its narrowest point, crossed by a high arched bridge. The Folly, an artfully built fake Gothic ruin that was going to be the backdrop for the wedding, was reflected in the pond's wide surface, shimmering golden in the light of the late afternoon sun. Concealed behind a grove of birch trees was the converted carriage house where the manager lived with his family.

To Bianca's immense relief, Franny answered her knock.

"Oh, what a precious baby," she cooed as soon as she saw Tia. "Come here, darling." She eased the baby out of Bianca's weary arms, handling her competently and with great gentleness.

Doris Ofstetler, the manager's wife and Franny's mother, bustled in from the back of the house, all smiles. "We have a cradle all ready for her," she said, leading Bianca into an alcove off Franny's room. "It's a family heirloom that we use for the grandchildren. You know, I thought maybe your own nanny would be able to make the trip after all."

"No, as it turned out, Gabrielle has mono. Doctor's orders are that no travel is allowed." Bianca had called before the diagnosis of mononucleosis to find out if Franny Ofstetler, whom she'd met the year before, was available to baby-sit. Fortunately, Franny had been willing, even eager.

"We like having a baby in the house, so please let Tia stay as long as you like," Doris Ofstetler said comfortingly.

"I've got a portable crib in the closet of my room, all ready to set up. I'll be back to pick her up after the rehearsal dinner," Bianca told them. She'd keep Tia all night and return her to the Ofstetlers in the morning. That way, no one would see her with a baby again. That way, her secret would be safe.

After leaving the Ofstetlers', Bianca walked slowly back to the hotel, her gaze lingering on the pairs of swans paddling so gracefully beneath the mossy gray stone bridge. Swans mated for life, she recalled with a certain degree of melancholy. Maybe, despite Neill's pessimism, the choice of Swan's Folly as a place to be married was a good omen for Eric and Caro.

"Bianca?" She whirled at the sound of her name. Eric was hurrying toward her, dressed in jogging clothes. He liked to run; she wondered if he still ran

every day. She used to know that kind of thing about
Eric, but everything had changed since he'd decided to
marry Caroline. Not that she was jealous; she was
happy for them.

She was relieved when Eric held out his arms and
enveloped her in a big bear hug.

"Let's talk for a few minutes," he said, keeping his
arm around her shoulders.

"Okay," she replied. They headed toward the
bridge, and Bianca wondered what Eric expected from
her. After she'd learned she was pregnant last year,
she'd phoned Eric from Rome to tell him; he'd been
flabbergasted. He told her that he'd never suspected her
secret crush on his older brother. Later, when he called
her and found out that she hadn't informed Neill that
she was carrying his child and didn't plan to, he'd been
furious. Fortunately she'd been in Rome at the time
and all she'd had to do was hang up. Then she'd cried.
She and Eric hadn't spoken since.

After they reached the top of the bridge, Eric stopped
and leaned on the railing. "I'm glad you're here,
Bianca."

"How could I miss your wedding?" she said, trying
to infuse the words with a lightheartedness that she
didn't feel.

Eric turned his head and looked at her, and in that
moment she knew he'd forgiven her. "How are you,
Bianca? I mean, really?"

"I'm fine. Just in case you ever want to try it, childbirth isn't all it's cracked up to be; I was only in labor
for a few hours."

Eric chuckled. "I think I'll let my future wife handle
that. How's the baby?"

"Tia is wonderful. Beautiful. Magical. I'd like for

you to meet her." Then she remembered. "But I'm not sure it would be a good idea. At least not during the wedding festivities."

Eric's expression clouded. "Why not?"

"Oh, Eric," she began, but she couldn't go on. She focused her gaze on a dragonfly hovering at the edge of the water.

"Is something wrong?" He sounded alarmed.

"Neill thinks the baby is someone else's," she said in a rush. The dragonfly flitted away and disappeared under the bridge.

"Another man's? Bianca, what have you done now?" Alarm had become exasperation. Eric had always been the levelheaded one.

"Oh, not another man's. I mean, the question hasn't come up, thank goodness. Neill thinks Tia is another *woman's* child. He saw me with the baby at the garden party and he walked over and I had a problem with my contact lens and Neill held her, and then he jumped to the conclusion that the baby belongs to Franny, who is actually the baby-sitter, and I thought it was better to let him think that." She paused, out of breath, and glanced out of the corners of her eyes at Eric to see how he was taking all this. He seemed floored.

He shook his head slowly. "Bianca, what will you do if Neill finds out the truth?"

"You're the only one here who knows I had a baby. Please, please, Eric, if I mean anything to you, don't tell Neill," she said in a low tone.

"But you brought the baby to the garden party. I assume everyone saw you with her."

"I was only there for ten minutes or so. Tia will be with the baby-sitter much of the time, and there'll be so much going on that no one will have time to think about whose baby it is.''

"Bianca, I can't believe you're doing this." Eric focused on her, his forehead knit in dismay.

"It's because I don't want Neill to find out I got pregnant after our one time together. You know Neill. He doesn't want permanence. He hates family life. I wouldn't want him to feel obligated, especially since I can provide for Tia myself.''

Eric remained silent. Under the surface of the water, little fish flashed silver in the sunlight. In that split second, Bianca was reminded of the Japanese carp in the pond in the backyard of the house in Lake Forest, Illinois, the suburb of Chicago where they'd all lived during the time that her mother was married to Budge Bellamy.

When Eric didn't speak, she said, "Remember the koi pond?''

Eric slanted a look in her direction. "You threw me in. Just like I want to throw you in right now.''

"That bad, huh?" She smiled ruefully.

"We're not kids anymore, Bianca. Adults make decisions and have to live with them. So if you really don't want my brother to know he has a child, I'll respect your wishes. But if it were me, I'd want to know I was a father.''

"Neill's different," Bianca said. "You've chosen to get married and I wish you and Caro every happiness in life and love and in raising a family, but we both know Neill's nothing like you. By the way, does Caro know I had his baby?''

Eric sighed. "You asked me not to tell her, Bianca, and I didn't. Fortunately, she's been focused on wedding plans.''

Bianca reached out and clasped his hand. For a moment, she gazed deep into her friend's eyes. They were troubled, but she didn't doubt his loyalty.

"I'll keep your secret, Bianca. Cross my heart and hope to die, on my honor never lie." It was their old vow, useful when it was just the two of them against the world, and it made her smile.

"You're supposed to cross your heart and spit over your left shoulder," she reminded him.

Solemnly Eric crossed his heart, and restraining a grin, spit.

Bianca laughed. "Oh, Eric, I've missed you."

He drew her arm companionably through his. "I've missed you, too."

"Why don't you and Caro come to Paris later this year?"

"I thought you didn't want her to know about the baby."

"After the wedding, once it's over and I'm far away from Neill and everyone else, you can tell her. Just don't tell her who the daddy is."

Eric was silent for a long moment before he spoke. "Bianca, do you honestly think this will work?"

"I hope so," she said fervently.

"You'll never tell Neill he has a daughter?"

"Eric, there's no reason ever to see him again once he's gone back to Colombia. Why should our paths cross? We live half a world apart, and we're not really family. Anyway, will you and Caro come to see us? My flat is big enough for all of us, and you could get to know Tia."

"I'd like that. I'll suggest Paris *after* the honeymoon."

"Where are you going?"

"Only Caroline knows. All I have to do is show up."

She slanted him an oblique look. "What's going on between you and Caro, anyway?"

Eric only rolled his eyeballs. "Aaah," he said, giving the impression of mustering a great deal of forbearance.

Bianca remained tactfully silent in case Eric wanted to unload his feelings. He didn't say anything, though, and she didn't want to pry. But Neill's words kept echoing in her head— *Bellamys aren't good marriage material...Bellamys aren't good marriage material....* She wanted to believe that, in Eric's case at least, Neill was wrong.

They had resumed walking and reached the place where the bridge met the path. Eric stopped and patted Bianca's arm reassuringly. "I'll leave you here," he said. "I know you probably need to rest after your long trip."

"And I'm ready for a bath. It's been a very long day."

Eric squeezed her shoulder. "Thanks for coming, Bianca. It means a lot to me."

She smiled at him, remembering all the fun they'd had as kids. "Me too," she said. And then he was off, disappearing around a curve in the path. Bianca stood looking after him for a few moments, her eyes misted with sentimental tears. She was glad to be here to see Eric get married. The hard part was all the other stuff— the bachelorette party, the dinner tonight, the rehearsal.

For which she wasn't at all prepared. Time, she thought as she squared her shoulders and sped up her pace, to have that bath and get dressed.

Bianca's room was located in the wing where she'd

stayed last year, and she reached it without encountering anyone else she knew. To get to her room she had to climb a narrow staircase, pass two utility closet doors, and climb three more steps. It was an unusually private nook, and she appreciated that. When Tia cried, it was unlikely that anyone would be able to hear her. Also, the room's separation from the others made it less likely that Bianca would be expected to socialize.

Not that the other members of the wedding seemed eager to hang out with her. At the garden party, Bianca had overheard Viv and that rather strange-looking girl who'd come to the wedding with Lizzie, the only other female bridal attendant that Bianca actually liked, talking about lunch tomorrow. No one had invited Bianca. After last year, who could blame them?

Genevieve and the others might think that she, Bianca, had a thing for Eric, but it simply wasn't true. It had never occurred to either Bianca or Eric to become romantic about each other. They had always been buddies, nothing more. So at the engagement party dinner right after the famous haircut episode, Bianca had been stunned when Genevieve stopped conversation cold by hinting that there was more to her friendship with Eric than anyone knew.

Caroline, who assured Bianca and Eric that she knew there was nothing to her mother's spiteful speculation, had stood up for Bianca. So had Eric. But it had been a humiliating moment for Bianca, and she'd fled the dinner. After which Neill had come upon her crying amid the lilacs and consoled her. In the gazebo. And the next morning, unable to face Gen or Eric or especially Neill, Bianca had run away. End of story.

Well, not quite. Tia was the end of the story. And

the end of any chance she might have had to build on whatever her relationship was with Neill.

All water under the bridge, she thought ruefully. And why had she ever thought it could be otherwise? Swans mated for life. People didn't. Her mother and Budge were certainly proof enough of that.

In her room, Bianca showered quickly. The rehearsal was at six, followed by the rehearsal dinner. As she was trying to decide whether to make a splashy state- ment by wearing a brightly flowered Italian knit or if she should stick with basic beige, she glanced at the clock and realized that she had time to lie down for a few minutes. The bed was wide and scattered with heaps of inviting pillows; it was covered by a plump duvet.

As tired as she was, Bianca couldn't resist. She tossed her towel in the hamper and crawled under the duvet, sinking into the soft, sweet-smelling sheets. She closed her eyes, letting darkness soothe her irritated eyelids. It felt so good to be off her feet; it felt won- derful to let her tense muscles relax.

She'd lie there just a few minutes, and then she'd get dressed.

"WHERE *IS* Bianca?"

Eric hissed the question at Neill, who was cooling his heels slightly out of the range of Winnie, who kept making eyes at him, and Nana, who was going the rounds of the men in the wedding party and asking them to save a dance at the reception for her.

"I haven't any idea," Neill replied. He'd worked out his frustrations over Bianca by swimming numerous laps in the hotel pool. He didn't know where she was, and he didn't care.

"But we can't proceed with the rehearsal until Bianca shows up," Caroline chimed in. She was looking lovely in a pale yellow linen dress that showed off her creamy complexion. She was also looking worried, probably because her mother was antsy. Genevieve had already declared that the dining room staff could hold dinner for forty-five minutes, max, and if they didn't start the rehearsal soon, they'd be late ending the rehearsal, and the beef Wellington would be ruined.

"Chill out, Caro," Eric said mildly, provoking a decidedly frosty rather than merely cool stare from his agitated fiancée.

The sinking sun poured a lambent wash of golden light over the honey-colored stones of the Folly, where they'd all gathered promptly at six. Through the crumbling structure Neill saw that a haze was forming above the pond, partially obscuring the swans. The scene was lovely and romantic, and Neill didn't want to see the evening ruined.

Eric, ignoring Caroline, said, "I hope Bianca's okay. I'll send Kevin to find her."

"Yes, do," urged the minister, a distant cousin of Genevieve's.

Neill thought fast. "I'd better go," he said, thinking he'd better leave the two not-so-loving lovebirds to patch things up. Besides, he feared the worst. He wouldn't put it past Bianca to walk out on this whole shebang, considering that she had done exactly that last year.

"Hurry," said Eric, casting an ominous look at Genevieve and another one at Caroline, who seemed undecided about whether to pursue looking miffed.

"Tell jokes or something to get their minds off things. I'll be right back. With Bianca, I hope."

"With Bianca. For sure," Eric called after him on a note of desperation.

AS NEILL STRODE away from the gathering, he suddenly realized that he didn't know Bianca's room number. He certainly didn't want to go back to the disgruntled group milling around in front of the Folly. So he confronted the desk clerk, a rosy-cheeked summer intern with a badge that gave her name as Suzie and who took her desk duties seriously. Too seriously, as it turned out.

Suzie confirmed that Bianca was still a guest at the hotel, which relieved Neill somewhat. But she wouldn't tell him where to find her.

"I'm sorry, Mr. Bellamy, we don't give out guests' room numbers, but you can leave a message," she said primly.

"Ms. D'Alessandro is late for the Knox-Bellamy wedding rehearsal. She's a bridesmaid."

"I'm sorry, but I—"

Neill clenched his fists and cautioned himself to be patient. "Let me talk to the manager."

"He's at dinner."

"The assistant manager?"

"On vacation."

Neill drew himself up to his full six feet three inches, pulled a twenty-dollar bill from his pocket, and waved it in front of Suzie's fascinated eyes. "Hainsworth Knox, who owns this hotel and is the father of the bride, will be very angry, Suzie, when he finds out that you haven't helped me find Ms. D'Alessandro. Mr. Knox will curse and yell at the manager. He will fire the assistant manager. And when I inform him that you, the desk clerk, did not give me my own sister's room number—''

''Ms. D'Alessandro is your sister? Why didn't you say so? She's in room 141. In the east wing.''

He tossed the twenty on the desk and slapped a fifty-dollar bill beside it. ''Do me a favor, Suzie. Send a tray of cocktails out to the wedding rehearsal, charge them to my room, and you keep the fifty. Got that?''

Suzie scooped up the bills. ''Got it, Mr. Bellamy.''

''Thanks,'' Neill said, taking off at a sprint.

Well, Bianca wasn't really his sister. But for fifteen months she *had* been his stepsister.

He flew down the hall of the east wing, adjusting his pace as the hall bent this way and that. He paused to listen for a moment at the door of room 141, hearing no sounds within.

''Bianca?'' he said.

No reply. Neill raised his hand to knock and noticed that the door wasn't locked; it wasn't even closed properly. He considered calling Security, but because time was short he didn't want to wait around for someone to arrive. Instead he nudged the door with a forefinger until it swung open.

In the big bed under the window overlooking the garden, Bianca was lying on her back, one hand flung outward, the other resting on the sheet across her chest. Her eyes were closed.

Neill was across the floor in two strides, grasping Bianca by the shoulder, shaking her awake. She opened her eyes slowly and saw his face only inches from hers, and then, incredibly, she lifted her arms and slid them around his neck.

''Neill,'' she whispered, her lips moist, her skin fragrant. She pulled him down to her, and his mind whirled with memories, and even as they chased through his mind, he found himself beside her on the bed. He registered that Bianca wasn't wearing much; only the sheet lay between him and her beautiful breasts.

Her breasts. They had been so pale in the moonlight that night in the gazebo, and the tips had been so taut, puckering invitingly beneath his fingertips, and when he'd kissed her there she had sighed and whispered his name.

But that was last year. This was now. The wedding party was waiting, and he broke the kiss. He wrenched himself from Bianca's arms and stood looking down at her for a brief moment during which her very vulnerability hit him somewhere in his viscera. In her wide pupils he saw his own reflection, miniaturized and desirous. *Careful,* he told himself. Because if it had been remotely possible, he would have stayed with her. He would have feathered his fingertips across those slightly parted lips, cupped his hand around the curve of her cheek, and joined her between those cool, soft sheets.

To hide his reeling thought processes, he threw Bianca's suitcase open and began tossing underwear and hose her way. Her bras and panties were delicate lace; of course Bianca would wear only the best.

"Get decent," he said tersely. "You're late for the rehearsal."

Bianca was now fully awake. Neill had startled her out of fantasy dreams in which they had both thrown their inhibitions to the wind. Thrown them right out of the convertible, which in her dreams Neill drove masterfully until he parked it in a dark unspecified place smelling of lilacs, and where she had reached across the seat to touch the nape of his neck while he pulled her sweater out of her waistband and slid her skirt up around her hips, and then he was kissing her and she was moaning and he was caressing her breasts, and then there he was beside her, really there, and the car had become her bed at the hotel and only a sheet separated her naked body from his. Only at that point it hadn't been a dream. When she'd pulled him down to kiss her, she'd found that out. He'd actually pushed her away, a complexity of emotions chasing across his face.

He must be angry with her. For good cause. She shouldn't have fallen asleep; she should have dressed right after her shower and gone downstairs and been sociable with whomever turned up.

Bianca was so shocked at the way she'd practically thrown herself at Neill that she didn't speak. She felt pale and shaken, unnerved by her loss of control. True, she'd been asleep. True, she'd thought he was only a dream. But Neill didn't know that. Bianca was sure that nothing she could say would improve the situation. Cautiously she reached a hand out from under the sheet and grabbed the bra that he'd tossed at her. At first she tried to put it on inside out and had to start over again. She felt all thumbs, clumsy and slow.

Bianca noticed that Neill kept an eye on her as she finally managed to wriggle into her bra under the sheet. When she reached around to fasten the clasp, the sheet slipped, revealing—well, nothing Neill hadn't already seen. She didn't know why she was so shy with him; it was ridiculous considering. He turned away as she shimmied into her underpants, still under the sheet, still not speaking.

Finally she found her voice. "Neill, I'm perfectly capable of getting dressed by myself."

"It was bad enough the day of the engagement party. You could at least be on time for the rehearsal."

Bad enough? What was bad enough? Disappearing with Eric, her dearest friend, for a little alone-time before he got completely caught up in wedding, wedding, wedding?

What had only moments ago been like a dream come true, with Neill in her arms, now seemed like a nightmare. Deciding that modesty wasn't important, Bianca stumbled out of bed. She was still tired, still jet-lagged, and clear on one thing at least—Neill didn't think much of her after all. To Neill she was still funny little Beans, not the sophisticated woman she'd become. Not the mother of his child. How could she be? He would never know about it.

"Another thing. The hotel has taken extra security precautions but they won't do any good if you leave your door unlocked."

"Yes, Neill. You're right, Neill. I won't do it again, Neill. Now will you please leave me alone?"

"What are you going to wear?" He spoke mildly, standing with his arms crossed over his chest. He might have been asking if she'd like to dance, and it was hard to stay angry with him when he was so appealing.

"Basic beige."

He plucked the dress out of her suitcase, handed it to her, and sat down on a chair at the end of the bed. Fortunately she had already stowed Tia's bags in the closet.

"You can go now," she said with as much dignity as she could summon under the circumstances.

"Nope," he said. "I'm not leaving until you do.

Hurry up, Gen's worried that the beef Wellington might fall.''

"Beef Wellington? Fall?''

"Or whatever it does when people don't show up to eat it.''

"Soufflés fall. Beef Wellington sogs.''

"And Gen rants. Plus the situation with Eric and Caro is iffy at best. Hurry up, Bianca. Or have I mentioned that already?''

Bianca didn't care if Genevieve ranted until doomsday, but concern about the situation between Eric and Caro spurred her into a faster mode. She struggled into the dress, mindful of Neill's watchful eyes. The dress was another clingy knit, the kind the Italians did so stylishly. It fit more tightly than it had before Tia was born; she'd gained a couple of pounds, which were all too evident when she wore something like this, but she had no intention of changing. It didn't make that much difference to her what she wore. All she wanted was for the wedding to be over and done. And to fly back to Paris.

Damn! The back zipper was stuck. She twitched at it and realized that the slider was hung up on a loose thread. What was worse, she was afraid if she pulled too hard, the knit might unravel.

"Neill, the zipper is stuck. Would you mind...?''

He stood up slowly and strode to where she was standing, assiduously avoiding her eyes. He zipped the dress in short order, but did she imagine that his fingers lingered too long on the silky skin of her back? Probably.

"Put on some makeup. Get rid of those circles under your eyes.''

"What difference does it make to you if I look like death warmed over?" she shot back.

"Not much, but it matters to you."

"The only thing that matters to me—" She stopped talking in midsentence. She'd been about to say that Tia was the only thing that mattered to her anymore. Which seemed like a jaded outlook, but true.

"The only thing that matters to you is what?" Neill followed her into the bathroom and leaned against the door, hands in his pockets.

"Is getting you off my case and me back to Europe."

"If I were really on your case, you'd know it. I'm merely trying to help. I said I wouldn't come back without you and I mean to deliver."

Bianca smoothed on foundation, considering how to reply to this. "For two cents I'd make a liar out of you," she said.

"Oh, great. Here I am, trying my best to get you on track, and this is all the thanks I get?" He was regarding her with a mock-tragic smile, and it was one of those expressions that had always made him so appealing to her. It was all she could do not to turn around and look at him, since his face was reversed. In the mirror image, the lopsidedness of that smile was disconcerting.

"You always were bossy," she said, smoothing her eyebrows. She picked up a brush and fluffed her hair. "Instead of merely standing there, you *could* get my shoes out of the shoe bag in my suitcase."

He rolled his eyes and went to dig around in her suitcase. Bianca breathed a sigh of relief. She felt as if she were fourteen again, the age she was when her mother married Budge, and Neill was once again the older stepbrother who never could understand what it was that was always cracking her and Eric up, who never joined in their fun and games, who put as much distance between himself and the two of them as he possibly could.

"Here," he said, handing her a pair of shoes. He'd found the right ones for this outfit; that was surprising. Bianca sat on the edge of the bed and slid her feet into them.

When she stood up, he said approvingly, "Nice. Let's go."

"I should wear jewelry," she said. She located her jewelry case, slipped on a gold bangle, and found a pair of spectacular earrings of her own design. No time to put them on now; she could do that as they walked.

"I'd better change purses," she said.

Neill appropriated her arm and walked her out the door. "No time. You'll do."

"Thanks," she said, but the sarcasm was lost on him. Bianca managed to slide the posts of the earrings through her pierced earlobes while skipping occasionally to keep up with Neill's long strides as they hurried through the maze of corridors to the lobby.

As they approached the bottom of the garden, he placed a guiding hand at the small of her back, and it was all Bianca could do not to lean into his touch. She didn't know whether he put his hand there to urge her along faster or whether it was a gesture of support and meant to give everyone else the idea that she was under his protection. Whatever it was, her skin tingled through the knit, but she didn't pull away.

The wedding party was waiting restlessly, and dusk was gathering in the shadows. Caroline and Eric greeted Bianca with relief, and Bianca murmured appropriate apologies, including the words *jet-lagged* and *hope you understand.*

Despite a few rancorous looks from Genevieve, the rehearsal proceeded under the tutelage of a wedding consultant who was cultivating a patient attitude. Following Fawn, Neill and Eric's five-year-old half sister, who was the flower girl, Lizzie Muldoon was the first bridesmaid down the aisle, followed by Bianca, followed by Petsy, followed by Winnie. Neill, as best man, was already waiting beside Eric as Bianca began to walk slowly between the lines marking where the chairs would be set up for the wedding guests. Bianca tried to catch Eric's eye and wink, but Eric was craning his neck to look past Winnie, the maid of honor, to where Caroline stood with her father, and it was Neill's eye that Bianca actually caught.

She couldn't help it. She felt her heart stop in her throat, and her hands, clasped around the artificial bouquet that she carried for the rehearsal, began to tremble. If only Eric wasn't watching Caroline and would smile back at her, but he was oblivious. Neill, however, was not. He raised his eyebrows as if to say, "Pay attention. Don't slack off."

Caroline and her father, the dignified Hainsworth, started toward The Folly. "Looks like there's going to be a wedding after all, doesn't it?" whispered Lizzie, the bridesmaid who stood next to Bianca.

"Is there some doubt?" Bianca whispered back.

Lizzie shrugged. Bianca turned her attention back to Eric, but he wouldn't look at her. He was focused on his bride-to-be.

But someone *was* looking at her, too. Neill Bellamy, standing beside Eric, was staring at her with an expression that she couldn't quite fathom.

When Neill caught her looking at him, he arched his brows emphatically as if to ask a question.

Bianca didn't dare think about what the question might be. Because it could never be the question she'd so often dreamed he might ask. Because she knew she could never be Mrs. Neill Bellamy.

Chapter Four

At the rehearsal dinner, held in Odette, the hotel's elegant dining room, Neill hovered no more than an arm's length away from Bianca.

"No martinis," he warned her under his breath when they first arrived.

She stared out one of the arched windows overlooking the starlit grounds. "I've only had two martinis in my life, and that was two too many."

"If you can still say 'two too many,' I won't worry about you."

"As I said, I've only had tee martunis in my life—" she began, hoping she could make Neill laugh, and he did.

"Uh-oh, you're starting to sound more and more like Genevieve," he said.

"Don't worry, I'm sticking to my usual wine," she assured him. Those two martinis had thrown her for a loop last year and might be part of the reason that she'd let her inhibitions slip. Well, okay, so there was more to it than that. On that night one year ago, she'd wanted Neill Bellamy. It was a time when it had seemed as if she'd have no better chance to live out her secret fantasies about him. The only problem was that she'd gotten something more than she bargained for, and that something was now sleeping in a cradle at the Ofstetlers' house.

Bianca turned to a waiter and pointedly ordered a glass of Chardonnay. She thought that once Neill realized that she intended to drink nothing stronger than wine and only one glass of that, he'd back off. She was wrong.

As Bianca was trying to figure out where she could turn next without bumping into Neill, she heard a small voice say, "You sure are a pretty lady." She glanced down and saw Lambie, short for Lambert Thorpe, Petsy's four-year-old son. He had wide brown eyes and a face like a mischievous monkey.

"Why, thank you," she said. She stooped to munchkin height so her face would be level with his. "I'm Bianca," she said.

"I know. My mother said you're a werry strange lady. I think you're a werry pretty lady. Because you have werry nice earrings."

"I designed these earrings myself, Lambie. I'm glad you like them."

"What's design?"

"It means I planned the way the earrings would look. I drew a picture and then the man who made the earrings built them exactly like the picture."

"Like with Legos?"

"Something like that," she said, trying not to smile.

"That's werry interesting," Lambie said solemnly.

"You know what, Lambie? I think you're the nicest boy here."

"I'm the only boy. Everyone else is big. Fawn isn't a boy. She's only a girl. But I like her werry much."

Fawn was Budge's five-year-old daughter by his cur-

rent wife, Rhonda. That made Fawn the half sister of
Eric and Neill.

"Did you say my name?" Fawn, a ringleted vision
in a full-skirted blue organdy dress, emerged from the
forest of skirts and legs.

Bianca, tired of crouching, sank onto a chair. "Lambie said he likes you," she said.

"Yep," said Lambie, looking wise. "But we're not
going to get married."

"*I'd* certainly advise against it," Neill said amiably,
pulling up a chair alongside Bianca's.

"I'm not getting married until I'm at least sixty-
eight," announced Fawn.

"I hope not," Neill told her.

"I'm not marrying Lambie, either. He's a meanie."

"Am not!"

"Are too! You pretended you were drowning in the
swan pool during the garden party and Joe and that
lady jumped in after you."

"I was swimming!" Lambie said stubbornly.

Neill put a man-to-man arm around the boy's slender
shoulders and adopted a friendly tone. "Tell you what,
Lambie. Tomorrow I'll show you some secrets about
swimming if you promise never to try to scare people
again."

At that moment an obviously inebriated Genevieve
announced that dinner was served, and Fawn and Lambie scampered away to be with their parents. The minister eyed Bianca as if he wanted to speak with her,
and she had no desire to sit with him. Bianca was preparing to bolt toward Vivian when Neill stood and offered his arm.

"Shall we?" he said.

"I don't think so, Neill. Besides, I planned to sit

next to your mother.'' She and Viv had always liked each other.

"Looks like she's sitting with Budge," Neill said. He took her arm and looped it through his.

Winnie, who had been slinging admiring glances in Neill's direction ever since the start of the rehearsal, was moving in their direction.

"Take pity on me, Bianca," Neill whispered, grinning down at her in his most charming way. "Protect me from Winnie."

Bianca had no desire to make meaningless conversation with Caroline's younger sister, so she put on a show of smiling delightedly up at Neill.

"I'll be glad to," she said as sweetly as she could, but behind her words, her teeth were tightly clenched.

Once everyone was seated, dinner commenced with innumerable toasts to the bride and groom followed by a parade of appetizers, salads, main courses and finally dessert and coffee. Viv, who managed to switch places with Fawn when the waiters were bringing in the cherries jubilee, settled in the chair across from Bianca and began to regale her with witty anecdotes. Among other things, she said that she was negotiating to sculpt someone that Lizzie had brought to the wedding, a muscle-bound young man named, of all things, Storm. Storm was trying to break into movies.

"And so I said to Storm, 'I don't suppose you've ever met Aaron Spelling,' meaning, you know, the famous television producer, and Storm said, 'Spelling wasn't ever my best subject.' Isn't that just the cutest thing?'' Viv was at her flamboyant best, and all Bianca had to do was listen and nod. Which was just as well, because other than Lizzie, Viv was the only grown-up present who seemed to notice that Bianca was alive. And Neill, of course.

Once they'd worked their way through dessert, Bianca was stifling yawns and looking forward to bed. Tonight she'd sleep and sleep and sleep. Until Tia woke up, which would probably be all too early in the morning.

Her attention was drawn to the head table, where Caroline was staring obdurately down at her empty plate. Eric whispered something in her ear, whereupon she pinned him with a look, and Eric suddenly threw down his napkin and stalked from the room. Caroline jumped up and ran out.

A sudden hush fell over the group. "I daresay they'll be back," Genevieve said into the rollicking silence just before she hiccuped.

No one knew what to say. The silence seemed to stretch on forever until people began to converse as if nothing untoward had happened. Bianca stared at the two empty chairs at the head table, her heart in her throat, a hollow feeling in the pit of her stomach. She wondered if she could go after her two friends and attempt to play peacemaker, then decided against it. Someone probably should, but it couldn't be her. Her interest would only invite speculation. Instead she opted for a quick trip to the ladies' room.

When she returned, people were starting to get up from their places and make polite leave-taking chitchat, and Vivian cleared her throat. "And so, Bianca, why don't you come to my room for a while after dinner? I'd like to show you pictures of my sculptures." Viv, after her second marriage to Budge Bellamy ended, had made a career out of sculpting nude men in life-size athletic poses.

"Well, um," Bianca stammered, trying to think fast. No way did she want to go to Viv's room. She certainly didn't want to be drawn into gossip about the bridal couple. Besides, she was tired and she needed to reclaim Tia.

Neill picked up on her reluctance. "Bianca has promised that she'll have a drink with me," he said helpfully. He draped his arm across her shoulders, much to her dismay.

"How nice," Viv said. She looked as if she meant it.

"To assure her that she's still part of this family," Neill continued.

He was a devil. He knew she didn't want to be part of his family. She was on the verge of saying something to that effect when Budge Bellamy, never Bianca's favorite person much less favorite stepfather, chose that moment to wedge his way into their little group. She steeled herself to endure his unctuous examination.

"Good to see you, Bianca," he boomed, all grin and eyebrows. "My, you've grown up." He'd said exactly the same thing last year; this year he actually pinched Bianca's cheek. She recoiled, and Viv, bless her, noticed.

"Budge, if you don't mind, I have some important things to discuss with you," Viv said abruptly, and led him away.

Neill said, "How about that drink?"

"No," Bianca said. "I can't imagine why you're doing this."

Before he could reply, Petsy Lambert Thorpe edged closer. She was wearing a white lace two-piece dress with a blue satin band around the hips that made her seem twice as wide as she really was.

"Hi, Bianca," she said breezily. "I didn't know you'd brought a baby until I saw you at the garden party." Her tone was honey laced with vinegar.

Bianca, taken completely by surprise, managed an offhand shrug and a laugh. "Well, I didn't bring any baby tonight."

Petsy eyed her up and down. "Well, I've heard that there's just no predicting what you will do," she said, all vinegar this time.

Bianca tried to think of a quick rejoinder that would quash the conversation and get her up and running for sanctuary, but Viv, back from her diversionary chat with Budge, chimed in with, "That's what people are always saying about me," almost as if she wanted to help by taking the spotlight off Bianca.

Bianca went limp with relief, and as the group began to break up, she drifted along with everyone else to the terrace. She half expected to see Caroline and Eric, but there was no sign of them.

Bianca began to plot her escape. She could slip into the darkness and hurry to the Ofstetlers' house; no one would see her go. As she was easing toward the shadows, Neill shouldered through the departing members of the group and grasped her arm firmly. "The bar is this way," he said.

"I don't want anything to drink," Bianca said stubbornly. "All I want is to go to sleep."

"So I'll walk you to your room."

There seemed to be no choice but to fall in beside him on the path that led to the front of the hotel; ahead of them, a man and woman laughed. Caroline and Eric? No, an older couple. Trailing smoke, they veered sideways into the darkness, the glowing tips of their cigarettes extinguished in the shadows. As Bianca and Neill passed the place where they had left the path, they heard nothing but silence, then a long throaty laugh.

"We need to talk," Neill said into the awkwardness.

"We haven't anything to talk about," Bianca replied quickly. She wanted to be rid of him. And his voice like dark brown velvet, not to mention the gleam in his eyes.

Overhead a zillion stars sailed in a cloudless sky; a fragrant breeze blew languidly off the pond. It could have been romantic, but with memories of last year still smarting, Bianca put the stars and the breeze out of her mind.

Neill glanced over at her, his eyes thoughtful. "Have you ever considered, Bianca, that we're the only two people here who are sensible about this wedding? And honest about marriage's pitfalls? I can't talk to anyone else about what's going on with Eric and Caro without worrying that I'm going to say something that will reveal my true feelings."

"What would be wrong with showing your feelings for a change?" she blurted. She was sorry for saying it immediately after the words left her mouth, especially when Neill's lips hardened into a straight line.

"In this company, quite a lot."

"You don't like these people much, do you?" she said. They were still walking, but their pace had slowed. The pale glow from the Japanese lanterns lining the path illuminated Neill's face.

"I like *some* of them *werry* much, as Lambie would say. And some of them more than that."

The way he said it, his tone loaded with nuance, rattled her.

"Yes, Fawn and Lambie are charming, aren't they?"

"I wasn't talking about Fawn and Lambie. Or my mother, delightful as she is. Or Caroline. Or Eric."

She grasped at this straw. "I talked to Eric today."

"Did he clue you in about what's going on with him?"

"No, he avoided a discussion."

"Well, the fact that you actually talked with him must mean that he's forgiven you for getting him into hot water last year, right?"

Neill and everyone else must think that her making him late for the engagement party was why relations between Bianca and Eric had been strained ever since. That was good; it was what she wanted them to think.

"Yes, everything's fine between us. Tell me, Neill, does your brother know you don't think his marriage will last?"

"No. You might as well admit it, Bianca. You don't like it that Eric's getting married any better than I do."

"That's ridiculous," she said flatly.

"I'm sure you have different reasons for not wanting him to marry." The way he said it made Bianca do a double take.

"What," she said with dawning comprehension, "are you saying?"

"I noticed the way you stared at Eric when you were walking down the aisle. And someone else might, too. So maybe you'd better guard against long lingering looks."

She stopped in her tracks. "Oh, no," she said, thunderstruck. "You can't actually think that Eric—that Eric and I—"

"Whatever happened between you and Eric in the past, it's over."

"Neill," she said. "There was never anything between Eric and me."

"Stop standing there looking as if you've just been struck by lightning. Are we walking or aren't we?" He looked back at her and frowned.

Bianca moved her feet; they felt as heavy as lead. When she reached Neill, she stared up at him. His eyes were shuttered, his face impassive. It was hard to tell what he was really thinking.

"I think I *will* fall over in a dead faint if you really believe that I ever wanted Eric for myself."

"Well, a few people may have that impression, especially after Genevieve brought it up last year. And," he said reasoningly, "you don't want anyone to jump to the conclusion that you're responsible for the problems Eric and Caro are having."

Suddenly this whole wedding seemed to take on a comic opera quality. A bride and groom who were barely speaking, and no one seemed to know why. People arriving, people leaving, people not talking to people for ridiculous reasons, people not knowing who was related and who wasn't, people skilled in the art of one-upmanship and people who let themselves be one-upped.

She laughed then, thinking that if anyone knew, really knew, her secret, it would put the scuttlebutt about her and Eric to rest. It would take the group's focus off Eric and Caroline, and it would certainly start more rumors.

"Excuse me, Bianca, but did I say something funny?" He hadn't, but by this time anything Neill said would have launched Bianca onto a new wave of hilarity wherein all her tension seemed to be vibrating at a new and higher frequency.

For a moment, although a brief one, Bianca actually wished that Neill were laughing along with her, but the sobering reality was that if he knew what she knew, he certainly wouldn't be laughing. But her own mirth was certainly cathartic.

"I—I—oh, Neill, it *is* funny. Though I don't suppose you'll ever get the joke." She had laughed so hard there were tears in her eyes.

"You and Eric always had jokes that didn't include me."

"You were hardly ever around, and even when you were, you never wanted to be included as far as we could tell," she retorted. "Besides, I'm not through talking about this—this supposed attraction between Eric and me. How could I act to convince you and everyone else that we've never been more than friends?"

"Look, I'm merely pointing out—"

"How about if I take up with someone else? That Storm fellow with all the muscles, the guy Viv was talking about, for instance. Would that let everyone know that I have no interest in Eric? Or how about the bellman? He's kind of cute with that thin little mustache, you know. Would that make it clear that the bride and groom's problems have nothing whatever to do with me?" She started to laugh again.

Neill said nothing. He was exasperating. He talked when she least wanted to hear what he had to say, and when she wanted him to comment, he kept quiet. Anyway, she was exhausted. "Lovely night," Bianca said, walking faster. "Lovely wedding. Lovely company."

"Must you be so sarcastic?"

"It's the only way I seem to get through to you."

They were approaching the front of the hotel, and several guests were exiting noisily from the bar.

"There's that bellman," Bianca said, spotting him inside the lobby. "Maybe I'll chat him up. Do you suppose he's off tomorrow? I'm not doing anything in the morning. I wish I knew Storm's room number. Perhaps your mother could tell me." Oh dear, she regretted that last remark, but too late—she'd already said it, which was a pity because she really liked Viv.

Neill narrowed his eyes at her. "That's enough, Bianca. I'll walk you to your room and then *I'm* going to have a drink. Maybe a double."

"Good idea. It might loosen you up."

They went inside the building and down the crooked little hall. She started up the narrow staircase, and Neill followed behind. "Don't feel as if you have to spend the weekend looking after me, Neill. Anyway, chivalry is already dead and crime at this hotel is nil."

"Don't be so sure. Everyone was talking about a burglary when I arrived. And Gen's hyper about kidnappers. She's alerted everyone at the hotel to be on the lookout for them. In fact—"

"I don't want to hear about any of this. Here we are at my room, and I hope you have a lovely evening. I hope—"

"Bianca," Neill said. "Will you please shut up." Without warning, he pulled her roughly into his arms and kissed her open mouth.

It wasn't just any kiss. It was thorough. It made her knees go weak and heart thump against her ribs. Before she could respond, and she would have if she hadn't been taken by surprise, it was over.

"Good night, Bianca," Neill said gruffly. He turned

abruptly on his heel and disappeared around the bend in the hall. She heard his footsteps on the stairs and then he was gone.

Bianca sagged against the wall. Neill Bellamy had kissed her. And it had been a real kiss, not merely lip service. And he'd left her wanting more.

But evidently one kiss was enough for him. Just like one night in the gazebo was enough for him.

It took her a few minutes to pull herself together. She was so tired. And she still had to go get Tia.

And then she'd have to get through the rest of this stupid wedding. Somehow.

NEILL WIPED Bianca's lipstick from his mouth with his handkerchief and headed for the Cygnet Club, the hotel bar, where he found Nana entertaining an audience of enthralled guests.

"And then there was the time I wore nothing but veils. It was in Paris after the war."

"What war?" someone called out.

"World War Two, of course. The Big One." She smiled beatifically at her questioner.

"It was in front of a fountain in the rain, very impromptu, but my fluter—that's what I always called the flautist who accompanied my dances—insisted that he sit in the automobile and play so he wouldn't get his flute wet. You can't play a wet flute, he said, and I only knew that I had to dance, had to emote, had to gather a crowd. The inimitable rain of Paris, so soft and gentle, and of course my veils became quite wet, but I danced anyway because I had to express the Truth of my Being. Afterward a man came up to me, he had been injured in battle, and he held my hand and told me he now understood the meaning of Life, which was..."

Kevin edged around a bar stool and leaned against the bar beside Neill. "She could go on like this for hours. Isn't it time *you* looked after Nana?" he said glumly.

Neill ordered a drink. "Where's Dad? Where's Hainsworth? Where's Joe? Don't they take shifts like we do?"

"Joe's already scooped Nana down from the bar, where she was doing the cancan. Dad and Rhonda and Fawn have retired to their suite for the evening. Hainsworth, I hope, is spoonfeeding Genevieve her tranquilizers. Anyway, I thought you might know what's going on over there." He gestured with a nod toward a far corner, where Lizzie was engaged in earnest conversation with Eric. Caroline was nowhere in sight.

"Sorry, I don't have a clue." As if he didn't have enough to think about, he told himself.

"Neither do I. Besides, big brother, I have a date. And it isn't with an eighty-something-year-old reincarnation of Isadora somebody."

"Isadora Duncan. A great dancer and a free spirit," Neill said, lifting his glass.

Kevin leaned closer. "It's my spirit yearning to be free at the moment. The desk clerk said she'd meet me after she gets off work, which was—" Kevin consulted his watch "—ten minutes ago."

"That cute little intern who works at the desk is meeting you? Suzie?" Suzie, whose palm he had greased so well in order to find out Bianca's room number.

"Yeah, Suzie. But not if I have to make sure Nana

doesn't break a hip while playing jump rope with her scarf."

Neill decided to take pity on Kevin. He'd been twenty-three once himself, although tonight it seemed like a long time ago. "What I want to know is why we Bellamy men have been charged with keeping Nana the wild woman in line," he said.

"Dad's idea. You have to admit he's dealt with his share of wild women."

Neill didn't feel like discussing Budge's many marriages. "Go ahead and meet your date, Kev," he said wearily. "I thought I'd have a chance to drink in peace and unwind, but I'll make sure Nana doesn't launch into her dance of the seven veils or whatever, at least not tonight."

"The dance of the seven veils was Salome, not Isadora, Neill. In the Bible. I do know that much." Kevin clapped him on the back and started to leave.

Neill grabbed Kevin's shoulder. "And it was John the Baptist's head she wanted on a silver platter. Let's make sure it's not either one of our heads that's served up after tonight. Watch out for that desk clerk, Kevin, and don't stir anything up. Under Suzie's prim exterior perhaps a tiger lurks."

"I should be so lucky," Kevin said before heading for the door.

Nana didn't seem to notice Kevin's departure. "And in Paris, you know, the Seine is so lovely in the moonlight, so my next performance was on a coal-hauling barge. What an inspiring sight to see people lined up along the riverbank and on the bridges watching, and I was dancing all in black with one white feather in my hair. Oh, and my hair was quite long. To my knees, like that country singer. What's her name?

"Must be Crystal Gayle," said one of her listeners.

"Crystal Gayle. Yes, that's it. It was that night that one of my children was conceived—can't recall which one. It took me simply ages to wash the coal dust off my feet. I always danced barefoot, you know. I couldn't bear any impediment to free expression. That's why I also refused to wear underwear. Still don't, if you want to know the truth."

"Nana," Neill said into the spellbound silence, "I'll be glad to walk you to your room."

She looked at him as if he were an insect. "Who *are* you?"

"Neill," he said. "Neill Bellamy. We went to the garden party together."

"You have something to do with jewels, don't you?"

"Emeralds. A mine in Colombia," he said.

"Oh, emeralds," she said dismissively. "No amethysts? They're my favorite."

"Only emeralds," he said with, he thought, admirable restraint.

Nana's face fell. "Well, no matter. I think I was going to teach you the cha-cha," she said. "We were going to practice."

"Not tonight," Neill said. He held up his glass, signaling the bartender for a refill.

During this exchange, some of the others in the bar drifted away, and two paid their checks and left.

Nana ordered a Manhattan and turned her attention to Neill. "You look dejected," she said, prancing over and hoisting herself on a barstool. "Don't worry. The cha-cha is quite easy to learn."

"I'm sure," Neill said.

"Or isn't it dancing that you're worried about?"

"Not exactly." He was thinking how soft Bianca's lips had felt on his; he was thinking how he'd felt the tip of her tongue against his teeth.

"It's a woman. Isn't it?"

Neill didn't want to talk about this, especially with Nana. "Maybe," he replied, but she pounced instantly.

"It *is* a woman," she said delightedly. "Now which one could it be? My lovely granddaughter Winifred? She's popular with all the young men."

Neill shuddered. "No, it's not Winnie. When you're through with your drink, let's call it a night."

"I haven't shown you my favorite bar trick," she said. She plucked the cherry from her Manhattan and popped it into her mouth. "Have you ever seen anyone tie a knot in a cherry stem with her tongue?"

"I don't think so," he said. The bourbon was starting to get to him, starting to numb his lips. And that was good; he wanted them numb. He didn't want to think about kissing Bianca.

"Watch," was all Nana said, and as he stared in fascination, she managed to contort her mouth this way and that and in triumph withdrew the cherry, its stem perfectly knotted.

"Well, I'll be," he said in surprise.

"*Now* will you tell me which young woman is the object of your affections?" Nana said slyly.

"I wouldn't say she's exactly the object of my affections. I don't think she even likes me much."

"But you'd like her to, is that it?"

He had a momentary vision of Bianca in bed with her arm outflung, the sheet pulled up over the rise of her breasts. "I'd certainly like more than I'm getting," he said in all honesty.

"Wouldn't we all?" she said, and then she laughed raucously.

Embarrassed, Neill contemplated his options. He could excuse himself and allow Nana to play herself out in the hotel bar. He could pick her up and carry her away to her room, but that might give her more of a thrill than he intended. He could reason with her.

The last option seemed the most sensible. If he left Nana in the bar, more than likely she'd end up dancing on the bar again. Picking her up and carrying her away was a caveman tactic and really not an option, though it would get this whole thing over with.

"Nana," he said, turning to her with his most persuasive smile. "Tomorrow is such a busy day. You'll probably want to shop in Lake Geneva; some of the other women have reserved the hotel limo for the day and would be glad to take you along, I'm sure. And then the bachelor and bachelorette parties are tomorrow night, so wouldn't it be a good idea to be well rested?"

"Oh, I will be! I never get up before the crack of noon at the very earliest. I always travel with my velvet sleep mask. It's lavender, specially sewn for me by my seamstress. Lavender's the only color I wear these days. Only color that speaks to me, as it were. But back to your problem. The young lady," she said.

"It's not exactly a problem," he hedged, wishing she'd stay on one subject long enough for him to make his point.

"The real problem is happiness," she said wisely. "Always has been, always will be. How do we find it? How do we keep it? For me, happiness is the dance." She pronounced it *dahnce*. "What's happiness to you, Kevin?"

"I'm Neill. And right now happiness would be seeing you to your room."

She laughed delightedly. "You wicked, wicked fellow," she said.

"I didn't mean—"

"Of course you didn't. Not when you're in love with someone. Who did you say it was?"

"I didn't," Neill said weakly. The drinks had been strong, too strong. Usually he would be able to hold his own in a conversation like this, but things seemed muddled. All he knew was that he wished he were with Bianca.

"Well, whoever it is, if she's the one for you, don't let her get away. Keep at her night and day until you convince her that you love her and only her, now and forever. Come to think of it, if you're in love with her, why aren't you with her?"

"Because she isn't interested," he said without much hope. It looked as if he'd be here for a while. And he wasn't in love with Bianca. Well, maybe a little bit.

Nana set down her drink with a clatter. "In that case, dear Kevin, it's time for us to go. Far be it from me to hinder true love."

"I'm Neill.

She patted his cheek. "Of course you are," she said. "Now are we leaving or not? Because if you aren't, I'll order another drink."

"Let's go," Neill said.

"Of course you must promise me that you'll go to your young lady and impress upon her the strength of your ardor," Nana said as he yanked her scarf off the back of the stool where it had become entangled.

"Anything," Neill said, barely keeping from groaning. "I'll promise anything."

"That's what everyone says," Nana said, and she chattered all the way to her room.

When he left Nana, Neill felt as if he had been squeezed through a wringer. He had no intention of going to Bianca and impressing upon her the strength of his ardor, as Nana had, in her good-hearted way, insisted he do. But as he walked through the moonlit garden toward the guest cottage where he was staying, he couldn't help wondering if happiness *was* really the central problem, and if it was, how did one get it and how did one keep it?

Chapter Five

True happiness, thought Bianca as she awoke slowly the next morning, was a good night's sleep.

She'd rushed straight to the Ofstetlers' house last night after Neill left and found Tia snoozing away, racking up the Zs she'd missed while traveling.

"She just dropped off a few minutes ago, poor little thing," Doris Ofstetler had whispered as they looked down at Tia in the cradle. "Won't you let her stay all night? It'd be better than waking her up and trying to get her to sleep all over again. Babies get jet-lagged too, you know."

Tia had looked so comfortable, the Ofstetlers had been so willing, and Bianca had been so exhausted that she'd agreed that Tia could spend the night. But she was going to pick her up as soon as possible this morning, so she'd better get moving.

Bianca had barely scrambled out of bed when the phone rang. She snatched the receiver up, thinking that there might be some problem with Tia. But it was Vittorio, her business manager, calling from Rome.

"Bianca," he said, sounding expansive. He also sounded as if he hadn't talked to her in months, but it had only been three days. She pictured him in his big office with the traffic of Rome snarled outside his window; the peace of rural Wisconsin seemed like a blessing at the moment.

"Yes, Vittorio?"

"I have found a supplier of rubies from Burma. Beautiful stones, lovely stones. And you know what he said? He said that the best emeralds, the biggest emeralds, are mined at the Viceroy-Bellamy mines in Colombia. He said that to me at the very moment that you and Neill Bellamy are together again. I think there is something fortuitous in your meeting."

"I haven't decided about the gemstone line," Bianca said cautiously. She didn't need pressure from Vittorio, who had no idea that to enlarge upon her relationship with Neill would cause havoc in her personal life.

"But you will decide soon, yes?"

"Oh, Vittorio, I can't think about this *now*," she said as a pounding commenced on her door.

"What a—shall I say—*golden* opportunity for a jewelry designer, that's all I wanted to point out. Your father thinks—"

"One moment, Vittorio." She held her hand over the receiver's mouthpiece. "Who is it?"

She expected to hear an impersonal voice announcing, "Housekeeping." Instead she heard Neill's deep and anything but impersonal voice announcing, "Tennis at nine-thirty, Bianca. I won't take no for an answer."

Bianca dropped the receiver onto the bed and, pulling on a robe of fine peach-colored silk, hurried to the door, opening it only a crack. "I'm on the phone long distance," she said into Neill's newly shaven and brightly inquiring face. "I don't have time for this."

"Of course you do," he said smoothly, inserting one very white tennis shoe between the door and frame.

A stream of outraged Italian emitted from the phone receiver on the bed behind her. Bianca glanced back at it wildly, then at Neill. It wouldn't do for Neill to hear his own name being bellowed across the Atlantic Ocean on too-clear phone lines. It would raise questions, and she didn't feel like explaining anything at the moment.

Realizing that she didn't have much choice, she released the door and went back to the phone, eyeing Neill all the while.

"Look, Vittorio," she said into the receiver as Neill nonchalantly sauntered into the room. "I can't talk now. I'll call you when I get a chance." Neill minutely inspected the pictures on the wall, the view from a dormer window, his own fingernails.

"Bianca," Vittorio said, taking off into a rapid discourse in Italian about why she should listen to him, why they needed the new gemstone line, why it was a prudent move to look for new markets, and why he wanted to retire again, this time for good.

Bianca had heard it all before. She switched to Italian, told Vittorio firmly that she appreciated his concern, and said again that she would call him later. He was still squawking when she summarily hung up.

"So," she said to Neill, regarding him across the room, which seemed much smaller with him in it. "You think I'm going to play tennis?"

He turned and lifted an eyebrow. "You *like* playing tennis."

"Not anymore." She hadn't played since Tia was born.

"You could humor me," he suggested, a twinkle in his eyes.

Bianca definitely wasn't in the mood to humor anyone. She gave herself something to do by scooping the crumpled dress she'd worn last night off the floor and tossing it into a hotel laundry bag. "Go away," she said, ignoring the sheer male charm that exuded from Neill Bellamy's every pore.

Before he could reply to his dismissal, she padded quickly into the bathroom and closed the door. She leaned over the sink to peer at herself in the mirror. The circles under her eyes had faded and the color was back in her cheeks. She pinched them anyway; she was too pale.

"You always said you wanted to play tennis with me," Neill said coaxingly. He was standing very close to the door.

In the old days, she *had* kept after him to play tennis with her; she'd broached the subject many times during their parents' brief marriage. But Neill was usually too busy.

"I didn't bring a racquet," she said. "Anyway, I told you to leave me alone. I mean it." She turned on the faucet and splashed her face with cold water.

There was a short silence. "I don't think so, Bianca. I'll be back in forty-five minutes and you'll be ready," Neill said over the sound of the running water. He paused. "I'll find a racquet, don't worry."

Forty-five minutes? She turned off the tap. Hitching her robe more tightly around her, Bianca flung the bathroom door open, but Neill had already gone. She heard him whistling as he retreated along the crooked corridor.

"Neill?" she said, dabbing at her face with a towel.

She kept her voice low in case someone in the room farther down the hall was still asleep. If Neill heard her, he kept walking anyway. She was pretty sure he'd heard her.

She resisted the urge to swear and slammed the door instead. A screw fell out of the strike plate in the door frame; another aggravation. She tossed the screw into a nearby ashtray. All she could think about at the moment was that in forty-five minutes, Tia would be with her. Tia, the baby that wasn't supposed to be hers. No way could she allow Neill to find Tia in her room when he returned.

So, Bianca would first play tennis, and then maybe Neill would leave her alone. Later she'd collect her baby and, perhaps, call Vittorio back and tell him that emeralds had no place in the gemstone line. *If* there was going to be a gemstone line. But no, she couldn't call Vittorio back. There was a seven-hour time difference, it was late afternoon in Rome, and it was a Friday to boot. Vittorio would already be en route to his villa in the countryside. So she had a reprieve from him, at least.

The one thing Bianca could do right now was to call Franny to tell her of the revised plans. "Give Tia a kiss from me," Bianca said before hanging up. She reflected that Franny and Doris Ofstetler were a godsend. And in Bianca's life, at least lately, godsends had been in short supply.

Bianca rushed through her shower and blow-dried her hair in record time. Why'd Neill decide he wanted to play tennis? And with her? And what kind of tennis was he into? Elegant tennis, like her mother had played at the spiffy tennis club in Lake Forest? Savage tennis, the way she and Eric had played as kids? Or bat-the-ball-back-and-forth pretend tennis where no one worked up a sweat, like Bianca used to play with Caroline?

But okay, so she'd play whatever kind of tennis was required with Neill if that was what it took to get through this wedding. This was Day Two. Once today was over, there would be only two more days to go. She'd make it. She'd have to.

And then she'd deal with Vittorio. And decide about D'Alessandro's gemstone line. And check on the fall previews for the fashion magazines and the show that was scheduled for New York in October to introduce a popular-priced line of jewelry and maybe, just maybe, she'd design a few new pieces. These thoughts reminded her that yes, she had her own life separate and apart from all these people at the wedding. And she'd be returning to it soon, thank God.

When Neill knocked on her door again, she threw it open with a sweet smile despite the fact that underneath she felt steely and resolute. She was more determined than ever that he wouldn't learn about the many conflicting emotions at play under the surface of her smooth facade.

Neill whipped a tennis racquet from behind his back. "It's Winnie's," he said. "You wouldn't believe what I had to go through to get it."

"Oh, wouldn't I?" Bianca said, again bowled over by the way he looked. She might as well get used to the idea that she couldn't make herself immune to his charm, not unless someone somehow produced a vaccination to protect women from men like Neill Bellamy. He wore his charm, good looks, and wealth like a talisman to overcome whatever resistance sprang up in his path. His rugged tan was set off by classic tennis whites, and a white cable-knit sweater was knotted around his shoulders. He looked like the old Neill, the one she'd known in the days before he'd run away to South America to make his fortune. Bianca's heart warmed to him, but then that was nothing new. Something was always heating up when he was around.

"I think you're supposed to either come out or invite me in," Neill said. He was looking at her with admiring eyes whose gaze swept her from head to toe, never mind that she noticed and he noticed that she noticed. She was wearing white shorts and a white polo shirt; nothing fancy.

To divert him, she adopted a lighthearted tone. "Let's face it—that Swiss finishing school didn't teach me anything about manners except how to pour tea and serve crumpets. I suppose you might as well come in for a minute. And let me see that racquet," she said. She unzipped it from its case and swished it through the air, trying it out. The racquet was nicely balanced and felt comfortable in her hand.

"Will it do?"

"I'll manage. Come on, let's go." Suddenly she wanted Neill out of her room. Sharing her personal space with him was too uncomfortable, and the unmade bed made her think thoughts that would be better off unthought.

"You used to be a pretty good tennis player," Neill said as she pulled the door to her room shut behind her.

"*Used* to be? I'll still beat the socks off you," she told him with a challenging grin over her shoulder.

"You always claimed that you could beat the pants off me," he said slyly.

Bianca felt her cheeks flush and was grateful for the

narrow hallway that didn't allow them to walk beside each other or see each other's faces. "I'll leave beating the pants off you to Winnie," she said.

Neill laughed. "No chance. I had to sit with her at breakfast and listen to an extremely boring account of her debutante ball. She wore the funkiest white dress, and it was the funkiest ball, and the men were funky, and she's sure that no wedding could top that funky time in her life, which is why she's never getting married. Come to think of it, maybe she's a pretty smart girl at that."

"Fun-*ky*," said Bianca.

Neill punched her shoulder playfully. "Don't say that word again upon pain of death," he told her, and she glanced back at him, unable to keep from laughing.

They had reached the lobby with its bowls of fresh flowers, highly polished brass doorknobs and collection of antique furniture. No one was there except the properly deferential assistant-assistant manager, thank goodness, so they didn't have to stop and make empty conversation with other members of the wedding party; they quickly moved through the lobby to the terrace. A brick path wound through a forested area toward the tennis courts and swimming pool. Once they were out of the building, it seemed awkward not to talk.

"So Winnie doesn't want to get married?" Bianca said.

"No, I think she just likes the chase."

"I predict that eventually she'll tire of it."

"Oh? Some people never do."

"Men. You're talking about men."

"Well, hey, it's a gender I know firsthand," Neill said.

"A lot of people—men and women—prefer to settle down after a while," Bianca said carefully.

"And get married?"

"Sure."

"Everyone to his own taste, said the old lady as she kissed the cow." Neill looked determined not to argue.

"My mother certainly likes being married. Her problem is staying married." Bianca offered this with a wry little smile.

"Maybe her current marriage will work. I've always liked your mother. She's interesting and fun."

"I don't think your father thought so," Bianca retorted.

Neill shrugged. "Who knows what their problem was? Unless it was Dad." He laughed, startling a couple ahead of them on the path. When they broke apart and started toward them, Bianca recognized Kevin and Suzie, the girl she'd seen working behind the desk in the lobby when she checked in.

"Where's everyone this morning?" Neill called to Kevin.

"If you mean Nana, I don't know. Some of the women are shopping, Caroline's with her parents, Eric's sleeping late and I have no idea where Lizzie or any of those odd friends she brought are. Joe is also missing. As for me, you haven't seen me." Kevin winked, and the girl smiled up at him. They ambled on through the woods, their shoulders brushing.

"Looks like we've got the courts to ourselves," Neill said as Bianca took her position on the opposite side of the net. "Too bad, because I'd like to have an audience to watch me win."

Bianca accepted the challenge. "In your dreams," she said. She met his first serve with a solid forehand swing, and after that she was so intent on the game that she didn't think about anything but winning. Since she hadn't played since the baby had been born and for some time before, her muscles had lost tone. Her serves were still at the top of her form, but Neill was a worthy opponent.

It turned out to be elegant tennis, reminiscent of their Lake Forest days. Neill won the first set, but she pulled herself together and won the second. In her first serve of the next game, a string on Bianca's borrowed racquet broke.

"Well," she said ruefully, "so much for tennis. Winnie's going to love me for this."

"Don't worry, I'll drop it off at a shop in town and have it fixed before she even knows it's broken. That was fun, Bianca. I don't get many chances to play tennis in the part of the world where I live."

Bianca wondered what he'd think about her game if he knew that she'd had a baby only three months before. But, "You did fine," was all she said. She wondered why she'd let herself be manipulated into playing tennis in the first place. Her knees were so shaky she couldn't believe Neill hadn't noticed. But she had proved she could still play, and she had gained Neill's respect. In this area at least.

She resisted the urge to suggest a moment's rest at one of the tables near the court. Instead she slid the racquet back into its case and handed it to Neill.

"Why don't we eat an early lunch? Or brunch?" Neill suggested, following her as she headed for the path.

Bianca was hungry; she'd barely had time to gulp down a cup of coffee in her room earlier, and playing tennis had taken every bit of energy she had. But there was Tia to consider.

"I don't think so, Neill," she said.

The woods as they passed through were quiet and provided a cool respite as they walked between leafy oaks and maples. From the swimming pool nearby they heard the laughter of children accompanied by much splashing.

As they traversed the terrace past the open door to the hotel dining room, Neill stopped. "Let's take a look at the menu," he said. It was posted on a stand next to the door.

"I really have to run along," Bianca said, although running wasn't a method of locomotion that was an option right now. Her calf muscles were protesting big-time.

Neill was apparently in no mood to take no for an answer. "There's eggs Benedict on the menu, and I'll bet the hollandaise sauce is great right here in the middle of Wisconsin dairy country. You used to love eggs Benedict, and Ursula would make it as a special treat when I was home from college. Remember, she and Dad always drank mimosas with it."

As he spoke Bianca was transported back to those days. During the warm summer months, the five of them had often eaten brunch on the patio of the big Bellamy house, and she had hidden her attraction to Neill Bellamy behind a charade of teenage flightiness.

"Once Eric and I poured champagne into our orange juice like Mother and Budge did, and they never even noticed," she said.

"Is that the time when you two decided to take a joyride on the gardener's riding mower and ended up lopping off the tops of Dad's prize bearded irises?"

Bianca was surprised that Neill remembered that, although she supposed that was one of their more memorable mornings as a family. "No, when we were sneaking champagne we didn't want anyone to know we'd been imbibing, so we acted very dignified," Bianca said, remembering. On the morning of the mower incident she and Eric had idly been waiting outside for brunch to be served and had wandered into the gardener's shed where the lawn mower was stored. They'd wanted to see how fast it would go. Too fast, unfortunately; Budge had been livid.

That time seemed so far away, so simple. And yet it had been anything but.

"Why, Ms. D'Alessandro, how nice to see you!" Franny's mother, Doris, wearing a pleasant smile to go along with her waitress uniform, finished setting a table on the terrace.

"I didn't know you worked here," Bianca said.

"Well, with two kids still in college and another set to go in the fall, every little bit of money helps. I hope you're planning to eat brunch with us this morning."

"Definitely," Neill said, and, with a flourish, he held out a chair for Bianca. Suddenly her hunger was overwhelming; she astonished herself by sitting down, and Neill joined her.

"I'll bring your water in a minute and send your server right out," said Mrs. Ofstetler. *Better send cold packs for my knees, too,* Bianca added to herself as she surreptitiously massaged one of them under the table.

Neill tossed his sweater across the back of a neighboring chair. "Now. How about explaining this nonsense that you and Eric knew how to be dignified?" he said, smiling at her.

Bianca made herself act as if his smile had no effect

at all on her, which was anything but true. She concentrated on his question.

"Oh, Eric and I managed to be dignified once or twice in those days, but the day we pretended we were racing the lawn mower in the Indy 500 wasn't one of the occasions."

Neill seemed eager to reminisce, which surprised Bianca. She wouldn't have expected someone so averse to family life to relish such memories. "Maybe," he said, "after all these years you can tell me why you pushed Eric into the koi pool that time. He was sure angry afterward."

"I pushed him because he was making faces. Like this," Bianca said, and she drew her cheeks in and opened her eyes wide, moving her lips in a perfect imitation of Japanese carp.

Neill started to laugh, and the waiter approaching their table stopped in his tracks and stared. Bianca quickly pulled a straight face and tried to look nonchalant, even though the waiter seemed transfixed.

Neill ordered mimosas and eggs Benedict for both of them, and after the waiter left, he leaned across the table. "That was a pretty realistic imitation," he said.

"You should see me do my impersonation of Petsy," Bianca said.

"Go ahead."

Bianca shook her head. "If I'm not mistaken, dear Petsy is heading our way. Let's hope she doesn't decide to be sociable."

Neill turned slightly and waved with a marked lack of enthusiasm. "She has Lambie and Fawn with her."

Bianca swiveled and treated them to her own lackluster wave. Petsy bared her teeth in what passed for a smile.

"We went to see the horses at the stable," shouted Lambie.

"This big, big horse named Maisie slobbered green stuff all over my hand," said Fawn.

"That's because Fawn gave her a sugar lump. Horses always do that when you give them a sugar lump."

"Yug," said Fawn, plainly disgusted.

Lambie shoved Fawn. "I'm going to ride that horse Maisie if they'll let me. She's for children."

"Both of you quit shouting, stop pushing and keep moving," Petsy said, clearly put out. They disappeared around the corner of the building.

"Talk about someone I'd like to slam-dunk into a fish pond," Bianca said.

"Me, too," Neill told her. "I pity Petsy's poor husband. He didn't come to the wedding, by the way."

"He found a way out of it? Smart fellow."

"Not too smart. He married Petsy, remember? However, they're splitting up."

"Well, he must have been in love with her once."

"Lots of people fall in love," Neill said as the waiter appeared with their order.

"I wonder if—" Bianca began, then reconsidered.

"Go ahead," Neill said. His eyes on her were steady, inquiring.

"If our parents loved each other when they got married," she said.

"Of course they did. They were nuts about each other. All you had to do was look at them in those days and you could tell."

"Was that love—or sexual attraction?"

"Both," Neill said. For a moment it seemed as if he

would elaborate, but then he appeared to think better of the idea and became quiet.

Bianca was feeling in a pensive mood as well, although it was time, she thought, for a change in topics. She delved into the food on her plate.

"The hollandaise sauce is good," she said after her first taste. "Not made from a mix. Rich and with exactly the right amount of tartness." *Like Neill,* she thought involuntarily, and she almost laughed.

"So I get credit for being right about the hollandaise at least?" Neill was teasing her again.

"You were probably right about Mother and Budge's being in love, too," she conceded, thinking before the words were even out of her mouth that she couldn't seem to stay off what was a touchy subject. "I don't remember much about their marriage. I suppose I was focused only on my own all-important teenage self."

"You were more or less insufferable at times," Neill said, and even as she bristled he smiled at her. "So was I," he added. "A big bad college man and intent on impressing everyone with my importance."

"You were—" But she couldn't say it. She couldn't tell him how she'd idolized him in those days. Even now she couldn't. Especially now. "You were hardly ever home."

"I think I was around enough to know that as far as Dad and your mother are concerned, things probably would have stayed all right between them if they hadn't gotten married," Neill said.

"Spoken from the perspective of a big bad college man? Or the wise adult you are now?" She smiled at him to show that she wasn't being confrontational, was merely interested in his opinion.

"This is the wise adult speaking. The jaded, outspoken adult who probably should keep his mouth shut."

"If our parents hadn't married, I'd never have met Eric. Or you," Bianca said, almost involuntarily. *Nor would I have had Tia,* she added silently.

"I'm not sure about that," he said. "What if Ursula and Dad had decided merely to live together? You and Eric and I couldn't have avoided knowing each other."

"So you're saying that it's better to live together— what's the phrase? 'Without the benefit of marriage'?"

"For a Bellamy, maybe so. I suppose Dad and Ursula couldn't merely cohabit; they would have worried about setting a bad example for us." He managed a curt laugh. "As it is, they turned into one more miserable example of why marriage can be a bad idea."

Bianca toyed with the napkin in her lap. "What is this Bellamy curse you keep harping about?" she asked. They were treading on shaky ground here, she thought, but she found herself wanting to know more about how Neill's mind worked. All those years admiring him from afar, all those years daydreaming about him, and she didn't really know the person he'd become. She was the mother of his child and she hardly knew who he was.

"You don't think my dad's a good example of the Bellamy curse in action?" Neill said, eyebrows lifted.

She struggled for a light reply. She'd never cared for Budge Bellamy. "Well, look at it this way. Budge is not cursed but blessed to have been married to four wonderful women."

"Uh, right," was Neill's response, but he was looking at her as if she were out of her mind.

Bianca decided to elaborate. "It would have been nice if Budge could have stayed married to your mother. It would be nice if all marriages worked out. But lots of marriages fail these days, Neill. Not just your father's. Not just Bellamy marriages.'' She thought about her mother, currently ecstatic about her new husband. It must be wonderful to feel so much in love—and so loved—that you'd want to spend the rest of your life with someone. Or would try to, anyway.

"Well," Neill said tersely, "this is one Bellamy who isn't going to marry. If it *is* a curse, it ends right here."

Bianca gazed over the tops of the trees. A few puffy white clouds hung suspended from a serene blue sky. "Then you'll never know if it could work for you," she said quietly.

"Why are we talking about me? You don't seem like the marrying type any more than I do."

She forced herself to look straight at him. "I haven't noticed anyone proposing," she said in her most matter-of-fact manner.

"Are you so busy with your business that you don't have time for men in your life?"

It was true that D'Alessandro absorbed a great deal of time. She was busy with Tia. And she hadn't been interested in other men since that night in the gazebo. How could she be when it was this man she wanted, this man she'd always wanted?

"Well?" Neill was staring at her from beneath a furrowed brow, his eyes so intent on her face that she almost flinched. And yet she found herself wanting him to look at her that way forever, to absorb his expression and create from it the hope that he might really care for her.

It would never happen, and suddenly she knew she couldn't stand any more of this. It was time to cut and run.

"I really have to go," she said. She stood and tossed her napkin down, unheedful of where it fell.

Neill stood too, polite and perplexed. "I'm going to drive into town for a while this afternoon. Why don't you go with me?"

Because when I'm around you, I can't think straight. Because my heart speeds up and my mouth goes dry and my knees turn to Jell-O. Well, maybe it was playing tennis that had given her the wobbly knees. And maybe not.

"There's something else I'd rather do. Thanks for the brunch, Neill." She was striving for pleasantry but her smartly clipped words ended up sounding aggrieved and snappish.

She walked swiftly across the brick patio. She'd eaten everything on her plate, but she was still hungry. Hungry for more than food.

BIANCA FLED straight to her room and called Franny, asking her to bring the baby to her. Bianca needed comfort, and in the past few months she'd learned that there was nothing more comforting than the adoration on her daughter's face when she looked up and saw her mother.

After Franny had left, Bianca nuzzled Tia's dimpled cheek. "Mommy has missed you," she crooned. "Mommy has missed you so much!" It was true; in her everyday life she was never far away from Tia even when she was working. Bianca always scheduled frequent work breaks in order to feed Tia, and she bathed the baby herself even though the nanny insisted that it was her job, not Bianca's. Bianca liked taking care of her baby. A baby was someone to love who loved you back. A baby was family, and to Bianca, who had never had a stable home life, Tia was a chance to establish one at last.

This afternoon Tia was in fine form and apparently recovered from her jet lag. She laughed out loud when Bianca playfully kissed her feet. Bianca held those two small feet in her hands; the webbed toes were a distinctive Bellamy characteristic. She'd always thought it pointless to attribute a baby's features to one parent or another, but she'd changed her mind once she had a baby of her own.

She traced Tia's brows with a forefinger. "These are like your uncle Eric's," she said. She touched Tia's chin. "I see your grandma Viv right here." She feathered her fingers down Tia's nose. "And this fine straight nose—well, that's so much like your daddy's," she whispered to Tia, who cooed as if overjoyed with this information.

Of course, Tia owed her pale hair, finespun as moonglow, to Bianca. And her eyes were blue like Bianca's, not dark like Neill's. Tia was a compilation of her parents' best traits. It was too bad that Neill would never know her.

When, after three hours together, Tia began to tire, Bianca opted to take her back to the Ofstetlers for a nap. And then Bianca headed for the swimming pool. She thought that perhaps an hour or so in the sun would provide a slight tan to offset the ugly pink of the bridesmaids' dresses. Oh, yes, and to provide a contrast with those cute little short white gloves Genevieve had chosen to go with them.

Neill had said he planned to go into town, so at least Bianca didn't have to worry about his showing up this afternoon. But as she entered the fenced swimming pool area, Neill Bellamy was the first person she saw.

Caught off guard, her heart swooped into the pit of her stomach and back up again.

He was wearing black swim briefs, which showed off every rippling muscle in his torso. And even though he was talking with a group of Lizzie's friends, he left them immediately and sauntered over to Bianca, who was arranging herself on one of the lounge chairs and wishing she'd gone for a long walk instead. Neill's very presence engendered a prickling excitement that she tried, by her very casualness, to dismiss.

"I thought you were going to town," she said as he approached.

"I changed my mind. Guess what?" he said brightly. Too brightly, it seemed to Bianca, and the smile on his lips was negated by the calculated manner in which he sat down on the chair beside her and narrowed his eyes.

Her heart started to hammer against her ribs. She coolly removed a bottle of suntan lotion from her tote bag. "I can't imagine," she said as though she couldn't have cared less.

Neill's lips curved into a thin smile. He leaned closer, invading her personal space. His eyes seemed to burn holes in her own.

"I had a little chat with Doris Ofstetler after you left the restaurant. And guess what?"

"What?" Bianca said, her voice no more than a whisper.

"Her daughter's name is Franny. And you know what else?"

Bianca didn't speak.

"She doesn't have a baby. Bianca, what the hell is going on?"

Chapter Six

The bottle of suntan lotion toppled onto the hard surface of the pool surround. Bianca bent to pick it up, grateful for the fact that Neill could not see the anguish on her face. This was it. Bianca wondered if Meryl Streep ever got sick to her stomach when she was about to act a big scene. And this was probably the biggest scene in Bianca's whole life.

"I never told you Franny had a baby." She was so cool that butter wouldn't have melted in her mouth. She was way beyond cool.

Neill subsided into what Bianca decided was shocked silence. She'd diverted him. But before she got to feeling too smug, she'd divert him a little more.

She rolled over on her stomach. "I don't suppose you could rub suntan lotion on my back," she mumbled.

She kept her eyes closed, but she heard Neill picking up the lotion, and in a few moments she felt his fingers administering the smooth cool liquid to the skin between her shoulders.

"So, Bianca, exactly what does Franny have to do with that baby you were toting around?" His tone was conversational, but he was rubbing her back too hard.

She made herself draw a deep breath. "You can put the lotion away now. Just drop it in my tote bag. Thanks, and now I'm going to clear my mind of everything, including this wedding and you."

Neill's deep voice had a hard edge to it. "You didn't answer my question. How about if we play twenty questions? You and Eric always used to like that game."

Twenty questions! He wasn't going to let her wiggle out of this. Her mind raced like a rat in a maze, frantic because it kept flinging itself up against painful dead ends. Neill already knew Franny wasn't Tia's mother. But he didn't know that she, Bianca, was. If she refused to tell him Franny's involvement in this mess, his curiosity might be so piqued that he'd start asking other people.

Okay, so no one except Eric knew that she, Bianca, had given birth to a baby. But Petsy might have suspicions. And Petsy didn't like her. On the other hand, no one in the wedding party had actually seen Tia since yesterday. Bianca, if pressed, might be able to make a good case for the baby's being someone's besides Franny's. But whose? And if Neill later caught a glimpse of Bianca with the baby, that would only inflame his curiosity even more.

Conclusion, reluctantly reached: she couldn't lie. He'd catch her.

A long silence, then longer. Finally, "Franny's the baby-sitter," Bianca said helplessly.

"If there's a baby-sitter, she must have been hired by the baby's parents. Or perhaps grandparents. And as far as I know, no one here is showing anyone else baby pictures. People do that, you know. So what we have is one baby, one baby-sitter, and no parents. Correct me if I'm wrong, Bianca, but I think I smell a rat.''

He was right about that. The rat was still running the maze. And there were still no outs.

Bianca squeezed her eyes tightly shut. Suddenly the sun seemed too warm, the sound of the children playing in the pool seemed too loud, and Neill seemed too...there.

She had been a fool to think this would work.

"All right," she said, keeping her eyes closed. She couldn't think of the best way to word this; she couldn't think, period.

"All right what?"

"The baby is..." she said, but the words stuck in her throat.

Neill snorted. "The baby *is*. An unrefutable fact. She's a lovely baby. But whose baby is she?''

"Mine," Bianca said in a small voice.

Neill didn't speak. Bianca kept her head hidden in the crook of her arm. The piña colada scent of the suntan lotion that he had spread on so liberally threatened to make her throw up.

Neill let out an explosive long breath, more than a sigh, less than an exclamation. He stood and began to pace to and fro.

"The baby is yours."

"Yes."

She could see his bare feet and characteristic webbed toes through the spaces between the woven ribbing of the lounge that now seemed to be cutting into her hips, her breasts, the tender skin of her ankles. She heard his quick indrawn breath and lifted her head to the red glare of the sun. Neill had stopped pacing. He was staring at her in disbelief, his eyes a flash of dark fire.

"You had a *baby?*" he said incredulously.

Through the buzz in her ears she said, "Don't say it quite so loudly. I wasn't planning on announcing it to everyone at this pool. I wasn't planning on announcing it at all."

"And whose baby is it?"

The words echoed in the hollow place in her heart. "Mine," she repeated.

This brought about a long silence.

"Right," Neill said at last. "It used to take two to make a baby. I'm aware that scientists are cloning sheep and frogs and who knows what else, but I think I can safely assume that you didn't clone your daughter. That brings up the inevitable question: Who's the father?" He stood before her, his hands resting on his hips, his eyebrows drawn together in an expression of intense scrutiny laced with something else—bewilderment.

It's your baby, stupid! Bianca's vision exploded into a crimson blur as the words careened through her head, and for a moment she thought she might have screamed them at him. How could he be so dense, how could he not know? And yet even as her mind grappled with the complexities of the situation, she knew that when she'd walked away from Swan's Folly a year ago, when she'd refused to have further contact with him, when she'd decided not to tell him that he'd fathered a child, she had let Neill Bellamy off the hook. Maybe he should suspect, but clearly he didn't.

"None of your business," she said flatly.

Neill raked a hand through his hair. He blinked, then shook his head as if to clear it. "I suppose you're right," he said finally. Bianca laid her head back down and willed him to go away. To get out of her space, out of her life. To let her experience her pain the way she'd been experiencing it all along—alone. Utterly, completely, and awfully alone.

"Does Eric know?" he asked in a low, urgent tone.

Bianca squeezed her eyes tight against the pain behind her eyelids. "Yes," she said.

"He never—" but Neill was interrupted by Rhonda of the teased and over-frosted hair, his father's present wife, who dashed up and clutched his arm.

"Neill, oh Neill," she said. "I have to run back to the hotel for a few minutes. Budge asked me to call his assistant and tell her to fax him some important papers, and I forgot all about it. Will you keep an eye on Fawn and Lambie? They're paddling around in the shallow end of the pool, and you promised you'd show them some secrets about swimming. I'll only be gone a few minutes." Rhonda looked harried; it was well-known that she was eternally grateful to Budge for promoting her from her position as his personal secretary to that of his fifth wife, and she always seemed to be trying extra hard to measure up to the role.

"All right," Neill said, anything but eager.

"Thanks, Neill. Fawn adores you. Lambie, too. Hi, Bianca. Maybe we can chat later," Rhonda added over her shoulder as she clomped away on her expensive European clogs, which were definitely at odds with her short polyester pool cover-up.

"And maybe *we* can chat later too," Neill said pointedly to Bianca.

"There's nothing to talk about," Bianca returned, injecting as much frostiness into her tone as possible.

"In my opinion there is." With that, Neill squared his shoulders and marched toward the swimming pool.

Bianca buried her face in her hands. Neill had taken

the news as well as could be expected, but what in the world would she say when he wanted to discuss the situation further? She felt depressed just thinking about it; there was no doubt in her mind that Neill would guess the truth. He must already have some idea that Tia was his child. Unless he had forgotten what happened in the gazebo that night.

Or unless...

Unless he thought he couldn't father a child.

Bianca's heart stalled, caught in a cage of memory, lost in a flurry of what ifs. Bits and pieces of forgotten conversation began to surface, floating to and fro in her mind like so many feathers.

There *had* been feathers on that day, and Ursula had forbidden the household help to assist in the task of stuffing them back in the couch pillows. Bianca and Eric had engaged in a no-holds-barred pillow fight earlier that morning, buffeting each other with the cushy down pillows from the couch, and one of the pillows had ripped open at the seam and filled the elegant living room with what seemed like buckets of white feathers.

Ursula had been furious, and Bianca and Eric had contritely gone about the task of cleaning up. When they had stuffed most of the feathers back inside the pillow, Bianca, who could sew in a rudimentary way, took upon herself the task of repairing the seam, and Eric had disappeared in search of a vacuum cleaner for rounding up the last little bits of white fluff from furniture, carpet and draperies.

That was when Viv, Neill and Eric's mother, had stopped by.

Viv and Ursula were friendly, and Bianca was accustomed to seeing Viv around the house, especially

when Viv came to pick up Eric for the weekends that
he often spent with her. But this time, instead of chattering about Neill's accomplishments at Harvard or
Eric's latest scrape, the two women had carried their
cups of coffee into the library and begun talking in
hushed tones.

Bianca listened unashamedly. And what she'd heard
hadn't seemed like any big whoop. She'd already been
disappointed to learn that Neill wouldn't be home from
college for spring break because he was sick. He had
the mumps. *Big deal,* Bianca thought. Mumps was a
silly childhood disease and hardly anyone got it anymore. All she could think about at the time was that it
was a stroke of bad luck for her that Neill wouldn't be
home. She'd been counting on the chance to impress
him in hopes that he'd be interested in her for once.

"He said he feels fine," Viv was saying to Ursula,
"but Neill rarely complains."

"I'm sure you did the right thing by telling him to
stay at school," Ursula replied in her slightly accented
English. "After all, we wouldn't want Eric to get
mumps, too."

"I thought both boys were vaccinated when they
were little, so I never dreamed that either one of them
was susceptible," said Viv. "Now I find out that Eric
was immunized but Neill wasn't. And I worry because
mumps can be so serious in a man."

"Ah, but Neill, he's very strong. I think there will
not be any problem."

Viv bent closer. "I knew someone who had mumps
as a teenager. He never could father children."

"Of course, there might have been some problem
with his wife's fertility."

"No, no, the doctor said it was his low sperm count."

"But Vivian, the disease must spread to—well, you know, a certain part of a man's anatomy—in order to affect sperm count." Ursula, though not prudish, had an aversion to naming specific male body parts, at least in English. She said they sounded better in German.

"It *has* spread. Both sides," and here Viv's usually strident voice dropped so low that Bianca couldn't hear the rest of the conversation.

This was the first Bianca had ever heard of mumps affecting a man's fertility. But the hush-hush aspects of the conversation had aroused her curiosity so much that she'd immediately looked up this fascinating sexual fact in a health encyclopedia from Budge's library. She'd learned that in men and postadolescent boys, mumps could spread to the testicles and cause problems with sperm production later.

Of course she'd confided in Eric about what she'd overheard and about looking it up in a book; of course Eric had thought Viv and Ursula were making much ado about nothing.

That summer Neill had come home and divided his time between their house and Viv's for a couple of months, and no one even referred to his bout with the mumps. Bianca hadn't thought of it since.

Well, now *she* knew he wasn't infertile. He was the only man who *could* have fathered her child.

But did Neill think he was incapable of having children? A thought occurred to her, one that was staggering in its implications. Maybe Neill's attitude toward family life wasn't only the result of his father's many marriage failures. Maybe he didn't think that having a family was an option for him and so he had either consciously or subconsciously chosen to avoid putting himself into a position where he'd have to prove himself.

In that case, she was dealing with a lot more here than she'd originally thought. And how she handled the situation would determine the outcome of her life and Tia's on so many levels that the implications were mind-boggling.

While she'd been running her mind through these hoops, Neill had been dealing with another kind of hoop. When Bianca finally lifted her head, she saw Neill coaching Lambie in the proper way to toss the basketball into the floating net.

He's good with kids, she thought in surprise. Somehow deep down she'd known this, but she'd never actually seen evidence of it. The fact made the situation—or what she now suspected the situation to be— even more poignant.

Lambie was standing on the wide pool steps, squealing every time he threw the ball. A determined Fawn was paddling nearby, oblivious to everyone else. Neill said, "Fawn, you're doing great. We'll practice breathing later, okay? Then you'll be ready to learn a new stroke."

"Okay," Fawn said, heading for the opposite side of the pool.

"I'm tired of basketball. I want to swim," Lambie said.

Neill relieved him of the ball and stowed it in the basket. "Just remember to kick hard, Lambie. If you do that, you'll be as fast a swimmer as Fawn."

"I'm going to be faster, not like yesterday in the pond when I fooled Joe," Lambie said before pushing off from the steps. Although he churned up the water like a hurricane, he was clearly not as proficient as Fawn, who was attempting something approximating a breaststroke.

While Fawn and Lambie swam, an older boy poised and prepared to dive from the high diving board at the opposite end of the pool. "Watch me, Mom!" he hollered at the last minute, and a woman watching from a chair nearby said, "Take it easy, son," as he flung himself into the air. Bianca's attention, like everyone else's, was riveted on the boy as he dived arrow-straight into the water. Bystanders clapped, and the lifeguard, who seemed to be a friend of the diver's, bent over to give him a congratulatory lift up the ladder.

At the other end of the pool, Bianca caught a glimpse of a small upflung hand in the middle of the maelstrom created by Lambie's flailing strokes. Her head swung around as her eyes scanned the surface of the pool searching for Fawn. But Fawn wasn't there.

Bianca bolted upright. If not swimming, Fawn should be clinging to the side of the pool. And no one was at that end of the pool—only Lambie, isolated in a patch of turbulent water, his expression one of sheer terror. Something was wrong, terribly wrong.

She shot out of her seat, but Neill was there first. It took him only a few well-measured and swift strokes to reach the boy, and as he did, Bianca saw Fawn's face surface immediately below Lambie's.

As Bianca ran, Neill pulled the two children apart, and only then did Bianca see what had happened. Lambie had latched onto Fawn and yanked her under.

"Easy," Neill said to Lambie, who was clinging to his neck and crying unintelligibly. With his free arm,

Neill eased Fawn over to the side of the pool where she clung gasping.

Bianca jumped into the pool beside Fawn. "Are you okay?" she asked.

"I was—swimming and—Lambie grabbed me. He—pushed me under. I couldn't breathe."

Neill, still holding Lambie, said quietly to Bianca, "Lambie panicked. He grabbed onto the first person he saw, and it happened to be Fawn."

The lifeguard, looking frantic, bore down upon them. "Is everything okay? I only looked away for a minute—"

"That's all it takes," Neill said sternly.

"Let's get you out of the pool, Fawn," Bianca said while Neill continued his lecture to the lifeguard. At that moment Rhonda clattered up, clearly beside herself. "I saw it. I saw it all! I thought my Fawn was going to drown, and she would have if it hadn't been for Neill." Her face was ashen.

By this time, Bianca had led Fawn up the steps of the pool. Rhonda bent and embraced her child, kissing her wet face, smoothing her hair off her brow, murmuring solicitously.

Neill, now that the chastened lifeguard had returned to his post, was working to calm the still-distraught Lambie. "It's okay, sport. Fawn's fine, but that was a dangerous thing you did. You've got to be more careful around water."

"I know," Lambie wailed. "Fawn, I didn't mean to hurt you. I got scared."

Rhonda, calmer now, said quietly, "I hate to think what might have happened if it hadn't been for you, Neill. I can't tell you how much this means to me."

A woman who had noticed the action in the pool walked up and congratulated Neill.

"That was a fine thing you did. No one else was watching the kids. The little girl might have drowned."

"I'd better take both kids back to the hotel. That's enough swimming for all of us for one day," Rhonda said.

"I'll go with you," Neill said. "Hey, maybe what we all really need is an ice-cream cone. I know someone in the kitchen of the hotel who makes the best ones ever. What flavor does everyone want?"

"Chocolate!" said Fawn, now recovered from her ordeal.

"Strawberry bubble gum banana!" said Lambie.

"Bianca?" said Neill.

The incident had shaken Bianca to the core. There had been so many people around, and yet in seconds, with everyone's attention diverted by the diver, the kids could have drowned. It made her own daughter's life seem all the more precious to her, and she wanted nothing so much as to hold Tia in her arms.

"I—I don't think so," Bianca said.

"You're sure?"

"Positive."

"I want to talk to you." Neill's eyes locked with hers for one interminable moment, and then, still carrying Lambie, he followed Rhonda out of the pool area.

Bianca knew without a doubt that there would be no avoiding a confrontation. The question she couldn't help asking herself was, if Neill were to find out that he was Tia's father, would he be delighted to know that he was capable of fathering a child?

"HEY! Aren't you Bianca?"

Bianca, who had showered and changed into a light

summer dress after leaving the pool, was passing through a fringe of trees on the way to the Ofstetlers' an hour or so later when she was hailed by a woman's voice from behind the Folly. She stopped in her tracks and shaded her eyes against the glare of the setting sun.

A head followed by a body popped around a corner of jagged masonry. The head wore long thick curly reddish hair; the body wore a scooped-neck smock made of crushed velvet. The zany effect was something like Little Lord Fauntleroy meets Knute Rockne, but Bianca had to admit that it was stylish—very stylish. This was one of the friends Lizzie Muldoon had brought to the wedding.

"I'm Saffron Schrempf. This is my brother Storm." The woman, smiling affably, held out her hand.

"I'm happy to meet you," Bianca said. She couldn't help staring at Storm. Even at long range, he'd been an amazingly fine physical specimen with those bulging biceps and undulating pectorals. Close up, with those assets spiffily displayed in a skintight white T-shirt, he was spectacular.

"Isn't this wedding a hoot?" he said. "You'd think Genevieve Knox walks around with an iron rod up her—"

"Storm," Saffron said warningly.

"You agree with me," Storm said, sounding slightly miffed.

Bianca suppressed a smile. "So do a few other people in this wedding party," she said. "What do you think of Swan's Folly?" she asked brightly.

"Pretty fancy place. I'm going back to the hotel and steam my dress for the bachelorette party tonight," Saffron said. "And I need to talk to Zurik." With a grin and a wave, Saffron set off in the direction of the hotel.

"Who's Zurik?" Bianca asked Storm.

"Alexander Zurik. A painter of the artsy-smartsy school. Lizzie hired him to paint a portrait of Caroline and Eric as a wedding present, but he hasn't finished it yet and came along with us to soak up wedding vibes."

"Oh, well...that's nice... If you'll excuse me," she said, turning resolutely toward the light-stippled path beneath the trees.

"Mind if I walk along with you?" Storm beamed his brilliant smile in her direction, revealing two rows of perfectly capped teeth. She nodded and Storm fell into step beside her. He regarded her seriously. "Have you heard the rumors about a jewel thief?" he asked.

"Jewel thief? At Swan's Folly?"

"That's what I heard. Rumors are flying. 'Course, I think it's a reaction to all this security at the hotel, you know, because it's a society wedding and the guests could be an easy mark. I heard somebody's going into peoples' rooms and dumping their jewelry out on the bed, but the funny thing is, nothing's missing."

"Neill did mention something about a burglary before he arrived."

"And get this—Caroline's mother keeps rattling on about kidnappers."

"What with the person who's going into rooms looking at jewelry, I'm not surprised Gen has jacked up security."

"Yeah, that Genevieve, she's a case, all right."

"Well, Storm, I couldn't agree with you more," Bianca said, wondering how to get rid of Storm before they reached the Ofstetlers' house. They hadn't yet arrived at the point where the path forked in that direction, but they would soon.

"Yoo-hoo! Storm! Bianca!" As they rounded the bend and emerged from the sheltering trees, they saw Winnie in a small rowboat skimming slowly across the pond. She shipped the oars and began to wave strenuously, threatening to sink the boat.

"Would you two like to take the boat out next?" fluted Winnie in her high clear voice. "I'm going to shove it up on the bank over there when I'm through."

"No, thanks. It's getting late," Bianca answered.

"Storm, maybe you and I should paddle around for a while." Winnie treated him to her trademark eyelash flutter.

"Not me, Winnie," he called back. Thankfully, before she could speak to them again, he and Bianca put several willow trees between them and the woman in the boat.

"So anyway, Bianca, it was nice to meet you. I think I'll check out the stables." Storm treated her to a fascinating ripple of his fabulous chest muscles and speeded up along the path, humming tunelessly as he left her behind.

Bianca was eager to see Tia, and maybe if she hurried, there'd be time to take the baby for a walk in her pram. She wouldn't head in the direction of the hotel; instead she'd explore the old apple orchard behind the Ofstetlers' house. There, at least, she'd be unlikely to run into Neill or anyone else from the wedding party.

Chapter Seven

After treating the kids to ice cream, Neill felt at loose
ends. He went to Bianca's room and knocked on the
door, but if she was in there, she wasn't answering.

Maybe she was out with the baby. He wondered
where the baby-sitter lived. He thought of asking at the
front desk, but he didn't want to create any problems
for Bianca, who had gone to such great lengths to keep
the baby out of sight.

Neill understood Bianca's thinking, or at least he
thought he did. Genevieve, who prided herself on being
able to recite chapter and verse of *Miss Primm's
Proper Etiquette Book,* would take a dim view of anyone who chose to become a single mother, especially
Bianca. Genevieve would take an even dimmer view
of her bringing a baby to Caroline's wedding. Also,
Genevieve would probably see the move as an attempt
on Bianca's part to upstage Caroline.

And then there was Eric. He wouldn't want the baby
around, either, especially if it was his child. Neill had
begun to harbor the thought that the trouble between
Eric and Caroline had to do with Bianca and her baby.
He tried to push the idea away, but it niggled at the
edges of his mind.

Like most of the other single male members of the wedding party, Neill was lodged in one of several picturesque small houses across the pond from the main hotel. When he couldn't find Bianca, he went to his lodging, cozily named Mulberry Cottage, and jumped in the shower, where he continued what might be a pointless conversation with himself.

Was Tia Eric's child? It was possible. Neill didn't know how to estimate a baby's age, but if Eric and Bianca had been together a year ago, it was possible for their child to be three months old. The baby didn't look as if she could sit up yet. How old did they have to be to sit up? At the same time that his mind was grappling with these questions, it struck him that Bianca would have to have a lot of gall to bring a child whom Eric had fathered to his wedding. He didn't think even Bianca had that much chutzpah.

Which opened up another possibility. Maybe Tia wasn't Eric's child. Maybe she was...his.

The thought caused him to drop the soap. He picked it up, letting the warm water spill down his chest and across his thighs, staring at the shampoo bottle on the shower ledge as if he'd never seen one before.

No. Tia couldn't be his child. It was impossible.

But was it? He and Bianca *had* made love. It had only happened one time, but it only took once to make a baby.

In his case, though, it was hard to believe that he could have fathered a child. Years ago, after the mumps he'd contracted in college, he'd wanted to know if he was capable, and his sperm count had tested so low that his doctor had deemed it extremely unlikely that Neill could impregnate anyone.

After he'd learned that fatherhood, for him, was only

a remote possibility, Neill had felt depressed and dejected, but later it seemed appropriate since he wouldn't be such a great candidate for fatherhood anyway.

His sperm count hadn't been nonexistent. It had been low. Very low. But...?

But.

Maybe the baby wasn't his. For all he knew, Bianca could have a boyfriend in Paris or Rome. Or even a husband. She'd been talking to someone named Vittorio on the phone when he'd gone by her room to pick her up for their tennis game.

Wouldn't Eric know if Bianca was involved with someone? Maybe not. Until this week, Eric and Bianca hadn't talked for a year. Maybe Vittorio was the reason. But why were Eric and Caroline barely speaking? Did that have something to do with Bianca, too?

Neill turned off the water and wrapped a towel around himself before he stepped out of the tub. For a long time he stood dripping on the bathroom floor, lost in thought as another mood stole in. It was too early to identify it, but it had something to do with Bianca and another man. He didn't like to think of her with Eric, but at least it would make sense. What Neill downright couldn't stand was the idea of her with some other guy. Vittorio. A playboy, no doubt. Someone who was only interested in her money and who wouldn't marry her.

Good thing the guy hadn't come with her. He, Neill, might feel honor-bound to flatten him. And, of course, that was exactly the kind of thing you'd expect at a Bellamy wedding, where anything could happen—and usually did.

BIANCA PUSHED the pram through a tangle of grass that had grown up in the largely unattended apple orchard and tried to think. It didn't help that Tia was fussy and refused her pacifier or that her diaper needed to be changed in midstroll. While Bianca was fastening the diaper and chattering distractedly to Tia to take the baby's mind off being uncomfortable, she couldn't avoid the thought that this year at Swan's Folly was certainly a lot different from last year at Swan's Folly. Or was it the same?

But last year! Last year had taken on a dreamlike quality in her memory. Bianca remembered how, after she'd stood for a moment on the bridge after leaving the engagement party where Genevieve had verbally attacked her, a breeze had sprung up, wafting with it the fragrance of lilacs. She'd walked slowly across to the shady area where the gazebo stood, and she'd found a bench in the shadows of the lilac bushes where she had slumped dejectedly, her hands covering her face. She couldn't help it; she'd dissolved into sobs. Genevieve had been so wrong. Bianca had never loved Eric, not in a romantic way. It had always been Neill who had fascinated her, titillated her—and ignored her.

Not that anyone knew how she felt about Neill. Eric would have made her feel ridiculous by hooting in amazement and disbelief if she'd told him she was madly in love with his big brother. Eric would have never let her forget that she'd told him, either. Ursula hadn't known, mostly because Bianca was sure she'd have confided in Vivian that her daughter was infatuated with Viv's son. And Viv might have told Neill, who would have pegged her for what she was, a silly girl in the throes of a teenage crush. On the night of Caroline and Eric's engagement party, she'd still felt like that teenage girl even though by most people's standards she was a sophisticated woman of the world.

On that night when she and Neill had ended up in the gazebo... Neill had startled her, coming upon her silently as she sat sobbing on the bench.

"Bianca?"

He had spoken so softly at first that she hadn't thought she'd heard him at all. Still, she'd know his voice anywhere. She lifted her face, tearstained and flushed, and looked directly into Neill Bellamy's eyes.

Glowing in the darkness, warm and tender in their gaze, they held a compassion that she had never noticed there before and had not considered to be a component of his personality.

"Neill, what—what are you doing here?" she stammered.

"I saw you leave and I came to see if you're all right." He moved closer so that his face, silhouetted against the moonlit Folly in the distance, became dark and enigmatic. She shivered, but not from the cold. It was because he was so close, only an arm's length away. And then he was closer because he joined her on the bench, which was so narrow that their thighs touched. A pulse started to beat in her throat.

"If it helps, I think you were right to get out of there," he said.

She glanced over at him and managed a smile through her tears. *"Thanks. Eric and I didn't mean to cause a problem this afternoon."*

"Genevieve's a nutcase. Everybody knows it," he said quietly.

Carefully blank-faced, Bianca said, *"I wish you hadn't left the party because of me."*

"I was ready. Hainsworth was preparing to offer another lengthy toast."

"And Genevieve?"

"Popping tranquilizers. As usual. Are you cold, Bianca? You're shivering."

She was trembling. She drew a deep breath, but it didn't quell the yearning that curled up from deep inside her, perhaps from the depths of her very soul.

"I'm warm enough," she said truthfully, but Neill slid a comforting arm around her shoulders anyway. The fabric of his jacket felt so good against her bare skin; she had worn a dress with slim straps and a gauzy full skirt that showed the outline of her legs when she stood in the light. Now the dress seemed heavy and weighted as well as too tight in the bodice. She felt a warm flush rising from her breasts to her throat, and she swallowed, hoping he didn't hear her.

The moon slipped out from beneath a cloud, spilling silvery light over the lilacs. Nearby a bird uttered a muffled cry, and Bianca wondered if it was one of the swans. She didn't know much about swans, how they sounded, where they lived when they weren't paddling serenely around the pond, how they mated. She imagined that swans would merge in a mighty rush of wings amid a turbulence of air but graceful all the same.

While she was thinking about the swans, Neill touched her cheek. *"Tears,"* he said.

She reached up to wipe away the moisture, and her hand met his. At his touch, she jumped as if startled, but he only twined his fingers through hers and smiled. *"There's another way to get rid of those tears,"* he said, and as she held her breath, hardly daring to believe this was happening, his lips descended, his breath warm upon her wet face. He touched his lips gently to

*her cheek, and she must have moaned because he said,
"Shh," and she did.*

*His lips were soft and warm, and she thought she
felt the tip of his tongue at the corner of her mouth as
he tasted her tears. She sat motionless, thinking that if
time were to stop at that moment, she wouldn't mind
at all. She had always wanted Neill Bellamy, and he
had always seemed unattainable.*

*And now he was kissing her and telling her she was
beautiful, and he was sweeping her hair off her neck
and letting the pale strands slide silkily through his
fingers, and he was pressing her toward him so that
their mouths met. Her eyes were wide-open at first so
that she could look into his, and she was savvy enough
to know exactly what she saw there. He wanted her,
was turned on by her, and she didn't know why or how,
only that her dream could come true. And this might
be the only chance in her lifetime that she could have
the man she'd always wanted above all others, and in
that brief but eternal moment she wanted him more
than ever.*

*He was insistent, pressing his thigh against hers,
gliding his hands around to her breasts. Trying to think
clearly, she pushed him away, surprised and then
touched to see the pain of rejection in his eyes. She
wouldn't have thought that a rebuff from her would
mean much to him. He cared. That meant everything.
She thought she should go back to the party to let
everyone know that Genevieve's remarks hadn't hurt
her at all. But they had, and here was comfort in the
person of Neill Bellamy. Why go back to what was sure
to be pure misery when she could have Neill instead?*

*She laced her fingers through his and stood, pulling
him along with her, propelled by the urgency of their*

*mutual desire. Her heart pumped, her breath quick-
ened, and the blood coursing through her veins seemed
to urge, Now, now, now!*

*When the two of them stepped into the gazebo, they
left the rest of the world far behind. She turned to Neill,
dreamlike, waiting to be enfolded in his arms, and once
there, she held her breath so that she could listen to
his heart beating beneath his clothes. It seemed to her
that her own heart sped up and synchronized its beat
with his, but that might have been pure fantasy. But
his mouth wasn't, nor was the way he pressed it to the
gentle rise of her breast above the fabric of her bodice.*

*"Oh, Neill," she said, or maybe she gasped the
words, and she pressed her hands to either side of his
face, his handsome face, and guided it upward until his
seeking lips found hers. She opened her mouth beneath
his, letting him taste her, letting him in.*

*When at last they mated, she thought she felt the rush
of air and the beating of wings, but the swans weren't
anywhere about. She was lifted out of herself, transported to a realm of grace and beauty and light. She'd
loved him in those moments; it seemed that she had
always loved him, and she knew then that Neill Bellamy
was the man with whom she wanted to spend the rest
of her life.*

*Later she had realized the hopelessness of her think-
ing. But she'd never been sorry about the time they'd
spent in the gazebo, not even when she found out he'd
made her pregnant.*

AFTER HIS SHOWER, Neill dressed and left Mulberry
Cottage. For a moment he stood watching the swans
swim along the far edge of the pond near the Folly. In
his opinion, the Folly was a foolish conceit. He'd heard

that Genevieve's great-grandfather had built it after traveling to England and observing that many English estates were embellished with similarly fanciful sham ruins. The Folly was a fitting background for Eric's wedding, though, since Neill believed that the marriage would crumble early on.

Hell, the Folly would probably still be standing in all its fake glory when the marriage was over.

Or maybe the marriage wouldn't take place. So many things could go wrong with Eric and Caroline not getting along and Bianca here with her baby and probably a lot of other things that he hadn't even heard about yet.

Who knows what to expect at a Bellamy wedding?

Neill didn't realize that he'd spoken the words out loud until he heard Eric's voice close behind him.

"Have you started talking to yourself these days?"

He wheeled around to see Eric standing there in his running shorts and a T-shirt, a damp towel draped around his neck.

Neill shrugged, trying to figure out what to say.

Eric saved him the trouble. "What's doing, big brother?" he asked, favoring him with his trademark easy grin.

"You sound relaxed," Neill replied with false heartiness.

"I'm going to get married in," and Eric consulted his watch, "about fifteen hours. Who wouldn't be?"

"A pessimist," Neill said, beginning to feel like Scrooge, W. C. Fields and Oscar the Grouch all rolled into one.

"That's you, not me."

"Last night you didn't seem so happy."

"Well, that was last night."

"So you and Caroline have made up?"

"Maybe you'd better ask Caroline. Believe me, I'll be glad when this wedding is over."

"That's understandable," Neill said. *So will I* was what he was thinking.

Eric sat down beside him. "Enjoying yourself at the hotel?"

"It's a great hotel. Mulberry Cottage and all."

"We put the groomsmen up in cottages, the women at the hotel. I thought you'd all like a little privacy." Eric winked.

"For what?"

"For whatever," Eric replied.

Neill rolled his eyes. He didn't want to engage in aimless chitchat; he wanted to ask Eric what was on his mind. But he couldn't force the words out of his mouth. No matter what was going on between Eric and Caroline and despite the fact that Neill didn't think Bellamys should marry in the first place, he didn't want to accept responsibility for the blowup of the wedding plans. At the moment, he felt like a jerk for even thinking that Bianca and Eric had ever been intimate.

Neill rose abruptly. "I've got to run, Eric."

Eric looked disconcerted. "Maybe we could—"

Neill cut him off. "No, I'm afraid not. Sorry."

He started to walk away, but Eric wasn't taking the hint. "Do you still exercise Black Jack for Winnie? Hey, why don't you exercise Winnie? She'd probably appreciate it."

"Cut it out, Eric. I'm not in the mood."

"Fine. Maybe I'll go for a swim. Leave you alone to contemplate whatever it is that's making you so damned irritable."

"What's making me so damned irritable is—oh,

never mind. Don't take it personally. Go swim." He felt jumpy, worried. He needed to marshal his thoughts before tackling Eric. Certainly he'd better censor his words.

Eric's expression was troubled. "Neill, we spend so little time together. Seems like we ought to get along for the short time we're going to be here."

Neill let out a long sigh. "I can't argue with that. All right, Eric, I'm going to lay it on the line. I want you to be straight with me."

Eric's eyes were unsuspecting. "You got it," he said.

"Bianca says she had a baby."

Those eyes shut down and clouded with a meaning that Neill wasn't sure how to interpret.

"She told you?" Incredulous words backed up by an incredulous expression.

"Yes. I saw the baby at the garden party."

Eric was silent. Neill waited, experience telling him that his younger brother would feel obligated to fill the silent void with words. But this time, that didn't happen.

"And what else did she say?" Eric was cautious, probing. As much as this surprised Neill, he forged ahead.

"The conversation was more remarkable for what she didn't say. Whether she has a husband or a boyfriend, for instance." He avoided mentioning Vittorio's name, wanting it to come from Eric.

But that's not what he got. "Damn," his brother said under his breath. Eric turned an unwavering gaze on him, and behind it Neill detected a smoldering anger. At what? Or whom?

"You're asking the wrong questions, Neill." Eric looked as if he could barely contain his fury.

"Would you mind telling me what are the right questions?"

"You're not going to find out from me," he said. He ripped the towel from his neck and started for the cottage where he was staying.

Neill clenched his fists at his sides. "Do you happen to know anyone named Vittorio?" he asked.

"I suggest that you talk to Bianca," Eric said, flinging the words back over his shoulder.

Great, thought Neill. It wasn't as though he hadn't been trying.

Well, this encounter had proved one thing. There was no point in enlisting Eric's help. His brother might as well be a total stranger for all the willingness he'd shown to tell Neill what he needed to know.

Also, Eric hadn't pinned fatherhood on the mysterious Vittorio, whoever he was. And, of course, that only increased Neill's suspicion that Eric was the father of Bianca's baby.

NEILL DIDN'T KNOW what the supremely ticked-off Eric had in mind when he stomped away from the bench in front of Mulberry Cottage, but he did know one thing and that was that he was more determined than ever to talk to Bianca.

He checked her room again, and again she wasn't there. He asked the bellman if he knew if she'd gone into town and received a negative answer. He was trying to figure out where to look next when his mother walked into the lobby.

"Have you seen Bianca?" he blurted without preamble.

"Not since the rehearsal dinner," she answered. "Come to think of it, I haven't seen you since then either. Want to go for a walk?"

"Good idea. We might run into Bianca along the way."

They went out through the French doors and Viv smiled up at him. "Good idea. It seems as if these events are really never long enough to get in all the visiting we need to do, are they?"

"Oh, I think these family events are long enough. *Quite* long enough," Neill said, but his meaning seemed completely lost on his mother. Anyway, there was no point in distressing her with what kept surfacing from deep in his soul—alienation, heartache, worry— all because family get-togethers brought home once again that he had lost so many people who were important to him over the years. Every time they all assembled as a family, it reminded him even more that they weren't one.

Viv chattered all the way to the Folly, where a flock of red and black orioles scattered at their approach. Neill hardly heard a thing she said until she declared, "It's getting close to time to get dressed for that silly bachelorette party, I can't imagine what we're going to do there unless it's eat bonbons and drink tea with our pinky fingers suitably elevated. Neill, I can't wait for you to see my new vintage motorcycle. It has a sidecar so we can go riding together."

This got his attention. "You rode up here on an old motorcycle?" he said unbelievingly.

"It wasn't such a long trip." Viv fumbled in her purse and pressed a set of keys into his hand. "Here, why don't you take a look at my most recent plaything? It's parked in the old shed behind the apple orchard.

You might even want to take it out for a spin some-time.''

Neill jingled the keys, scarcely aware that Viv was still speaking. ''Mom, do you have any idea how old babies are when they sit up?''

That question coming from nowhere stopped Viv cold. ''Why, Neill,'' his mother said slowly, focusing on him as if she were seeing him for the first time. ''Why on earth do you ask?''

WITH TIA NOW CONTENT in her new dry diaper, Bianca navigated the pram through the orchard to the very back of it where it tapered off into the woods. At the edge of the trees behind a screen of bushes nestled a small wooden outbuilding, and out of curiosity she rubbed a circle of dirt from the lone window and peered inside.

When her eyes adjusted to the shed's murky light, she saw that the only occupant of the building was an old but shiny motorcycle complete with a sidecar. Well, maybe there were a few spiders around as well, judging from the cobwebs in the corners of the window.

Interesting. Maybe Franny's father was into vintage transportation.

She paused to tuck the light blanket around Tia's legs and then resumed her walk. It was almost time to get ready for that stupid bachelorette party, an ordeal that Caroline had insisted required her attendance.

AS HE APPROACHED the orchard, wending his way between the old gnarled trees, Neill mulled over his mother's answer to his parting question.

''I don't remember exactly what age babies are when

they sit up," she'd said. "Seems like maybe it's six months or so before they can hold their little backs straight enough."

Neill knew she was itching to interrogate him; Viv wasn't the kind to let such a significant query from her eldest son go by the board. In order to accomplish a quick getaway, Neill had made the excuse of being eager to see Viv's motorcycle and left her standing beside the Folly looking clearly puzzled. And now he was required to follow through by searching out the shed behind a low growth of shrubbery, unlocking it, and staring down at the new acquisition of which his mother was so proud.

Well, how many other mothers Viv's age would ride on a vintage bike? With a red sidecar? Not many. Neill had to admire her spirit.

The orchard was quiet and peaceful, and after he'd relocked the shed, Neill strolled aimlessly through the weeds and vegetation for a few minutes, trying to figure out the next logical step in finding Bianca. He saw rutted tracks and decided to follow their wandering path, and eventually the orchard opened up into the rambling backyard of a small two-story stone house. It was the old carriage house, if he wasn't mistaken. He walked around to the front of the house where a gray pram occupied a narrow porch.

He recognized the pram immediately. It was the same pram that Bianca had been pushing at the garden party. It was a clue. A major one.

Neill psyched himself to march up the path and knock on the front door with its gaily beribboned wreath of dried flowers. He would ask if Bianca were there. If she wasn't there, he'd ask when she'd be back.

But as he raised his hand to knock, the pram jiggled.

He heard a rustle and a noise. He wheeled around and bent over the pram. Inside was Bianca's baby.

He looked at the baby. The baby looked at him. The baby smiled. He smiled back. The baby made a kind of meowing sound. No, *cats* meowed. This was a *baby*.

Neill supposed that if he thought about it, he'd have to classify this noise as a coo. He didn't know much about talking to babies. He'd tried it yesterday in the car and the conversation had gone nowhere. Yet here was this baby blinking at him expectantly. She looked kind of cross-eyed. Did that mean anything? Did they all look like that? Or was there something wrong with this baby, this Tia?

He crossed his eyes at her in fun, and she smiled. She didn't have any teeth. He could see her gums, all pink, and her tongue, so tiny. She screwed up her face, and for a panic-stricken moment, he thought she might be going to cry. Instead, she sneezed.

"Gesundheit," Neill said automatically. Did one say gesundheit to babies? Tia wrinkled her nose. He wondered how they blew their noses. They couldn't do it themselves, could they? How could they hold a handkerchief? He took his out of his pocket and looked from it to the baby.

Tia sneezed again and began to bicycle her little legs energetically under the blanket. Her pacifier was sitting off to one side. He wondered how she would sneeze if her pacifier was in her mouth. Her Binky. Or maybe the pacifier acted like a plug and kept her from sneezing, preposterous as that sounded. *Jeez, how did you learn these things?*

"Want your Binky?" he asked her. Tia stared at him. He saw a droplet of moisture at the edge of one of her nostrils. Maybe she did need to blow her nose.

Keeping his eye on her, he folded his handkerchief; it was so big. Did they make baby-size hankies like they made baby-size shoes and baby-size hats? He'd never seen any baby handkerchiefs.

"Will you blow your nose if I hold this up to it?" he said in a low tone. He felt kind of stupid asking.

Tia kicked the blanket off and chortled. At least he thought it was a chortle. It didn't qualify as a coo, and he didn't think it was a gurgle. And her nose was running.

He was bending over the pram to wipe her nose, hoping it wouldn't make her cry, and thinking that he had a lot to learn about babies when the door behind him scraped open.

He didn't have time to look around before he heard a gasp. And then a panic-stricken voice he didn't recognize bellowed behind him, "Mo-*om!* Call Security! Some man's trying to hurt the baby!"

Chapter Eight

An arm grabbed his and wrested the handkerchief out of his hand. He didn't fight it; he wasn't doing anything wrong.

"Hey, wait a minute!" Neill protested. "Her nose is running!"

His skeptical assailant danced away with his handkerchief and glared at him from beneath a fringe of frizzy bangs. She was chewing gum and couldn't have been more than seventeen.

Clattering footsteps closed in, and Bianca and the Ofstetler woman burst from the house. Bianca took one look at Neill and closed her eyes in weary disbelief before waving the girl away. "It's okay, Franny. I know him. He's—" She bit her lip, but not the way she clamped down on it when she was trying not to laugh. This was entirely different.

"I'm Neill Bellamy," he said, jumping in to make things better.

"He is. I know him," Bianca quickly assured the two wary onlookers, regaining some of her color and also her poise. "Franny, Neill is the groom's brother and best man in the wedding. Neill, Franny. Neill, you already know Doris Ofstetler, her mother, from the restaurant.''

So here Franny was in person. Mrs. Ofstetler was nodding cordially in recognition, but Franny moved away and folded her arms across her chest. "I thought he was putting chloroform on Tia's face. I thought he was a kidnapper. There's been all this talk about jewel thieves and kidnappers, you know.'' Franny popped her gum and managed to look chastened.

Bianca put an arm around the girl's shoulders. "I'm glad you're so conscientious about looking after my daughter, but really, it's okay. And it's time for me to get back to the hotel." She appropriated the handkerchief from Franny and gently wiped the baby's nose before handing the hanky back to Neill. Tia gurgled. Neill was sure it was a gurgle, not a chortle or a coo.

"Well, I'll just stay out here and enjoy the fresh air with Tia," Franny said as she dumped herself into a hammock swinging at the other side of the porch.

"That's fine, Franny, and I'll be back to pick Tia up after the bachelorette party," Bianca said. She dropped a light kiss on the baby's forehead before heading down the porch steps. Neill followed Bianca, who by this time was steaming toward the hotel full speed ahead.

"I was only trying to get the baby to blow her nose," Neill said as he pulled even with her. He figured that to Bianca's way of thinking, he had some explaining to do.

"They don't actually blow their noses when they're this age," Bianca said tightly. "You're supposed to use this little suction thing with a bulb for that."

"A syringe?"

"I think it's called an aspirator, and later, when

they're old enough to understand, you hold the tissue for them and they blow their noses into it."

"Well, how was I to know?" Neill asked plaintively.

"I can't imagine how you would know that. I can't imagine why you were even there. On second thought, maybe I can. Tell me, Neill, aren't you a little old to be playing spy?" Disapproval was inherent in her tone, and perhaps there was a bit of panic, too.

"I wasn't spying. I happened to be passing by."

"Right. You happened to be passing by that out-of-the-way house on the edge of the Swan's Folly property. I don't buy it, Neill. Besides, you have no business following me around."

He hadn't been following her, but he might have been if he'd known where she was in the first place, so he decided to let this pass. "How else am I going to get to talk to you?" he said.

"Go talk to someone else. You'll get as much information out of any of the other people in the wedding party." She forged ahead of him, her hair flying out behind her. It was beautiful hair, shining with golden highlights, fragrant with the scent of expensive shampoo.

"Eric said—"

She inhaled sharply. "You've talked to Eric?"

"Briefly," he acknowledged. She wrapped her arms about herself as if to ward off a chill. The temperature at this hour of the day wasn't cool but warm, and a light refreshing breeze swept in from the direction of Geneva Lake. It smelled of sun-dried reeds and cool freshwater, scents familiar to him from the weekends he'd spent in Lake Geneva with a friend from prep school when he was a boy.

Bianca tossed back her head, making her highlights shimmer in the light of the dying sun. "I wish you'd get off my case," she said.

"If you only knew it, Bianca, I'm your best friend here."

Her wide eyes focused on him, and he noticed for the first time that the deep blue pupils were edged in silver. He also noticed that they shone with pure exasperation.

"The more I think about it, the more certain I am that I have *no* friends here," she said vehemently.

"The way you're acting, it's no wonder," he said, trying to inject a note of reason.

"I came because Caroline insisted and because I wanted to be here for Eric on his wedding day. I didn't come because I wanted to."

"You didn't have to bring the baby," he pointed out. "If it was going to keep you upset all the time."

The look she shot him was incredulous. "Do you think I wanted to put either of us through this? Gabrielle got sick with mononucleosis at the last minute. Otherwise Tia would be in Paris."

"Is she—is Tia okay? With her nose running like that?" What if a baby got mono? Was it serious? Or didn't they get mono? Again, he wished he knew more about babies.

"She's fine. She's doing better than I am. Why all the questions?"

You know why, he almost said. *She might be my daughter. I have an interest in her welfare. I want to know more about her, what she eats, what she likes, everything.*

At that moment, he could hardly bear to think about the more likely possibility that Tia could be the child

of Bianca and another man. Neill unclenched his jaw
and mentally warned himself not to move too fast. Tia
might be his daughter, the child he'd never thought
he'd have, but Bianca was skittish and unpredictable.
In order to learn the things he longed to know, he'd
better handle her with care.

Lots of care. And at that moment, even though she
walked as far away from him on the path as possible,
even though she kept her face averted and her head
down, he cared for Bianca very much.

"Look, couldn't we sit down somewhere and talk?"
he said.

"No. Anyway, I have a horrific headache."

She looked pale, but he'd attributed that to anger.
Perhaps Bianca wasn't angry as much as she was in
pain.

She kept talking nonstop. "I didn't bring any aspirin.
Maybe one of the others has some medicine for headaches, but I hate to bother other people with my trivial
problems. Eric never takes medicine for headaches, so
he's no help, and—"

"Bianca, you're babbling," he said.

She cast him a blank look. "So?"

"I have some superstrong pain tablets that I use for
everything from sprains to hangnails. Come to my cottage and I'll give you one. Two if you need them."

Her look was skeptical. "Do you promise this isn't
a ploy to manipulate me into having this conversation
you've been threatening?"

That was a toughy. They had to talk, yet he was
aware that there was no point in trying to get the information he wanted when she was in this mood. "All
right," he conceded. "You can take the pills and go

back to your room." *For now,* he added in his thoughts.

She followed him silently. When they reached Mulberry Cottage, she hung back on the doorstep.

"Come on in," he said, holding the door wide to show her that there were no traps, only a small sitting room complete with wing chairs in front of the stone fireplace; the bedroom was out of sight behind a closed door.

"I'll wait here," she said firmly.

"Suit yourself," he said. "I'll only be a minute, but there's a bench by the pond if you want to sit down."

She nodded and he went inside. As luck would have it, he had tossed a packet of the pills into his suitcase at the last minute before leaving his house in Colombia, and he hadn't unpacked them when he unpacked everything else. Finding them meant hefting his large suitcase off the closet shelf and discovering that he'd snapped the lock earlier, which meant experimenting with half a dozen combinations before he hit on the right one and clicked it open. Then he had to explore all the little pockets inside the suitcase before he finally found the pills stuck between one of the zippered sections and the frame.

He heard the commotion as he was filling a glass with water from the tap, and as soon as he realized what was happening, he ditched the water and the pills before running outside where Bianca was in full retreat near the pond.

"Stop! Go away!" Bianca was saying as she switched her skirt at one of the swans. It was advancing on her with grunts and hisses, its frenzied wings beating the air. The two of them looked so ridiculous that he might have laughed if he'd thought Bianca would laugh with him. He didn't think she would, though, so he tactfully concealed his amusement.

Bianca jumped up on the small bench where he'd earlier visited with Eric and unleashed a stream of Italian, which affected the swan not one bit. In fact, if anything, the Italian curses, if that's what they were, infuriated the swan even more.

Welcoming this chance to be regarded as heroic, Neill grabbed a fallen tree limb and rushed toward the swan, flailing the limb as he ran. Never mind that he looked as ridiculous as Bianca; he would protect her. The swan, in full attack, wove its head back and forth and darted its bill at her, lurching ever closer. Bianca, fresh out of curses, uttered a small "Eep!"

"He's trying to scare you, that's all," Neill shouted.

Bianca shouted back, "Well, he's doing a fine job of it!"

Neill, brandishing the limb, stomped his feet sharply on the ground, and the swan, arrested in full attack, stopped flapping and hissing. It uttered one more guttural grunt before grumpily folding its wings to its side and splashing awkwardly into the shallows of the pond. Once there it swam rapidly away without so much as a blink backward. For the first time, Neill saw the other swan gliding serenely at a safe distance.

Bianca, looking ruffled, hopped down from the bench. "Admit it. You put that awful bird up to this."

"Torture by swan? I don't think so." He had to laugh because the idea was so absurd.

Bianca smoothed her skirt, but he could tell by the way she sucked in her cheeks that she was trying not to laugh along with him. "I know you think I must have done something to provoke an attack, but I didn't. I was standing and watching the other swan in the water, and suddenly the mean one came thrashing toward me out of the reeds.''

"That was the cob, or male swan. He must have thought you were a threat to his mate, the pen."

"A pen might be a good idea, but only to put him in," Bianca said ruefully. Neill chuckled, and after a brief moment, she gave in and laughed, too.

"Thank goodness you came along. I was afraid he was going to start nipping at me with that vicious orange bill of his."

"How's your headache?" he asked.

"Worse," she said.

"I'll go get the pills and the water," he told her.

When he returned, Bianca was sitting on the bench looking as demure as Bianca could look, which wasn't very. Wordlessly Neill held out the glass of water before dropping one white pill into her other outstretched hand.

She gulped the pill down. He fought for a handle on this situation, trying to figure how to build on this little bit of goodwill and gratitude while the two of them were together and alone.

"I didn't know swans could be so mean. They look so peaceful and happy when they're swimming," Bianca said.

"Swans can be nasty. There were two pairs in the park near where my mother used to live when I was a kid. I did a fourth-grade science project about them. I remember that once Eric got too close and they raised their wings and hissed and chased him in typical busking behavior. He was pretty young at the time, and he was terrified."

"What sets them off?"

He shrugged. "The cob is very protective of the pen.

Last week I saw the cob chase a dog that wandered onto the property and barked at the pen. The dog went yelping away, and I never saw him again.''

"Perhaps the swans have a nest nearby. What are the babies called? Chicks?''

"Cygnets. As in the Cygnet Club at the hotel.''

"Of course. I should have known that. Do these swans have names?''

"I don't know. Any suggestions? We could name them after a famous couple, like Romeo and Juliet. Or Arthur and Guinevere.''

"Did Godzilla have a girlfriend?''

He laughed again, but she was still thinking names. "The pen looks kind of prissy, swimming around in circles and acting so aloof. How about Godzilla and Priscilla?''

"That'll do. Godzilla and Priscilla they are.''

Bianca stood and handed him the empty glass before turning to go. "Thanks again for the remedy. And the water.''

"Maybe we could get together later,'' he said on a note of desperation.

"Caroline's holding me captive at the bachelorette party. You'll be a hostage at the bachelor party on that boat out in the middle of the lake. What's the name of it?''

"The *Truelove*. Corny, isn't it?''

"Not really. Anyway, it's going to be a late enough night as it is. Just be glad you'll be on a boat having fun with the guys and not in the private dining room being annoyed by Gen. Talk about Godzilla! Well, thanks again.'' Bianca shot him a quick and wary smile, then tossed her hair back over her shoulders and set off along the path. There was nothing, Neill thought unhappily, that he could do to keep her.

Unbidden, Nana's words came back to him. *Impress upon her the strength of your ardor.*

The advice had a hokey ring to it, but it might be sound. The only trouble was that every time he thought he was making headway with Bianca, something happened. He never seemed to be able to get close to her.

It was time to concentrate on a new approach. He'd have to come up with something if he was to win her over. Time was growing short: only two more days left.

And two more glorious and romantic summer nights, including tonight.

THE *TRUELOVE,* the sixty-foot yacht that the late, great Swanee Lambert had presented to his wife as a gift in the early 1900s, was rocking with the bachelor party by the time night fell. Neill, though chafing to do something, anything, to resolve his doubts about Eric and Bianca, waited patiently for the other attendees to be caught up in the merriment and exhilaration brought about by plenty of expensive Scotch and a prize heavyweight fight on closed-circuit television.

Eric stood alone at the bow railing when Neill approached. In the stern of the boat someone howled like a wolf, and a glass shattered as it fell. The elegant mansions on the bluff provided a stately counterpoint to the high jinks on the *Truelove,* the golden reflections of their lights rippling among the stars on the lake's surface.

"Just think," Eric mused without turning around as Neill joined him. "Tomorrow at this time I'll be married." He stared into the clean white waves folding back into the boat's wake, possibly a little drunk.

"Yeah, I know," he said. "Look, Eric—"

"Hey, Neill, maybe I got too hot under the collar this afternoon," Eric said in a troubled tone. He focused slightly bleary eyes on his brother.

"I came to you for answers, and I didn't get them," Neill said.

Eric seemed to be trying to pull himself together. "Neill, I told you. You're asking the wrong questions of the wrong person."

"Bianca isn't exactly forthcoming with information."

"I can't break a confidence," Eric said firmly. "Don't ask me to do that. Bianca means a lot to me."

"And the baby?" Neill held his breath. He looked to see if Eric's knuckles where he gripped the railing turned whiter. They didn't.

"Why are you asking me about this?" Eric said carefully. The words didn't slur, but they came close to it.

"I should think it would be obvious."

"Not to me. Nope, a lot of things are obvious in this very interesting situation, but not to the right people."

"You've always had a stubborn streak. I used to have to apply physical force to get you to cry uncle."

Eric looked startled and then cracked a wry smile. "Very funny," he said as if enjoying a private joke.

Uncle. If Tia was Eric's child, Neill was Tia's uncle. Neill pretended that he didn't get it.

"I don't think any of this is funny. And I don't expect you to own up to everyone here, much less to Caroline and her family, but if you're the father of that baby, I want to know."

"You think *I'm* the father of Bianca's child?" Eric looked flabbergasted.

"The thought presented itself. I'm merely considering it."

"Bianca didn't—?"

"She said only that the baby is hers. She wouldn't say who the father is."

Eric ran a shaky hand through his hair, causing it to spring up in little spikes. "Jeez, Neill, I love Bianca, sure. But there's never been the slightest bit of romantic interest between us. She's like a sister, a sweet little sister." Eric took two steps away from the railing and whirled around. "I can't believe this," he said. "I'm about to be married to a woman who isn't speaking to me at the moment. I've spent the past year calming her mother down and convincing her that Bianca and I weren't up to anything when we disappeared together before the engagement party. And now my own brother is accusing me of bothering a child—I mean fathering a child—with a woman I've never even kissed except on the chic. Cheek." His face contorted in anger.

"I wasn't accusing. I'm merely asking." Neill moved closer to Eric, meaning to placate him.

He'd misjudged Eric's mood, that was for sure, and belatedly he recalled that Eric had never been able to tolerate Scotch. Still, he was stunned when Eric, blundering and intense, grabbed him by the lapels of his blazer.

"I'm *not* the father of Bianca's baby," Eric said.

Neill pushed him away. "Chill out, Eric, I'm sorry I mentioned it," he said, but Eric, who was waxing red in the face, grabbed his arm. A cuff link went flying, but Neill couldn't tell at the moment whose it was.

"If you had any sense, Neill, you'd know whose baby it is. And you'd know how Bianca has suffered. But no, you're too high and mighty, too far above it all to see what's right in front of your face. Let me tell you, I know how hard it is to decide on the right woman, but I don't know how much longer I can stand aside and let you ignore the truth.''

Neill tried to shake the belligerent Eric off. ''That's what I'm trying to get, Eric. The truth. Which in this family seems like a mighty scarce commodity.''

''Maybe we need to rough up that smooth veneer of yours,'' Eric said as Neill tried to sidestep his brother's long reach. Eric took a wild jab at him and he ducked.

Neill was outraged. ''Hey, wait a minute,'' he said, dodging another of his brother's swings. He was relieved to see Kevin and Joe materialize out of the darkness. As Eric lunged toward him again, Kevin collared Eric and Joe grabbed Neill.

''Take it easy, guys,'' Kevin interjected in a conciliatory tone.

''Tell that to my brother,'' Neill replied in disgust.

''Yeah, tell that to my brother,'' Eric repeated, glaring at him.

''Hey, in the interest of family unity, can't we all go sit down?'' Joe asked plaintively. ''Maybe smoke a cigar with your dad?''

Neill, released by Joe, brushed lint off his lapels. He considered his options. He could hit Eric, which might mess up his face for the wedding. He could act as if nothing had happened and smoke a cigar, but he hated cigars. Or he could bug out. It wasn't hard to make up his mind.

''Cigars stink, and so does this party,'' he said heavily. ''Have the captain stop at the next dock.''

''The captain takes his orders from me, and he's not stopping,'' Eric said.

"You're not thinking of jumping ship, are you, Neill?" Kevin asked in surprise.

"Just watch me," said Neill. Before any of them could reach him, he was up and over the rail. He poised gracefully before diving into the water.

"Hey!" cried Kevin. "What the hell do you think you're doing?"

Going to Bianca, Neill thought as he surfaced and shook the water out of his eyes. He set off for the nearest dock, stroking through the dark, star-shimmering water. Behind him the *Truelove* motored on, the captain oblivious to the fact that he now had one less passenger on board.

Neill thought he heard a splash behind him, but he figured it was only an empty bottle tossed overboard. At the moment, he was more concerned about ruining a perfectly good pair of new Gucci loafers.

A DECOROUS CAROLINE, wearing delicately flowered crepe georgette and sitting beneath a canopy consisting of hundreds of pink and white balloons, had barely distributed the bridesmaids' gifts at the bachelorette party when Nana jumped up from the table in the hotel's elegant ballroom where the party was being held.

"Now *I* have a present for *you,* my lovely Caroline, a dance that I've titled 'Ode to a Bride.' I brought a tape of the music and everything." She winked at her speechless granddaughter. Members of the string quartet suddenly stopped playing.

The silence of the other women present was deafening. Genevieve half rose from her chair, the bell-shaped sleeves of her lace frock quivering. "I'm sure you're too tired to even think about dancing, Mother," she said hastily and none too gently.

"*Au contraire*, my dear. I slept for quite a while this afternoon," and Nana turned with a devil-may-care flourish to the mirrored armoire behind her. She threw open the elaborately carved door to expose a rack of stereo components. "Now," she said, producing an audio cassette tape from the flowing folds of her lavender chiffon gown, "I'll just pop this in," but she froze. "How strange," she murmured. "There's already a tape in here. I wonder whose it is?"

Bianca folded Caroline's bridesmaid gift to her, a silver-backed mirror engraved with her initials, into its blue velvet case. At the same time, a loud knock rapped on the door nearest the head of the table.

"Are we expecting anyone, Mummy?" Caroline asked as all the women's faces turned expectantly.

"If so, I'm not aware of it," Genevieve said.

The door sprang open to admit an enormous wedding cake on wheels. It was decorated with a mass of gaudy tissue-paper roses, and Caroline's and Eric's names were entwined in sparkly silver letters across the top. The straight-faced busboys who wheeled this monstrosity through the door guided it carefully to the middle of the room. Genevieve stared, her mouth hanging open in an uncharacteristically undignified way. Caroline's hand fluttered to the perfectly matched string of pearls at her throat.

"There must be some mistake," Genevieve said, recovering slightly. "We didn't order this."

"Mummy, the cake must be meant for some other party," Caroline said uncertainly, but Genevieve's reply was lost in a sudden blare from stereo speakers signaling the popping of the top off the cake.

Bianca, like everyone else present, stared in disbelief as the figure of a man, a muscular and singularly attractive man, burst in glittering splendor from the wedding cake. He was painted from head to toe in gold body paint and wore a gold lamé loincloth along with a stiff white collar, a black-and-white polka-dot tie, and white cuffs complete with rhinestone cuff links. As the female members of the wedding party and other female guests watched, he leapt free of his conveyance and began to gyrate in time to the ditty known as "The Stripper."

When Bianca had recovered slightly from the shock of his appearance, she stole a peek at Genevieve, whose face was turning an unbecoming shade of puce. Caroline's hands flew up to cover her mouth, her eyes bugging out of her head. Genevieve's quiet, unassuming social secretary, Anne, looked as if the hinges in her jaw had given way.

At first, because the gold paint effectively camouflaged his features, Bianca had no idea who their dancing man might be. But as he sprang to the tabletop, almost dashing several flutes of champagne to the floor, she recognized him.

It was Storm Schrempf stirring up a tempest. No way had Genevieve Knox requested him to entertain at her daughter's bachelorette party.

And entertain he did. First he ripped off his tie and draped it around Genevieve's neck. She didn't know where to look, down at the tie or up at his grinding pelvis. Then he removed his cuff links. Next he ripped off the cuffs and, after posing with them held above his head to better display his muscular torso, he chucked them into a potted palm. The last article of clothing to be removed was his stiff white collar, which he held aloft before placing it gently on Caroline's head like a crown.

Caroline gasped and wailed, "Mum-*my*," but the apoplectic Genevieve was in no condition to help. She was fanning herself through a hot flash with one of the hand-printed menu cards.

Storm dipped and wheeled, his pelvis still rocking rhythmically. "Anybody wanna dance?" he shouted over the swell of the music.

"I thought you'd never ask!" shouted Nana, and Bianca watched in shock as she shimmied over to the gold-painted man and proceeded to match bump for grind right along with him.

Caroline dissolved into hysteria. Bianca rose with the intention of escaping to the ladies' room as Genevieve, her eyelids fluttering as if she were about to keel over in a dead faint, stood up. And suddenly Bianca, who knew that Gen had already pegged her as a troublemaker, knew what was coming.

Genevieve pointed an accusing finger. "You...you..." she said, mustering her strength.

And that was when Neill Bellamy, soaking wet from head to toe, threw the door open and walked purposefully to Bianca, his eyes fiery, his lips in a grim line, and water squishing from his shoes at every step. Not far behind was an equally waterlogged Joe heading toward Lizzie....

Chapter Nine

Bianca didn't know what Neill's watery presence at the bachelorette party meant, but she had never been so happy to see anyone in her entire life.

Genevieve ignored him, and as was her wont at any provocation, lit into Bianca. "Who else but you, Bianca, is outrageous enough to force a disgusting spectacle like that on the rest of us?" The words were delivered in tightly controlled tones, but Bianca had the impression that Genevieve was distinctly blotto.

Bianca's feet rooted themselves to the spot. "You think *I* invited a stripper to come here and jump out of that cake?" she blurted.

Neill stepped forward and cleared his throat. "Of course she didn't," he said, injecting a note of sanity, if you could call it that when he looked as if he'd just been ejected from a Maytag, and before the spin cycle.

"Of course I didn't," Bianca repeated firmly. Something about Neill's deep voice and the determined jut of his jawline gave her confidence. Caroline's mother might want to squash her like an ant at a garden party, but Bianca was in no mood to allow it. She had run away last year; this time she'd stand her ground.

Genevieve acted as if neither of them had spoken.

"First you ruined the engagement party, now you're trying to sabotage the wedding," she sputtered, her fury on the upswing. "There is a limit to how much more we can bear." The royal *we* did not escape Bianca.

"*I* thought the young man was rather fun," said Nana. "We needed something to pep us up. I don't want to hurt your feelings, Genevieve darling, but your parties are, well, rather boring. Stuffy, and worse."

"They are?" Genevieve said in a small voice. "You think I'm stuffy?"

"Ever since you were a little girl, you've tried to compensate for having a mother who is a free spirit, a lighthearted being, and oh, I know it's been hard for you, but there's no need to act as if—" began Nana.

"Hush, Nana," interjected Winnie. "*I* thought Storm was really funky."

"Did you ever think that the man might have done this on his own?" Bianca asked, striving to keep her voice down.

Genevieve had recovered enough to jump back into the argument. "Why, I saw you talking with him earlier. Winnie remarked that you two were in deep conversation."

"In deep conversation?" Bianca was mystified.

"Near the pond today."

"Oh, *that*. Storm and I were only chatting, Genevieve. We weren't plotting anything."

"Of course they weren't," said Winnie, jumping up from her seat. "Kevin and I, um, thought it might be fun to let Storm entertain. After all, it's what he does for a living, so we paid him to jump out of the cake. He's a professional."

"A professional *what* is what I'd like to know," huffed Genevieve.

Caroline, her nose blown and her eyes wiped, jumped in to soothe. "Certainly he was a surprise, Mummy. And yes, I was stunned, but I can't say that his performance was offensive. I've seen worse on television, really I have."

"*I* wish he'd have danced longer," Winnie said, whose eagerness was barely concealed.

"Dear God," said the beleaguered Genevieve, collapsing in her chair.

Caroline inserted herself into the breach with an aplomb that did credit to her good breeding. "Bianca, please sit down. Mummy was wrong. And Winnie, don't worry, it *was* fun." She nodded at one of the astonished waiters, who had hovered motionless near the door since the evening's entertainment commenced. "Now perhaps we could have dessert," Caroline added.

"I think," said Nana, "we've just had him... Er— *it*, I mean." She looked as if she were about to let loose with a big guffaw.

Genevieve did not say a word.

"Bianca, let's go," Neill said, linking her hand through his arm.

Bianca couldn't wait to leave. "Thank you, Caroline. The dinner was delicious, and the engraved mirror is lovely. I'll see you all tomorrow." She forced a pleasant smile through gritted teeth. After that, with the obligatory thank-yous out of the way, she could think of no good reason not to accompany Neill out of the room with her head held high, her arm looped through his.

"I wonder why Neill's clothes are all wet," piped Winnie.

"Caroline, darling, do *you* think I'm dull?" they both heard Genevieve murmur plaintively as they escaped.

Once outside the ballroom, Bianca removed her arm from Neill's and stared at him. His hair hung over one eye, and something that looked suspiciously like algae was twined around the gold button on his blazer.

"Yikes," she said. "Where did you come from? *The Poseidon Adventure?*"

"Actually, it was more like *Jaws*. Eric and I got in a fight—"

"A *fight!*"

"—and I dived off the boat and swam to the nearest dock—"

"*Swam!*"

"—and Joe jumped in after me, since he thinks he has to save everyone in sight—"

"*Joe!*"

"Another former stepsibling of mine, as you might recall. He's lurking around here somewhere—"

"Lurking?"

"Apparently he and Lizzie have something going."

"What on earth—! But how did you get back here?"

Neill rubbed his chin, considering this. "I hitchhiked."

"*Hitchhiked?*" She was mystified. "You shouldn't have left the bachelor party. You're the best man."

"Tonight I'm satisfied to be second-best man. I left Kevin to do the honors, which as far as I can tell mostly involve keeping Eric from getting drunk and out of trouble on the night before his wedding. Not that it seems to be working, I might add."

"Oh, great. That's one more thing to worry about." Not that she was surprised; anything could happen at a Bellamy wedding. She knew it and Neill knew it.

"Bianca, let's not think about it. It's not our problem," Neill said. He whipped off his wet tie and stuffed it in his blazer pocket.

Bianca paused a moment before answering. "No," she agreed finally. They had other concerns, and she didn't know how much longer she was going to be able to avoid them, even though she *was* grateful for Neill's timely appearance.

"Come on, let's get out of here. I'm dripping all over the carpet." He took her arm and began to hustle her past the door of the Cygnet Club.

As they hurried past unobserved, they caught a glimpse of Storm describing his dance, complete with gestures, to a captivated audience.

Neill pulled her into an alcove in the lobby where they were effectively shielded from view by a potted palm. "Look, Bianca. Can we go somewhere? Just the two of us?"

He spoke the words with quiet intensity and was looking at her so earnestly that she didn't want him to stop. She wanted him to go on looking at her that way forever. It was the openness of his expression that was so disarming, and it made her feel as if she could keep no secrets from him. And that was ridiculous; she had one big secret that she must hold in her heart forever. She pushed the thought into a separate part of herself, isolating it from what was happening here and now.

"You," she said, "are soaking wet."

"The palm tree needs watering." He pulled his soggy tie out of his pocket and wrung it into the foliage.

At least this afforded Bianca the chance to escape. Neill moved to block her, but she effectively side-stepped him. She heard his footsteps slogging along behind her as she darted out the front door of the hotel.

"I feel like I'm being followed by the Creature from the Black Lagoon," she said over her shoulder.

"You're in the mood for a movie tonight, aren't you? *The Poseidon Adventure, Jaws,* and now," and he lowered his voice to a tone of deadly menace, *"the Crea-turrre."* Behind her, he lifted his arms above his head and snarled.

"Act like a grown-up," she said, almost ready to laugh. "Besides, you mentioned *Jaws,* not me."

"Somehow, a Bellamy wedding doesn't seem like an event where anyone acts like a grown-up. Stop by my cottage with me and we'll see what videos the hotel has supplied. There's a whole case full of them, and a VCR, too."

"I don't want to see any videotapes," she said.

"Not even of the biggest emerald ever mined at Viceroy-Bellamy mines?"

He *would* dangle that in front of her as bait. He *knew* she was thinking about starting a gemstone line.

"I really need to pick up Tia at the baby-sitter's," she said, knowing even as she said it that Tia wouldn't know if she were picked up now or later. Tia was probably sound asleep.

"You know, you're hiding behind that baby," Neill said.

She attempted a laugh but didn't carry it off very well. "Don't be ridiculous," she said.

"Since you're a jewelry designer, I thought you might be interested in the marketing video we use at the mine. I could change clothes while you watch it, and afterward I'll walk with you to pick up Tia. I don't like the idea of your walking around alone in the grounds at night.''

"Don't be ridiculous, Neill. With all the extra security precautions, Swan's Folly is perfectly safe," she said.

"I've heard rumors of a jewel thief, Genevieve is worried about kidnappers and today you were almost flattened by a swan," he reminded her, raising one eyebrow.

"I'm not concerned about thieves or kidnappers, and don't swans sleep at night?"

"Maybe, but why don't you indulge me?" he said lightly.

"You're shivering," she said.

"All the more reason for me to get out of these wet clothes."

Bianca sighed. "Okay. We'll go to your cottage. But it had better only take a few minutes."

"A few minutes," he agreed solemnly.

She walked beside him along the moonlit path. Above them, the trees swayed sensuously in the caress of a light summer breeze. At Mulberry Cottage, Neill held the door for her so she could precede him inside. The interior, a small living room that she'd only glimpsed briefly earlier, was all English country, with chintz prints and mullioned windows and even a pair of Staffordshire spaniels flanking the oak mantel. Bianca stepped inside wordlessly, her heart speeding up. She didn't think that being alone with Neill was the wisest thing to do, but why think at all?

Neill flipped on the TV set, popped a tape in the VCR, and excused himself to the rear of the cottage, where she presumed there was a bedroom. Bianca sat down on one of the wing chairs while distractedly watching the videotape of emeralds from the Viceroy-Bellamy mine. Behind the closed door, she heard Neill moving around. Doors opened and closed, a bedspring squeaked. She imagined she heard Neill sliding out of wet clothes and into dry ones and pictured the way he'd look without any clothes on. It grew quieter, but she kept listening, all the while keeping track of some of the most gorgeous jewels she'd ever seen as they were paraded through the video by models wearing emerald rings, earrings and necklaces.

Her interest in the emeralds grew as she watched. The stones were beautiful, but the jewelry designs were stodgy. If she were the designer, she'd incorporate more gold and platinum, mix the emeralds with semi-precious stones, try avant-garde settings for the rings.

"What do you think of our products?" Neill said, sticking his head out the bedroom door. His hair was wetter now, and belatedly she realized that of course he would have showered before changing clothes.

"Amazing," she said. "I had no idea your mine produced such stunners."

"Some of our best emeralds aren't on the video because they were mined after it was filmed. Keep watching, I'll be back in a few minutes." He closed the bedroom door again, and she heard the sound of a hair dryer.

She made herself watch the rest of the tape. Business was, after all, business, and with a source like the Viceroy-Bellamy mine, Bianca was sure that she could keep a roomful of jewelry designers busy for the foreseeable future, not to mention a few master gem cutters, a couple of new marketing people and miscellaneous administrative assistants. If she expanded into gemstones with emeralds like the ones on this video, she'd have more than enough business to open that new office on this side of the ocean. It was exciting to think about. Although she'd known that the mine Neill owned was a major one, she realized as she watched the final segment of the video dealing with mining operations that she hadn't had any idea how large the mine was or how broad in scope its business.

Neill emerged from the bedroom, his hair sculpted into its natural waves, his eyes bright with interest. He stood and watched the closing moments of the video with her. The moment it started to rewind he said, "Well? What do you think?"

She stood up. "I'm impressed. I want to see some of those emeralds myself."

He smiled and reached for her, and unwittingly she realized that she'd left herself wide-open. He might think that she wanted to see the emeralds for other than a purely professional reason; he might think she wanted to see *him*.

Well, didn't she?

Yes. And no. She didn't want another fling with Neill Bellamy. And he would never be ready for anything permanent.

She pushed him away. "I told you I didn't want to stay here longer than it took to watch that tape. We'd better go, Neill."

He let his hands drop to his sides. "All right, this is it," he said. A resolute expression came over his face, and she knew in that instant that nothing she could do or say would keep him from saying whatever he meant to say. A sick feeling stole into the pit of her stomach, and she turned away in an attempt to hide her anxiety. This time if Neill asked her who Tia's father was, she wasn't sure she could put him off again. She steeled herself for the worst and wished that she were anywhere but there.

Neill moved around her so that he was looking her full in the face.

"I'm going to lay it on the line. Bianca, are you married? Or do you have a boyfriend?"

This was so unexpected that she could only stare at him. "What *are* you talking about?"

He regarded her intently, his gaze delving deep into hers. "I want to know if there's a man in your life. If you're in a relationship."

She mustered the poise that seemed to desert her whenever Neill was around. "Is it any of your business?"

"I think it is."

She closed her eyes, then opened them. "My life is complicated enough without answering off-the-wall questions. Now if you'll excuse me, I'm supposed to pick up Tia."

She tried to brush past him but his arm shot out and pulled her back. She avoided looking directly at him.

"Not so fast," he said. "You haven't answered me."

"And if I don't, so what?" She summoned all her bravado and made herself look directly into his eyes.

"Here's what," he said, pulling her into his arms. She braced herself against his chest and pushed. He budged not an inch.

"Let me go," she said, but she was effectively boxed in. Not that it was unpleasant. His arms around her were a barrier between her and the rest of the world, and part of her wanted to enjoy that. The other part of her wanted to hit him over the head with something.

His face moved closer until it was only inches from hers. "I don't think you want me to let you go. I think you want me to do this," and he lowered his lips to hers.

His mouth was soft at first, but as it became more demanding a flood of sensation swept through her, over her, around her. She breathed in sharply and savored the scent of him: a subtle aftershave and the fragrance of a strong, virile man. There was no way she could not respond to him.

Her arms went around his neck and her eyes fluttered closed. At the moment she couldn't think, she could only feel. She couldn't pretend that she wasn't still attracted to him.

He stopped kissing her as abruptly as he'd started. She felt his lips close to her ear.

"I think you've answered my question. If there were another man in your life, you wouldn't be kissing me like that."

"I really have to get Tia from the Ofstetlers'," she mumbled into his lapel, embarrassed about letting her guard down.

He laughed, a short outburst, and she made herself step away. Maybe she should let him think there was someone else. It might make it easier for her. But she had already lied enough. There was no point in making things even worse.

"All right," he said. "We'll go to the Ofstetlers' because you keep insisting. But the night isn't over yet. Not by a long shot."

She allowed herself one last look at him, standing there and looking so determined and so heartrendingly handsome, and, heart in her throat, she rushed out of the cottage, Neill right behind her. She flew past cottages with the picturesque names of Dandelion, Pennyroyal, Thistle, repeating them in her mind as a kind of mantra to keep away unwelcome thoughts. Somehow she knew that when she looked back on this wedding weekend, all she would remember was running and being pursued by Neill Bellamy. Once that would have been the stuff of dreams, and maybe it still was. Only in real life, she'd better hope that she could succeed in holding him at arm's length. She felt the sting of tears behind her eyes and blinked rapidly to dispel it. How could she want him and not want him, how could she love him and not let him know?

She was almost grateful when he caught up with her so that she wouldn't have to pursue this confusing line of thought.

"Tell me about the baby," Neill said as he caught up with her.

She struggled to keep her voice under control. "What would you like to know?"

"Do they have personalities at that age? I'm afraid I don't know very much about babies. Well, you already know that," he offered in a tone that approached apologetic.

Bianca rallied and realized that she could talk about this; her child and her new status as a mother were topics she loved. She drew a deep stabilizing breath before she spoke. "You could have written all I knew about babies on the head of a pin until I had one. It's amazing, Neill. Tia had a personality right from the start."

"I don't see how they can have personalities when

they can't talk or let you know what they're thinking,'' he said.

"Oh, babies have ways of communicating.''

"Cooing? Gurgling? When I was with her today, I couldn't figure out what any of it meant.''

"You could if you were around her for any length of time. You know, the week I took Tia home from the hospital, the pediatrician suggested that I offer her water in a bottle now and then. She hated it from the first. She'd push it away and look at me like I was crazy for even thinking that she'd be interested. I knew what she meant without her making a sound.''

"I've heard mothers say that their kids had personalities of their own from the time they were born.''

"Tia did. She's cheerful and energetic and she likes people. And she's easygoing most of the time. She's happy to see me in the morning when I pick her up out of her crib. I can tell because she waves her little arms and kicks her little legs, and she smiles. She has a wonderful smile.''

"She sounds like fun,'' Neill said. He sounded mildly surprised.

"She's my life,'' was Bianca's simple reply. It was the truth.

"What made you decide to have a baby?''

She didn't know what to say. She could hardly tell Neill that she hadn't planned to have a child but that for her, once she was pregnant, there was no other choice. She kept her silence, thinking that it was the better virtue and knowing full well that virtue had nothing to do with any of this.

They walked on for a few more moments when Neill said, "Sorry. It's none of my business.''

She felt as if she were suffocating under the weight

of her secret. It *was* his business, or at least it could be.

She made herself respond, and in the only way she could, which was straight from her heart. "I chose for Tia to maintain a low profile at this wedding, but I love her more than anything in the whole world."

The Ofstetlers had left the porch light burning, and it lit Neill's face as they approached their house. He looked serious, thoughtful. "I know you love her," he said evenly.

Bianca didn't expect him to walk her up to the door, but he did, his footsteps ringing out on the wide boards of the porch floor. A moth flitting around the porch light dive-bombed her head; Neill brushed it away. Bianca knocked on the door, feeling awkward. Maybe Neill did too, but if he did, he didn't show it. He was hard to figure and always had been.

"Do we put the baby in the pram to take her back to the hotel?" Neill asked while they waited for Franny to answer their knock.

Bianca shook her head. "I'll carry her."

"But where will she sleep?"

"I have a crib set up for Tia in my room."

Franny opened the door, her shape outlined against the cozy interior of the house. She held the baby in her arms. "Hi, Ms. D'Alessandro, Mr. Bellamy. Tia was a good girl tonight. She drank every bit of her formula. Want to come in?"

"No, I'm tired, Franny, and tomorrow's the wedding. We'd better be on our way."

When Franny placed Tia in her waiting arms and went to get the baby's bag, Neill moved closer. The three of them stood encapsuled in the golden rectangle of light from the doorway.

Like insects trapped in amber, Bianca thought as she dropped a kiss on top of Tia's head. However, unlike the insects, they would not be there forever. They would be moving on, resuming their own busy lives and pursuing them in places as far apart as possible while still living on the same planet.

"The baby looks so heavy for you. Won't you let me carry her?" Neill offered.

Bianca didn't think she could bear to see the baby in Neill's arms again. Last time he had held Tia, it had made her think of too many might-have-beens, should-have-beens, could-have-beens.

"I'm used to it," Bianca said carefully. "You can bring her bag if you like."

Neill grunted but didn't say anything. When Franny returned, he wordlessly took the bag that held Tia's extra diapers and formula and followed Bianca as she called out goodbyes over her shoulder.

Bianca held Tia close, but the baby seemed overly interested in the man who walked beside them so silent in the moonlight that sifted through the sheltering trees. Past the willows, past the pond, past the darkened Folly. Bianca was grateful for the dim light because it afforded her welcome privacy. The silence between them lengthened; Neill didn't speak and neither did Bianca.

Bianca knew that it was because neither of them knew what to say.

And because even if they knew precisely the right thing, neither of them would say it.

NEILL FOUND THAT, after the shadowed grounds of the hotel, the lights of the deserted lobby seemed altogether too bright. As they entered it, Tia whimpered and stirred, and Bianca, who much to his surprise was as attentive and loving as a mother could be, calmed the baby with a few soft words.

"Does she always do that?" Neill whispered in the hall.

"Do what?"

"Make noises."

"All babies do."

"I thought they only ate, slept and cried. Oh, and cooed and gurgled."

"Well, they do a couple more things, too. One of which I'm pretty sure I'll have to deal with when I get her to my room."

"Oh. I get the drift," Neill said, and he was grinning as he took her key from her to unlock her door, which swung open before he had a chance to use it.

Bianca walked into the room and began to settle Tia in her crib, which was set up in one of the dormer window alcoves. As she began to change the baby's diaper, her face was alight with the glow of maternal love, and Neill wished she'd look at him with as much devotion. The thought engendered a feeling of such longing that he knew it must show on his face. Quickly, before Bianca took note, he turned back to the door and studied the lock and the plate with its missing screw.

"You really should have called somebody to fix this lock long before this, especially since there's someone around who seems to be going in peoples' rooms," he said over the murmured reassurances that Bianca was giving the baby.

Bianca looked up from her task. "Yes, I know, but I keep forgetting to call whomever I'm supposed to call."

"Some of this beefed-up hotel security, for starters."

"I'll call first thing in the morning."

Neill didn't like to think of Bianca and her baby in this room unprotected all night, and furthermore, Bianca's cavalier attitude toward safety bothered him. He suspected that she didn't ever have to deal with such inconveniences as broken locks; she had people for that. Well, so had he until he decided to make his life more real by moving away from Lake Forest and the comfortable cocoon that his family's wealth and position provided.

Without thinking about it, he let his gaze rest momentarily on the tiny bundle in the crib. Not only was Bianca a concern, but he wasn't willing to take the chance that anything could happen to such a sweet baby. Such a helpless baby.

He fiddled with the doorknob. "I have just the thing to take care of that lock," he said. He reached his other hand into his pocket and closed his fingers around the familiar and comfortable shape of a Swiss Army knife. When he pulled it out, Bianca moved closer.

"I remember that knife," Bianca said in surprise. "I gave it to you for Christmas shortly after Budge and Mother were married."

Neill had owned the knife for so long, had depended on its built-in gadgets for so many things, that its origins had long been forgotten.

"I don't remember that," he said. Then, thinking that he'd sounded ungracious, he added, "I've taken this knife everywhere. It goes down into the mine with me and on vacations with me, and I suppose I'll carry it in my pack when I climb Mount Everest."

"Mount Everest? You're climbing Mount Everest?"

"I'm thinking about it."

"What on earth makes you want to climb the highest mountain in the world?"

"There are no Knoxes or Bellamys at the top of Mount Everest," he said wryly.

Bianca shook her head and lifted her eyes to the heavens. "You must want to be away from here almost as much as I do."

He let that pass, mostly because he wasn't so sure he wanted to be away from here. Away from *her*. He doubted that she'd want to hear it, however. *She* was the one who didn't want to have anything to do with the Bellamy tribe, up to and including him. He wondered what it would take to change her mind. He wondered if he was up to the job.

Bianca silently repositioned a lamp on a nearby table so that the light fell directly on the work area. He made himself concentrate on the plate, which was loose and misaligned so that the latch bolt was not able to engage properly.

He saw the missing screw in the ashtray on the nearby console table. Once the striker plate was realigned and the missing screw attached using the knife's screwdriver, the lock engaged properly. He opened and closed the door experimentally a few times, then stood up and folded the knife, his fingers lingering on its worn finish. How could he have forgotten that it was a gift from Bianca? Or had he buried the memory like so many other memories of his turbulent young adulthood?

Without speaking, without looking at Bianca, he went slowly to the crib and stood staring down at Tia, who had fallen asleep. Her eyebrows were pale, but her eyelashes were dark and cast feathery shadows on her plump pink cheeks. He thought that she must look a lot like Bianca had looked when she was a baby. Or did she look like another man, perhaps Vittorio? In the dim light he couldn't be sure. And in that moment it didn't matter. All that mattered was that Tia was part of Bianca.

He heard a soft rustle behind him and felt Bianca's presence. He also smelled her perfume: Joy.

"She's such a pretty child," he said.

Bianca was silent. "I'm glad you think so," she replied finally, and there was a slight catch in her voice. He looked at her quickly. She was biting her lip, and he thought he caught the glimmer of tears beneath her lowered eyelids.

Funny little Beans, he thought to himself. He'd never known how emotional she was before, or how vulnerable. In that instant he wanted to take her in his arms and press her head to his chest. He wanted to make sure that she never wanted for love or happiness or companionship or money.

Or a decent lock on her door.

He turned away, confused by his emotions. And hers, which were something of a mystery to him. What was she thinking just now, what was she feeling?

"Bianca," he said, then stopped. He looked back at her, his heart melting when he saw the complicated emotions playing across her face. "I think I don't want to be away from here as much as I did." There. He'd given her an opening if she chose to take it.

She walked quickly to the other dormer window, hugging herself and looking somehow forlorn. "Why?" she asked bluntly.

He followed her. "Good question."

"What kind of answer is that?"

"The kind you might expect from someone who wants answers to his own questions."

She was silent.

He touched her shoulder. She didn't move, and he thought she might be holding her breath.

"We're talking in circles," he pointed out unnecessarily.

She wheeled around and tried to brush past him. He blocked her way.

"Bianca, you shouldn't have left so suddenly last year," he said.

She gazed at him, her eyes deep and soulful. Did he read regret there, or was it something else?

When she would have bowed her head, he tipped a finger beneath her chin. "Don't look away from me," he said softly. "It's another way of running." He framed her face with his hands so that he was gazing full into her face, such a lovely face that he couldn't imagine why, when they were younger, he hadn't realized how beautiful she was. Soft pale brows, wide-set blue eyes, a small perfect nose, full lips with a sensual quirk at the corners. She was so familiar, yet so new to him. He marveled at the softness of her skin. It was the texture of gardenia blossoms, dewy and fresh and inviting.

"I *should* run," she said half to herself.

He traced her cheekbones with his thumbs and lifted her chin. Her lips parted slightly, and he felt his head dipping toward hers. When their lips met, hers were trembling, and he slid his arms around her to hold her tightly, wanting her to know the warmth and strength and protectiveness that he could provide.

She hesitated before she returned his kiss, and he remembered that night in the gazebo when she had been so passionate that he'd ultimately lost control. Now he wanted to take it slow and easy, to show her how tender their lovemaking could be.

When his lips released hers, he was stunned to see that tears glistened in her eyes. In that moment his hopes were dashed, but somehow he couldn't believe he had misread her.

Words, in this instance, were obligatory. "If you don't want this, we won't," he whispered.

One tear spilled over and trickled down her cheek, a tiny crystalline droplet. "The baby," she said.

He glanced at the crib. "Sound asleep," he murmured into her ear. She brushed the tear away and looked as if he'd misinterpreted her meaning. He drew slightly away. "Is something wrong, Bianca?"

"You could say that," she said, not very loudly. He was on the verge of insisting on an explanation, but to his immense surprise, she distracted him by taking his hand and placing it firmly on her breast. Her hand remained on his, leaving no doubt that she wanted it there. Her eyes were closed, her nostrils flared, and her expression was one of intense longing.

His head swam with the possibilities, and before he could sort them out she was kissing him again, this time so thoroughly that all he could think was that he'd been a fool for staying in Colombia and not seeking her out long ago, baby or no baby. And if he'd gone to her and found her pregnant? It would have made no difference. He would have wanted her anyway.

She unbuttoned his shirt, carefully and deliberately, her eyes intent on the task. While he stood motionless, she loosened his tie and slipped warm hands inside his shirt. Neill managed to come to his senses and tug the zipper down on her dress. The silky fabric slid to her waist, and with an expert twist he unfastened her bra. Her breasts were even more perfect than he remembered them. He teasingly flicked the firm pink nipples with his thumbs. They stiffened at his touch.

"Beautiful," he said, his breath stirring little tendrils of hair in front of her ear. He bent and touched his lips to one erect peak, then the other, and then her dress puddled to the floor so that only a brief snippet of lace remained between her body and his. He knelt and shimmied it down past her hips, kissing her knee and then her softly rounded hipbone on his way back up.

He had wanted her to be totally revealed to him, and he especially wanted to know what she was thinking and feeling in those moments. Her expression gave him no clue. He traced the line of her ribs until his hands reached her backbone; she pressed against him so that their bellies were flat against each other. When she offered her lips, he tasted them slowly and gently, nibbling, sucking, beginning to own the feelings that welled up from somewhere deep inside his soul.

He hadn't known he could feel so much for one person. He couldn't have known, because none of the others were Bianca. There was something so special about her, something that engendered a kindred expectancy in him. He sensed that she knew and understood exactly how he felt about all the important life events that had molded him into the person he was.

She had been through so much of the same. It hadn't been easy for either of them.

He swung her easily into his arms. She was featherlight, and his head swam with the reality of the moment. Bianca had been the subject of many daydreams and a few impassioned night dreams, but never had his fantasies approached such pleasure.

He laid her on the soft feather comforter, his eyes caressing her as he rid himself of the last of his clothes before he switched off the light. They hadn't drawn the curtains, and moonlight streamed into the room, touching lightly upon the sleeping Tia in her crib, upon Bianca with her arms upstretched to receive him, and then upon the two of them, man and woman, as they melted together in sweet pleasure.

"It's been so long," Bianca sighed.

"Too long," he agreed. Then he smiled at her and strung a chain of hot-and-hungry kisses from her earlobe, down her neck, across her breasts and up again to capture her lips in an intoxicating kiss.

"I don't think it's only Eric we have to worry about getting drunk," he murmured before turning her over so that she was on top.

Her hair slid seductively across his face. "What are you talking about? And why are you talking?" she said, pressing her lips to his throat.

"I'm drunk with kisses. Drunk with passion."

"You're awfully talkative when you're drunk," she said playfully, and he laughed low in his throat as he slid his hands down her back to cup his palms around her sweet curves.

Her flesh was firm and yet yielding. So many times as he lay in his narrow bed in the house near the mine he had thought of Bianca—of her face, which he had often tried to sketch but couldn't; of her eyebrows delicately winging toward her pale, pale hair; of the slim, sleek lines of her and what it felt like to sweep his hands along the curves from hips to stomach to breasts and upward to tangle in her hair. Since he couldn't have her body, he had steeped himself in the memory of her, living her and breathing her, for to inhale her meant that she was made part of him, and then he could know her in every cell of his body. Sometimes his heartbeat pounded out her name, *Bianca, Bianca, Bianca,* and his mind had caught on fire with the refrain so that sometimes he couldn't sleep at all on those long, humid nights. And when he had slept, his dreams had often been of her.

But now as Bianca slid her knees upward until they embraced his thighs, he knew that this wasn't a dream. No dream woman could have risen above him in such pale beauty, nor could a dream woman lean forward and rest upon him, her breath stirring the hair on his chest as she nestled her head in the hollow of his shoulder. It fit exactly, like a missing puzzle piece.

He stroked her hair gently, wanting to touch her elsewhere but reluctant to relinquish the tenderness of this moment. Bianca was a capable woman, a strong woman, but he wanted to protect her like the male swan protected the female. He wanted to wrap his wings around her and take her into his heart.

She lifted her head and smiled quizzically. The smile said so much. It said, *Do I please you?* It said, *Are you glad?* It wasn't necessary for her to speak the words. He knew. And he tried to think if he'd ever experienced that degree of knowing with any other woman, and he couldn't think of anyone with whom he had even come close.

"Of course," he said simply, gazing deep into her eyes.

They widened. "What?"

"You know what. You know what I'm thinking." There was a catch in his voice.

"Of course," she said in a tone of wonder.

"How could we not have known this years ago?"

She shook her head slightly, shrugged those bare shoulders, bit her lip.

"Come here," he said, moving his hands upward to press them against the back of her head.

She said, half laughing, "I'm already here."

To which he replied against her lips, "So you are, my dear Bianca," and then his mouth covered hers.

He wanted to be consumed by her, ravished by her, and as his arousal sought her softness he thought that perhaps it was possible. But no, it wasn't possession of her that he wanted but union, that exquisite melding of bodies and communion of souls that had always eluded him. In the gazebo they had been ravenous for each other and unwilling to wait. Now they had time to explore and appreciate. There was no hurry, only discovery, and if that seeking proceeded slowly at some times and more passionately at others, it established an ebb and flow of rhythm that seemed perfectly natural.

And if the rhythm surged deeper than they could have imagined, if the getting turned to giving, if the giving gave to them both, it was no more than they each expected. And no less.

The first climax was hot and long, lost in the sighs and murmurs of utter contentment. And later they found themselves caught up again in sweet shivering passages of delight, in shuddering moans and whispered endearments and the impassioned slow silkiness of flesh upon flesh.

They made love. It wasn't mere sex, this honest-to-goodness mating of two who knew how to pleasure each other, body and soul. It was more, much more. At last, when they finally lay sated in each others' arms, the comforter and the sheets had been consigned to the floor and all pillows jettisoned except for the one that cradled both their heads. Bianca slept, but Neill remained half-awake. He was too overjoyed to fall into a deep sleep; he was full of plans and ideas and musings, all of which concerned Bianca.

When the baby began to stir, he came fully awake with a start. Tia wasn't cooing; she wasn't gurgling. This sounded more like a snuffle. No doubt about it, the noise the baby was making was definitely identifiable as a snuffle. All kinds of thoughts flew out of nowhere and settled on his mind; a snuffle meant a stuffy nose, and Tia couldn't blow her own nose, she was a baby, and her nanny had been diagnosed with mono, which meant that perhaps Tia was sick. Maybe he'd better make sure she was still breathing.

He thought for a few seconds about waking Bianca, but he didn't want to bother her unless there was real trouble. Bianca was sleeping the sleep of the truly exhausted. He could take care of this himself, probably. Maybe he'd need one of those aspirators to suction out Tia's cute little nose, and if that was what it took, he'd find one if he had to call 911 or the state police or whomever. He, Neill, could deal with this.

Full of good and noble intentions, he disentangled himself from Bianca, and with one last lingering look at her lovely hair spread out upon the pillow, he went to see what Tia needed. He'd given Tia a bottle and burped her on the day of the garden party, and he didn't think that changing a diaper could be much more difficult.

Sure enough, the baby was soaking wet. He found disposable diapers in that big bag that accompanied Tia everywhere and inexpertly fumbled with the adhesive strips that held the old diaper on. Somehow he managed to encase the baby in the fresh diaper, eyeing her with trepidation all the while. She waved her arms and smiled around her pacifier, so evidently what he was doing met with her approval.

Another problem—Tia's gown was drenched. He stripped it from her, taking care not to hurt her. She seemed so delicate. She began to whimper, and he didn't want her to break into a full-grown fit of crying, so he carefully picked her up and cradled her against his bare chest. She quieted right away and stared up at him. She felt so warm against his skin, and so cuddly. It occurred to him that she might have been cold without her gown on.

"Is that what it was?" he whispered to her. "Were you too cold? Well, I'm warming you up, aren't I? Just a minute and we'll have you all set."

Tia blinked at him a few times, then her small rosebud mouth stretched into a very wide, very wet yawn. He smiled at this. He didn't think he'd ever seen such a charming baby.

Using one hand, he dug around in the diaper bag until he found a clean gown. Carefully he laid Tia in the crib before painstakingly shoving Tia's little arms through the sleeves. The gown was the kind with a drawstring on the bottom, so he tucked her feet securely inside. It was only when he was preparing to pull the drawstring tight that he noticed—really noticed—those feet.

They were small and pink and utterly adorable, but they had one feature that was unmistakably meaningful. The toes were webbed.

These were Bellamy feet, that was certain.

That left only one possibility.

The shock of recognition drenched him in cold sweat. He was unable to doubt any longer. *Oh, God,* he thought as his world reshaped itself. Why hadn't Bianca told him?

Neill felt numb. All his emotions seemed suspended in the light of his discovery. An ache seized his throat reminding him of all that he had loved and lost in his lifetime, too much for any one man. Stepmothers, half brothers and sisters, stepsiblings, Bianca—in that moment his grief at losing all of them flashed through his mind. It squeezed the air from his lungs, it paralyzed his brain, it tightened its fist around his gut.

All of those people he had loved and lost. And he had lost his child, too.

In a daze he tucked the blanket around the baby and stood staring down at her mother. Bianca slept on, unaware that his heart was pounding and his mouth dry.

Bianca, how could you?

He couldn't fit his present emotions into the ones he had felt last night. Last night had been perfect, wonderful. He was pretty sure that Bianca had thought so, too.

He wanted to shake her awake and hold her accountable for her secrecy and her lies. He wanted to make her defend her decision and to apologize. He wanted to break her heart open and find out, at long last, what was inside. He wanted—he wanted so much.

Maybe too much.

As usual, he considered his options. He could wake Bianca, or he could climb back into bed beside her, or he could leave.

So in the end what he did was put on his clothes and, without a backward look, he walked out the door.

Chapter Ten

Bianca woke slowly. She had so often dreamed of staying with Neill deep into the night and opening her eyes to find herself sleeping beside him. Sleeping together seemed like the ultimate intimate act, a closeness more meaningful than even sex because two people must let their guard down completely while asleep. And she and Neill had no need to erect barriers between them. Today she would tell him everything. All of it.

The sun streamed across the crib with the sleeping baby in it, and the hotel was slowly coming to life around her. Around them. She reached across the bed for Neill and found—

Nothing. No one.

Her eyes flew wide-open then, and she bolted upright in bed. At her first waking, she had gloried in the natural rightness of it; Neill beside her, their baby sleeping in a patch of sunlight beyond. And now everything was wrong. Again.

His clothes were gone, and his jacket had disappeared from the back of the chair. She slid out of bed and pulled on a kimono, checking the bathroom just in case. Nope. No Neill.

She grabbed the phone to call him at Mulberry Cot-

tage. But before she could place the call, Tia started to
fuss, so Bianca replaced the phone in its cradle and
went to attend to the baby.

"My, aren't you dry this morning!" she said to the
baby in surprise. But then she noticed the clumsy way
that the disposable diaper had been stuck together at
the sides. And Tia was wearing a different gown from
the one she'd been wearing when Bianca put her in her
crib last night.

Then it struck her: Only Neill could have changed
Tia's diaper. The thought that he had done it was en-
dearing, not to mention surprising.

But then she realized that he couldn't have changed
the baby, he couldn't have put a new gown on her
without seeing Tia's feet. *Bellamy* feet. He would have
recognized those webbed toes.

He must know that he was her baby's father.

The thought stilled her heart. After last night, she
wanted Neill to know everything about her. They both
knew that they belonged together; it had been implicit
in their actions and interactions, in their loving and in
the communion of their bodies. They *knew*.

And she had so desperately wanted to tell Neill herself about what she'd been through in the past year. To
hold his hand and break the news softly, to watch the
gentle, fierce pride of fatherhood leap into his eyes, to
soothe away his anguish at the lost year, the lost
months when they could have been together.

A sob caught in her throat. She'd been denied what
she wanted—again. She'd screwed up—again. And
Neill was gone—again.

She knew, of course, why he'd left without waking
her, without a word. He'd run as she'd run last year
from him. And she had to talk to him, to tell him that

she'd done what she thought best at the time, and that she regretted shutting him out of her life and Tia's, and that she'd been wrong, and that she loved him.

She loved him. Oh, yes. And she had to tell him. She might have to miss the wedding breakfast, but she *had* to tell him.

She pulled on jeans without benefit of underwear, shoes without benefit of socks, and a shirt without benefit of bra.

It didn't matter. The only thing that mattered was finding Neill. And, finally, daring to bare her soul to him once and for all.

"COME ON, let's *go,*" Bianca said, poking her heels into Maisie's considerable girth. Her urging didn't do any good, so she resigned herself to the horse's slow pace and tried to think of how she might best find Neill. Franny, when she'd dropped Tia off, had told her that she'd seen Neill earlier riding Black Jack, the horse he exercised for Winnie.

Unfortunately, by the time Bianca had arrived at the stable, all the horses except for this sweet-tempered elderly mare were gone; someone had reserved them for a trail ride. Bianca had thought that riding Maisie would be faster than walking. She was wrong.

At the first possible opportunity, she angled Maisie off into the woods and eventually found herself being borne along slightly faster than the speed of molasses across a landscape composed of gently rolling hills and a farmhouse in the distance. Bianca headed for the farmhouse, thinking that maybe someone there had seen a handsome stranger ride past.

The farmhouse seemed deserted. She reined Maisie in for a few minutes, then urged her into the woods on the back side of it. She doubted that Neill would have stuck to any of the main trails.

Eventually the woods opened out onto a large, flat meadow, and then she saw Neill. He was riding a huge black horse and goading the horse to run faster than fast, fast as the wind. The animal was magnificent, his coal-black mane and tail streaming in the wind, his ears forward, his mouth straining at the bit, his hooves pounding the grassy turf.

Bianca watched in awe as man and horse streaked across the landscape. Neill moved at one with his mount, leaning forward to whisper in the silky black ears, and the horse galloped as if the devil were chasing him. They raced around the perimeter of the meadow, riding now in Bianca's direction. For the first time since she'd mounted her, Maisie pranced sideways and gnawed the bit. Bianca was surprised to learn that there was still life in the old girl, and she patted Maisie reassuringly on the neck.

It wasn't until Neill was approaching the small creek that lay between them that Bianca noticed the bee. It hovered above a clump of wildflowers, and as it prepared to land, Maisie, wary of the approaching horse and rider, whinnied and lowered her head. The surprised bee whirled upward, hitting the horse's nose, and Maisie reared back and blew out her breath with a snort.

Bianca hadn't expected this, and she was quick to rein the horse in, but not before the sudden movement caught Black Jack's eye. That eye rolled backward so that she could see the white as Neill prepared to jump the horse over the creek, and without warning Black Jack dug in his front hooves and refused to budge.

Black Jack stopped, but Neill didn't. He went flying

over the horse's head, landing on the ground with a solid *thunk.*

Oh, my God! Was he hurt?

Her heart in her mouth, Bianca scrambled down from Maisie's back and ran to where Neill lay on the soft bank in a place thankfully cushioned by dried sedge. One of his boots had flown off and landed in the creek. Black Jack, sides heaving, had found shelter under a nearby tree.

And Neill wasn't moving.

"Neill!" cried Bianca. She knelt and felt his head. He was breathing, thank goodness, and she saw no blood.

Bianca pulled the scarf from around her neck and dipped it into the cool water of the creek before wringing it out. She tried to remember elementary first aid; she couldn't think. She wondered if there was a phone at that farmhouse and how long it would take her to run there and if she should leave Neill alone to do it. She wondered if any other riders would come this way and how soon. And she laid the cloth across Neill's forehead, trying to figure out if this was the prescribed treatment.

He stirred and pushed the cloth away; was this a good sign?

"Neill? Are you all right?"

He opened his eyes and regarded her laconically. "I'd be a lot better," he said, "if dirty creek water wasn't running in my eyes."

Then Bianca realized that Neill hadn't been unconscious at all. While she watched, still unable to comprehend that he was really all right, he wiped a rivulet of water off his cheek with one hand and sat up.

"You tricked me!" she accused. She fell back on

her heels and stared at him—at the tousled hair falling across his forehead and the dirt stain on the sleeve of his khaki shirt. Considering the fact that she had only a few moments ago thought he might be seriously injured, this seemed like a minor miracle. No—a major miracle.

"Black Jack doesn't like it when other horses act up. You should have kept your horse under control. And in case you're interested, it looks as if she's deserting you." He nodded toward the place where she'd left Maisie, where Bianca saw the mare's hindquarters disappearing into the woods at the fastest pace the horse had exhibited so far.

She started to clamber to her feet. "Stupid horse," she muttered.

"Not so fast," Neill said. She felt his hand clamp around her wrist and slowly sank back down again. Overhead, a faraway plane droned, or was it the bees in the honeysuckle, or was it her pulse in her ears? She swallowed, her mouth suddenly dry.

"Your horse frightened mine," he said.

"Everyone knows Black Jack is a handful. A bee scared Maisie. And shouldn't you tie him up or something?" She gestured toward Black Jack, who was now grazing calmly some distance away.

"He's fine, and he won't go anywhere. I often bring him here and let him enjoy an hour or so of freedom. Black Jack and I are alike. We don't like being cooped up. By the way, I saw you watching me from the edge of the woods before Black Jack got spooked," he said.

"I came out here to find you."

"Interesting. After all that time avoiding me."

Her heartbeat seemed to echo inside her head. Perhaps last night hadn't made that much difference in their relationship after all. She cautioned herself to remember that Neill had just found out he'd fathered her child. Of course he wouldn't act normally.

"You shouldn't have pretended you were hurt," she said falteringly. "You scared me half to death."

"Some injuries don't show." He treated her to a long penetrating look.

She didn't know what to make of this. She bit her lip, knowing that anything she said was bound to be the wrong thing.

For a long time Neill didn't speak. He only stared at her, his dark eyes gleaming. At last he said, "Tia's mine, isn't she?" The anguish welling in his eyes gripped her soul and tore at her heart.

"Tell me the truth," he demanded. She thought his eyes would burn right through her.

"Oh, God," she said brokenly. "This wasn't the way this was supposed to happen."

"And how was it supposed to happen, Bianca?" He sounded dangerously calm.

She waited for the words to occur to her, tried to think of how to explain. She felt on shaky ground here; she didn't know how to say what she wanted to say.

When he spoke, it was with barely concealed outrage. "What was your plan? How did you intend to let me know that I'm a father who wasn't living up to his responsibilities?"

She gaped at him. She had expected him to rail about her keeping a secret from him or perhaps to register bewilderment at the fact of his being a parent. She had even prepared herself for his rejection.

She stared at him blankly. "Responsibilities?"

"Fathers have responsibilities," he said tightly.

"I can provide for Tia," she retorted, utterly failing at keeping the edge out of her voice.

"Oh, there's no question about that. But after my father's cavalier attitude toward all his kids, don't you think I'd want to do better? At least Dad provided for us all financially. I wasn't even allowed to do that." He sounded bitter.

Bianca drew a deep breath. "I—I wasn't exactly thinking along those lines. I've known all along how you feel about families," she said, plunging ahead. "I know you aren't the kind of guy who wants a real home. You live at the back of beyond and you want to climb Mount Everest, for Pete's sake. You—"

His words were swift and urgent. "All of that has been true, but Bianca, listen to this and listen well. I never wanted to be like my father. And that's one reason why I've always been glad that I would never have a child. Whatever causes the Bellamy curse, I wanted it to stop right here, with me."

She lowered her gaze, unable to meet the intensity of his. Inside she felt about two feet high. "I'm not sure I believe in this Bellamy curse that you're so adamant about, but I knew you didn't want to settle down. That's why I—I couldn't bear to burden you with a baby."

The fierceness burned out of him all at once. He looped his arms around his knees and gazed off into the distance. "Burden me? God, Bianca. I never thought I *could* have children. I never dreamed I would. But now I have the chance to break the Bellamy curse by being a good father. That's something I never expected."

Bianca was conscious of the stream purling along in its bed, of the hawk circling overhead. She didn't, couldn't look at Neill, but his voice was insistent, yet calm, pouring out like the stream across the rocks. She took heart from it.

Neill turned his face toward her, and on it was an expression of wonder. "This morning I got up and stood by your baby's crib. And because she was yours, she was special to me. She was part of you. But then I realized Tia was mine, and I wanted to laugh and cry and scream to the world that Neill Bellamy has a daughter. And you would keep that from me?" He couldn't hide the incredulity that he was so obviously trying to keep in check.

"I didn't know you'd care," Bianca said helplessly. "How could I?"

"You didn't even tell me when you found out you were pregnant," he said.

"And if you'd known?" she shot back.

"I'd have come to you," he said.

"Out of duty? I didn't want that."

"It would have been more than duty."

"I was nothing to you. You were only being kind the night of the engagement party."

Something tightened in him; she could sense it. She saw his force of will playing out across his face as he leaned forward and gripped her shoulders so tightly that she winced. His eyes were steely, his voice emphatic. "Bianca, it was more than that, but you never gave me a chance to tell you. I couldn't believe how you just walked out after our night together last year. Why did you do it?"

She thought back to that night and was engulfed by the feelings she had felt then as if she were experiencing them for the first time. She'd been so embarrassed, shocked, stunned when Genevieve accused her of wanting Eric. She'd been humiliated, even though Caroline had tried to set her mother straight. And she'd felt guilty. Bianca *had* kept Eric out that afternoon.

Neill suddenly released her shoulders and Bianca dropped her face to her hands, wearily rubbing her eyes.

"Careful of your contact lenses," Neill warned.

She lowered her hands and smiled at him—a tentative smile, but a smile nonetheless. If he could think about her contact lenses, he couldn't be all that angry. He'd listen, and that was all that mattered at the moment.

She sighed. "All right. Let me try to explain how it was for me. I've never mentioned this to another soul, and I wouldn't now except that I know you'll understand. On that day Eric was overwhelmed with the enormity of cementing his engagement to Caroline, and he was showing signs of cold feet. I was trying to be a true friend to him while he talked out his feelings. And all the while I felt as if our childhood had truly ended and that I'd never have another friend as close as Eric, and I wanted to hold him close to my heart on that day, if only for a few hours."

"I didn't know Eric was worried."

"He didn't want anyone to know. We talked for a long time, and not just about his marriage but about me and my dreams and—well, afterward I was ready to release him to Caroline and participate wholeheartedly in the celebration of their engagement that night, happy for them both. But I never had the chance. Genevieve ruined it for me."

Neill nodded, his eyes intent on her face as she continued. "You know that on the night of the engagement party, I couldn't face everyone, and that's why I ran, and that's why you came out of the hotel to find me. And—and when I woke up the next morning, I was embarrassed about my behavior the night before. I practically threw myself at you, Neill, and I've never been so...so..."

"So passionate?" he supplied. In that moment, much to her surprise considering the serious nature of this conversation, he looked as if he were suppressing a grin.

"I guess that pretty much sums it up," she said ruefully.

To her surprise, Neill reached out and pulled her close. His lips were close to her ear as he spoke. "You were beautiful and exciting and so very, very sweet that night, Bianca. The next morning I couldn't wait to see you again, but you were gone. I was going to ask you to come to me in Colombia, to stay a while so we could get to know each other."

She could hardly believe he was saying these words; she shook her head clear. "You—you were?"

"You are—you always have been—someone special to me. Last year I began to realize it, but I thought you didn't have the same feelings about me. How could you when you split, not even leaving me a note? I thought I meant so little to you that you couldn't even stoop to say goodbye." His features were taut with passion, but there was something else, too, an emotion with which she was all too well acquainted. In that moment, Bianca knew that Neill's heartbreak had been as painful as her own.

Her eyes misted with tears. "That wasn't the way it was," she said, fighting for control. "I wanted you to know that—that—"

"What, Bianca?"

She expelled a long breath. "That I cared for you. That it was something special."

"After last night, I know that. Last night was exceptional, Bianca. When I think of how much I've wanted you this past year, I can't imagine why I didn't come looking for you," he said.

In weaker moments since the night in the gazebo, she had dreamed that Neill Bellamy might suddenly appear in her life, but she'd always come to her senses, and for good reason. "I wouldn't have wanted to see you. I was as big as a house," she said.

"Because you were carrying my child. And you would have been beautiful to me. You should have let me know." He sounded reproachful.

"I didn't want you to feel obligated," she whispered. "I didn't want you to think I wanted anything."

"And how about what *I* wanted?"

"I didn't know what *you* wanted."

"My point exactly. And let me tell you what I want right now. I want to make love to you again the way we did last night, to feel my lips on yours, my hands caressing your breasts."

She thought she would never forget his face as it was in that moment: dark eyes utterly earnest and lustrous with desire, tiny laugh lines fanning outward from their edges; strong straight nose, nostrils flared; a sensuous lower lip that she longed to nibble. "Then we both want the same thing," she said shakily.

"Which is amazing, isn't it?" he said mildly. "Do you know how seldom people actually want the same thing at the same moment? In the human experience, it's really quite rare."

He pulled her to him and rolled her over so that she lay pinned beneath on a bed of ferns. The earth was solid and warm beneath her head, and the air was filled with the rush of flowing water and the round, full-bodied notes of birds singing in the woods.

"Wait a minute," she said, straining against him, but he laughed low in his throat.

"I've been waiting a whole year. Isn't that long enough?" Neill, straddling her, was already shrugging out of his shirt. He swiftly folded it to make a pillow for her head and began to unbutton her blouse, making such slow progress that she finally nudged his hands away and finished the job herself.

"A woman after my own heart," he said. "No bra."

"I didn't take the time to put it on," she said, faintly apologetic.

"You got a slight sunburn yesterday," he said.

"Only enough to give me some color. I haven't been out in the sun since the baby was born." It was hard to carry on a conversation as if nothing else were going on; she spared a wary glance for Black Jack, still munching in the distance and paying absolutely no attention to them.

Neill curved his hands around her breasts, teasing the nipples until they stood erect. "Quite a bit of you is going to be exposed to the sun today," Neill said.

"If someone comes, they might see," she whispered.

"The only people who are going to come are you and me," he said, His hands moved downward, and he trailed a string of kisses along her throat.

"Neill," she began, but he silenced her with a kiss on the lips. By the time he released her lips, she couldn't remember her objections.

"Don't worry, Bianca, I ride Black Jack in this meadow all the time," Neill said reassuringly, his breath warm against her skin. "No one lives at the farm, and in more than a week I've never even seen evidence of one other person. And I've always wanted to make love to you on the banks of a creek hidden by tall grass and sweet-smelling fern.''

The warm, sun-washed scent of him filled her nostrils, and his beard was rough against her breast. She closed her eyes and abandoned herself to the exquisite sensitivity of the moment. She trembled in anticipation as his hands feathered across her breasts and then lower.

''What's this?'' he said.

She opened her eyes. He was looking at the faint lines webbed low on her abdomen.

''Stretch marks,'' she said, somehow embarrassed. ''I gained a lot of weight with Tia.''

''Will they go away?'' He sounded alarmed.

''No.'' She moved as if to turn on her side, but he held her there.

''Don't be ashamed,'' he said. ''You have them because you were carrying my baby. *My* baby.'' The word was infused with a sense of wonder. He touched his lips to the stretch marks, but she wound her hands through his hair and pulled his face up to hers.

''I hate it that you had to go through pregnancy and childbirth by yourself. Was it a difficult pregnancy and birth?'' he said, gazing deeply into her eyes.

''I had morning sickness a lot during the first three months, and I was exhausted most of the time. From what I can tell, it's that way for a lot of women. The birth was normal in every way.''

''I should have been there,'' he said.

She was touched by his sincerity. ''I can't really imagine you in the delivery room coaching me to breathe,'' she said, smiling at him.

"I'd be good at it. I've been breathing all my life."

She giggled but sobered quickly when she realized that he was only halfway joking. "I was fine, and I wasn't alone. I had my mother. And Tia."

"And Tia. I'll have to get to know her better."

"Mmm," she said, not ready to think about that yet. Her mouth sought his, blossoming beneath his lips. The stubble of his beard bit into her cheek, and she fumbled ineptly with the fastening of his jeans until he took over and slid out of them. At the same time she shimmied out of the rest of her clothes, and then he pressed her backward into the fresh verdant greenery where they lay silently for a long time, glorying in the exquisite sensation of intimacy.

Sunlight dappled his dark hair and skin; it dazzled her. Or he dazzled her, and she wasn't sure which. She didn't know how many women ever got to live their dreams, but she was living hers now, this very moment.

"What is that word you say to Tia, the one where you call her something that means she is dear to you?" he murmured close to her ear.

"*Cara,*" she said unsteadily.

He lifted himself up on his elbows. "*Cara.* I like it," he said.

"And '*cara mia*'—my dear."

"*Cara mia,*" he repeated, looking down at her with ineffable tenderness.

Bianca thought that in that moment, she must be experiencing the fullest measure of happiness allotted to anyone in one lifetime. As Neill slid his body over hers, he said, "I wonder if any other two people in the world ever enjoyed lovemaking more than we do."

"I doubt it," she replied, sure of the truth of this.

"Why is it so good with us?"

Because I'm crazy in love with you and have been since I was a kid, she wanted to shout.

All she said was, "Could we please stop talking about it and just plain do it?"

He chuckled deep in his throat. "We don't 'just plain do it.' You make it sound simple, like frying an egg. We're talking gourmet here, Bianca."

She could feel his arousal, and she didn't want to wait any longer. "We're talking entirely too much," she said as the pulse quickened in his neck and her body arched to fit his. Reality slipped away as her softness engulfed him, and after that they didn't talk at all for a very long time.

"DO YOU HAVE any idea what time it is? We've missed the wedding breakfast," Bianca said, sitting straight up.

Neill lay with his arm across his eyes. His skin gleamed in the bright sunlight, and she thought she had never seen a more perfect physique.

"I can tell by the way my stomach is rumbling." He rolled over on his stomach and rested his head on her chest. His arms went around her, his fingers caressing her spine slowly.

"Haven't you had enough?" she said.

"Have you?"

She thought about this. In terms of a lifetime, maybe not. Could she say that without making it sound as if she expected him to hang around for the rest of her life? Probably not.

"I asked you first," she said.

He snorted. "We sound like kids. We sound like you and Eric in the old days."

"We are children, in a way. We're hesitant and unsure, looking to each other to find out what we're supposed to be doing.''

He kissed the tip of her nose. "What we shouldn't be doing is overanalyzing. Let's have a picnic.''

"You brought food?''

He lifted a shoulder and let it fall. "I wasn't planning to go back to the hotel until it was time to get ready for the wedding. The kitchen made me a few sandwiches and I brought some fruit. Let's see what else they packed.'' He pulled on his jeans, smiled at her, and walked over to Black Jack where he dug in one of the saddlebags.

He returned triumphant, holding out a small lunch pack. "They even threw in a couple of sodas,'' he said.

Bianca dressed quickly, and they settled on a large flat rock overhanging the stream. Neill spread the food out in the sun, and they downed the sandwiches and some of the fruit before lighting into the fudge brownies for which the hotel was famous.

Afterward they dangled their feet in the water and let little minnows nibble at their toes. A vociferous chipmunk chattered at them from a tree stump, and Neill chattered back at him until Bianca laughed. Neill kissed her until she stopped laughing, and then he held her hand and they lay back to gaze at the clouds so high above. Neill lifted her hand, studied the lines in her palm, and pressed his lips to it. He placed her hand over his heart where she could feel it beating, and then he closed his eyes.

She turned her head toward him and studied the firmness of his jaw, which reminded her of Tia's. She wondered if Neill would ever love his daughter; wanting to be a responsible father wasn't the same as loving her. Certainly it was part of it, though.

And did he love her, Bianca? If he didn't, would he someday, given the chance?

She sighed, knowing that all of this would have to be worked out later. But when, she didn't know. She was scheduled to leave tomorrow. As if he could read her mind, Neill opened his eyes and propped himself up on one elbow.

"Will you and Tia come to visit me in Colombia?" he said.

A year ago she would have leapt at the chance. And she certainly wanted to be with Neill. She wanted to see how he lived, spend time with him, laugh with him, love with him. But reality was rearing its intrusive head, and she had to take other facets of her life into consideration.

"We could come in October after I introduce the new line of popular-priced jewelry," she said reluctantly.

"October! That's months away! Tia will be four months older by then." She could feel his dismay.

"Neill, I can't just abandon my business after taking time out for this wedding. And I'll need to bring a nanny, and I'm not sure if the one we have now would want to go to Colombia even if she's well enough, and she might not be."

Neill looked so disheartened that she tried to think. "Maybe if I could persuade my mother to take a more active part in the company, I could come in August," she said. Ursula was a member of the board of directors of D'Alessandro, and both her business and design sense were impeccable. Also, she was good at dealing with Vittorio.

"In August, I'm climbing Everest," Neill said.

His words pricked her bubble, and it burst. If she

was willing to adjust her schedule, couldn't he do the same? He would if he really wanted to get to know Tia, as he'd said. He would if he loved her.

But he hadn't said he loved her. He'd said he wanted to get to know Tia better. He'd said he wanted to be a responsible father. All well and good, but not what she longed to hear. And she couldn't make him love her, nor could she force him to see things her way.

She felt slightly sick. "I think we'd better go back to the hotel," she said. "It's time to get ready for the wedding."

"Bianca, I've planned to climb Everest for a long time," he said slowly.

She turned to face him, not wanting to throw cold water on his plans but knowing that she needed to make her stand clear.

"And you've said *I'm* running. Neill, Mount Everest is about as far as anyone can run and still stay on this planet. But you know what? When you come down, the people you're trying so hard to leave behind will still be here. And so will the problems associated with them." She made him look at her, made him blink. He flushed angrily and walked swiftly to Black Jack, leaving her alone at the edge of the creek.

When he led the horse to her, she was dusting off the seat of her pants. She didn't speak and neither did he. He hoisted her up on the horse first and swung into place behind her. And although she rode in front of him on Black Jack, even though she felt the warmth of his body through their clothes, they seemed miles apart. It was as though he were already high on a lofty mountain and she was back in Europe, and it was as if they had never shared their feelings or talked about plans or even made love.

But they had, and that was as much of a problem as everything else.

When they reached the stables, she slid down from the horse immediately.

"I'd better get back to my room and make sure my dress is in order for the wedding," she said.

"Bianca..." He sounded exasperated, but so was she.

"I'll see you later," she said, not entirely succeeding in keeping the chill out of her voice.

"Right. We'll see each other at the wedding. There's no avoiding it, is there?" he called after her. If he cared for her at all, she couldn't tell from his tone of voice.

Bianca blinked tears from her eyes as she made her way back to the hotel. She was hoping she wouldn't run into any other members of the wedding party, but as she was sneaking into the lobby through the doors leading out to the garden terrace, she spotted Caroline hunched in a chair in the corner near the French doors and crying her heart out.

"Caroline," Bianca said. "Are you all right?"

"There's not going to be a wedding," Caroline sobbed.

Bianca knelt beside Caroline. "If Eric has hurt you, Caroline, I'm going to give him a good talking to. How can he be such a fool, that's what I want to know. Why would he—"

Caroline blinked wide blue eyes at her. "Eric?" she said slowly.

By this time Bianca was fuming. "Yes, Eric, just another no-good Bellamy when you get right down to it."

"But Bianca, Eric isn't the reason the wedding is off. Mummy fired the minister. We don't have anyone to perform the ceremony."

Chapter Eleven

"Oh, yes we do," said Kevin, who happened to wander in at just that moment.

"Who?" chorused Bianca and Caroline.

"Saffron." He was carrying a putting iron and was clearly just back from the putting green.

"*Saffron!*" chorused Caroline and Bianca.

"Saffron," Kevin repeated smugly. "She's a licensed minister." He leaned on the golf club and grinned.

"I thought Saffron was the co-owner with Lizzie of The Velvet Fig. It's a mail-order company," Caroline said in bewilderment as she dabbed at her mascara with a damp handkerchief.

"Well, I don't know about that. All I know is that Saffron told me she's performed marriage ceremonies before."

Caroline was out of the chair like a shot. "I'd better go talk to her. I think I saw her headed toward the pool. Excuse me, both of you."

Kevin and Bianca stared blankly at each other.

"Well, what could you expect," Kevin said with a twinkle. "It's a Bellamy wedding. Anything can happen—"

"And usually does," Bianca chimed in so that they repeated the words in unison.

"Well, Beans, do you have time for a cup of coffee?"

Bianca remembered Kevin from when he used to come to visit Budge at the Lake Forest house. He had been an annoyance then, always wanting to tag along when she and Eric were teenagers and he'd been a little kid.

"Maybe later," Bianca told him. "I've got things to do."

"Do you think I should follow Caroline? Help her to find Saffron?"

"You might as well," Bianca called over her shoulder. Kevin disappeared out the French doors again, golf club over his shoulder.

All right, thought Bianca. Next problem. Whatever it might be.

Well, it wasn't the dress, which was hanging freshly pressed in the closet, but it might be the message light on the phone, which was blinking. She checked her messages and learned that Vittorio had called.

While she removed the dress from its protective plastic bag, she tried to figure out if it was too late to phone Vittorio in Italy. She decided it wasn't, especially since she was sure he'd want to know that she'd seen the video of emeralds from the Viceroy-Bellamy mine.

She called Vittorio at his villa and was delighted when he answered. Quickly she told him about viewing the video of the Viceroy-Bellamy emeralds.

"Ah, Bianca, you are right to start a gemstone line! With quality stones in the family, how can you go wrong? Tell me, do you have a problem with going ahead? With hiring the people we'll need, setting up the paperwork?''

''No, Vittorio. Have our people call their people and get on the case.''

Vittorio laughed. The ''their people, our people'' line was a joke between them, since she and Vittorio were ''the people'' at D'Alessandro. ''When Ursula comes back from her honeymoon, I will suggest that she call the Viceroy-Bellamy mines. Perhaps she will want to go there. She is an intrepid traveler, your mother, and she loves to shop.'' He laughed again.

''Well, Mother will probably love it, and she'll drag Claudio along, and he'll enjoy it, too.''

''I am glad you called, Bianca. I have missed you.''

''I miss you too,'' Bianca said before she hung up. There was an ache in her throat. It was true. She did miss her work. Until she had this conversation with Vittorio, she hadn't realized how much. More than ever she realized that her work was her link to another life, one that made sense, one without any Bellamys in it whatsoever.

AT LONG LAST—at very, very long last, it seemed to Bianca—it was time for the wedding of Miss Caroline Lambert Knox to Mr. Eric Bellamy. The garden at Swan's Folly had been transformed into a confection of pink and white roses and pink-and-white-striped tents and pink and white streamers marking off the reserved rows.

Guests had already been seated and the bridesmaids were lined up on the terrace ready to proceed to the Folly for the wedding ceremony. As they waited for Genevieve's cue to proceed down the aisle, an airplane swooped low over the grounds, momentarily drowning out the sedate strains of the string quartet sawing its way through a Bach trio.

"Damned reporters," grumbled Hainsworth, standing behind them with Caroline on his arm. "Rivals of Eric's magazine, no doubt. You'd think they'd let the wedding proceed in peace."

Over Lizzie's shoulder, Bianca saw Saffron emerge from the Folly. She was wearing a yellow velvet dress, long and sleeveless, and she'd topped off the ensemble with an enormous matching hat. Bianca, who liked things simple and elegant, would have called Saffron's outfit the Scarlett O'Hara Just Snatched My Dress From the Drapery Rod look.

Saffron situated herself under the bower of white roses erected for the occasion, and Eric and Neill took their places to one side of her, both of them gazing expectantly toward the terrace.

"Good grief," said Petsy, looking askance at Saffron's getup.

Bianca whispered to Lizzie, "What church is Saffron ordained in?" Genevieve turned around and glared at them, but Bianca didn't care.

"Church?" said Lizzie, looking puzzled.

"Kevin said she's a minister!"

"Shh," hissed Genevieve.

"Saffron isn't ordained in any church. She's a member of the Cloister of the Goddess of Universal Bliss and Sunshine. They're into bliss and joy. That's why they love weddings." Lizzie shrugged. "I think all of them perform ceremonies."

"Cloister of the *what?*" Genevieve asked loudly. "Did you say..." Her voice grew fainter. "Did you say *goddess?* Good Lord."

Lizzie bit her lip, and Bianca stared blankly.

At this point, Kevin tugged impatiently at Genevieve's arm, and they started off down the aisle.

Bianca giggled; she couldn't help it.

"Okay, this is it," hissed Lizzie.

"It had better be," Bianca said. The words couldn't have been more heartfelt.

In front of the Folly, Eric waited expectantly as the bride started down the aisle. Eric was much more nervous about the wedding than Neill had expected him to be, which was why it was a good thing that he and Neill had patched up their quarrel earlier. Just before the ceremony, Neill had told Eric that he now knew that Bianca's baby was his own.

Eric had seemed relieved. Well, he ought to be. It couldn't have been fun for Eric to know that his own brother suspected him of fathering a child by a bridesmaid, and Bianca at that. Maybe that very suspicion on Caroline's part is what had fueled the arguments between bride and groom. Who knew? One thing for sure, Eric sure wasn't talking. In fact, he didn't look at all like a bridegroom should look, which was slightly nervous but totally in thrall to his bride. Eric didn't have that enthralled look. He looked—well, resigned.

Neill glanced at Bianca, who stood on the other side of Saffron. Bianca was avoiding his eyes, and he knew why. She wanted commitment. But was he ready for that? He could barely admit that he was half in love with her, and commitment required being totally, completely and irrevocably in love.

Caroline emerged from the hotel for the march down the aisle. She wore a lacy gown and a frothy full-length veil flowing as long as her train.

He sneaked another look at Bianca. In that moment he was sure that no bride could hold a candle to her,

putrid-pink dress or not. She stood calm and erect with
a small wistful smile playing across her lips, those lips
that he had so recently enjoyed kissing. She had always
been a striking woman, but today she was even more
so. She managed to look cool and collected despite the
heat of the day, and she was so sensationally beautiful
in that ridiculous fluffy dress that the sight of her made
his throat catch. Would their little girl look like her?
He hoped so.

Hainsworth, advancing with Caroline on his arm,
was playing the part of the proud father, and Genevieve, for once, smiled benignly as her daughter
reached the place where her bridegroom waited. The
guests were suitably hushed, Saffron looked solemn,
and there was a helicopter homing in overhead.

A helicopter?

Neill looked up at it as he felt the down rush of air
from its blades. *Whoppeta whoppeta* they went, and the
guests were all gaping, too, even as the intrepid Saffron, as officiating minister, went into a spiel about
bliss and joy that Neill could barely hear because of
the noise. Out of the corner of his eyes, he saw Bianca
looking at him, eyebrows slightly lifted in a question
mark. He shrugged, and Bianca quickly looked away.
Another helicopter appeared from somewhere, and he
saw a photographer leaning out the door. Stupid paparazzi; he didn't know why they or anyone else cared
about these nuptials, major society wedding or not.

Neill's mind wandered as he thought how proud
Hainsworth had looked as he walked his daughter
down the aisle. In his split-second imaginings, Neill
saw himself romping on the beach with a two-year-old
Tia and admiring her drawings at her grade-school
open house and shooting videos of her dancing at a

teenage party. He realized how hard it would be to see a daughter off to college knowing that she would never live at home again. He even imagined himself handing his daughter into the protection of another man, her future husband.

In his reverie, he forgot Eric. He forgot Bianca. He even forgot the helicopters. He knew in his heart that fatherhood couldn't be taken lightly. It was serious business, and he broke out in a cold sweat just thinking about it. He wasn't ready to be a father. He might never be ready to be a father.

Suddenly he understood what his own father must have felt when he was a baby, and in that moment the mists of confusion peeled away and one of the great mysteries was finally revealed to him.

He finally understood that happiness actually was the central problem, and that the way you found it and the way you kept it was by forming meaningful relationships with the other people in your life. With his heart in his mouth, he mutely sought Bianca's eyes, wanting to tell her, wanting her to know.

But she wasn't looking his way. She was looking up at the helicopters, and so was everyone else.

BIANCA STRAINED to hear Saffron's words. Saffron had reached the part of the ceremony where she asked if anyone knew of any reason why this couple shouldn't be joined in holy matrimony. There was a definite pause. Saffron looked at Lizzie, and Lizzie looked at Saffron. Saffron looked at Bianca, and Bianca stared back. Finally Saffron looked at Eric and Caroline.

Saffron had to shout to be heard over the noise of the helicopters. "Do you, Caroline, take Eric to be your lawful wedded husband?"

Caroline said nothing. Bianca shifted uncomfortably in her dyed-to-match shoes of pink peau de soie. They hurt; she'd have a blister before the day was over.

Caroline still wasn't saying anything. Saffron tilted her head quizzically, and Bianca frowned. Something struck her as not being quite right.

"Caroline?" Saffron said, but because of the noise, they only saw her lips move.

Genevieve, in the front row, leaned forward and hissed, "Say it, Caroline!"

Caroline blinked, looked at Eric, and shouted "No!"

"OH, HELL," said Hainsworth. The wedding had erupted into a melee. After her startling pronouncement and the ensuing shock when everyone was saying something, half of which was accusatory and none of which Bianca could remember, Caroline had hightailed it into the hotel followed by Petsy. While everyone was gawking at the spectacle of the bride defecting from the ceremony, a skydiving photographer had parachuted right into the middle of the gathering and landed on top of Lizzie. Joe, fireman that he was, carried her away, presumably to revive her. Neill punched the obstreperous sky diver in the stomach, after which the sky diver had jumped in the pond and was attacked by a furious Godzilla. Nana was still running around and asking, "What did Caroline say? Can anyone tell me what's the matter?"

"Plenty," Neill growled under his breath. He nursed his sore hand, then stuck it in his pocket. He wondered where the helicopters had gone; they'd disappeared in the direction of the swimming pool.

Bianca glanced at him, not sure whether she should be exasperated with him for hitting the sky diver or not. She decided not, considering. Over to the left of the Folly, Genevieve was sobbing loudly and interspersing her wails with dire predictions of kidnappers. Bianca couldn't see Eric anywhere, and there was something else to worry about. Someone had knocked over a huge vase of pink and white roses at the end of one of the rows of seats, and the resulting flow of water threatened to swamp her hated pink shoes.

Delicately she lifted her voluminous skirts and tiptoed clear of the stream of water before sinking down on one of the chairs and watching the confused guests as they tried to figure out what had happened.

"Do you know what's going on?" asked Lambie, who as ring bearer was all decked out in formal wear. He hitched himself onto a chair beside Bianca.

"I don't think Caroline and Eric are getting married," supplied Neill helpfully.

Lambie thought about this. "Well, Mr. Frog says that's okay," he said.

"Mr. Frog?" Bianca had in mind a cute stuffed animal, something green and soft and cuddly.

"Yeah, he didn't want to come to the wedding anyway." With some effort, Lambie pulled an ugly brown toad out of his pants pocket and held it aloft. It immediately escaped his grasp and hopped directly onto the front of a round matronly lady who jumped and screamed and ran. Lambie howled with laughter.

"Okay, sport, no more of that," Neill said, looking as if he was holding back laughter.

"Aren't we going to have the party?" Lambie asked after a few seconds.

"I don't know anything," sighed Bianca, gazing dispiritedly down into her wilting bouquet and sliding the offending shoes off her feet.

"Of course we're having the party," Hainsworth barked somewhere behind them. Bianca turned around so she could see him. Looking grim but determined, the beleaguered father of the bride jumped up on a chair and clapped his hands. It took a while, but everyone finally stopped milling and began to pay attention.

"Thanks to all of you for coming today," he said. "Now I don't know what the problem is exactly, but one thing I do know. The Swan's Inn hotel chain is famed for its hospitality, and we won't turn any guest away unhappy. I have decided that the reception will go on as planned! No matter what!" This announcement was greeted by an uncertain round of applause and a collective sign of relief.

Nana, poor thing, finally heard something. She shimmied in delight and yelled, "Let's party!"

Suddenly a band started playing in one of the tents, and as if on cue a long line of waiters marched from the hotel bearing enormous trays of hors d'oeuvres. Guests straightened their clothes and fluffed their hair, and Genevieve blotted at her running mascara gingerly with her hanky in one hand while reaching for a Rob Roy on the rocks with the other.

"Well, Bianca," Neill said, looking down at her with an air of resigned amusement. "Shall we go to the reception?"

Bianca slid her feet back into her shoes. Her heels were halfway to a blister, and her longline bra was biting into her rib cage, but, with a sense of perverse fascination, she couldn't wait to see what happened next at this Bellamy wedding. Or non-wedding. As it were.

THE SILVERY STRAINS of Leo Lavin's Orchestra, the band of choice for society weddings from Lake Forest to Grosse Point, filled the pink-and-white-striped tent on the wide level part of the lawn below the hotel terrace.

Neill, after investigating and learning that Eric was nowhere to be found, wanted nothing so much as to hold Bianca in his arms.

He'd seen her dancing with others, and her grace of movement on the dance floor had caught him off guard. He couldn't recall that they had ever danced together, and he intended to remedy the situation immediately.

He pushed his way through the crowd of men surrounding Bianca. Every unattached male at the wedding seemed enchanted with her, pink butt bow notwithstanding. Neill hovered at the edge of the crowd, unable to make any progress toward his goal but close enough to hear what was being said.

Bianca was regaling her admirers with news about D'Alessandro. They seemed to be hanging on every word, eager for details about the fall line, about sales last year, about her expansion plans for the company. He didn't quite catch the context, but he distinctly caught the word *Vittorio*.

At that, he shouldered into the group, but his position was slightly behind Bianca and he was sure she didn't see him. Her hair hung down her back, shimmering whenever she tilted her head. It was all he could do not to reach out and touch it.

She paused in what she was saying, and he cleared his throat.

"Bianca, let's dance," he said into the air somewhere in the vicinity of her left ear, and she whirled around. A few strands of her hair brushed his cheek.

She lifted a hand and tucked the renegade strands

behind her ear. "Neill," she said. "I didn't know you were there." Her eyes were wide, and he could tell nothing about what she was thinking from their expression.

But for him, everyone else in the room disappeared and it was only Bianca. He wanted to drown in those blue eyes, to dive deep into their depths and never surface. He took Bianca's hand and led her to the dance floor where the band was winding up a slow ballad. He had just taken her in his arms, when, without warning, the music segued into a mind-walloping beat that seemed to combine rap, rock and roll and disco into one tune.

He looked down at Bianca and she looked up at him, and suddenly they both broke into laughter. Several much younger couples as well as Fawn, who was dragging a protesting Lambie onto the floor, began to gyrate in time to the music, arms and legs flailing wildly.

"I hate dancing when the people don't touch," he said.

"So do I. You might as well be dancing by yourself."

"Which seems pointless, doesn't it? Bianca, maybe we'd better sit this one out."

"Maybe." She looked toward the long table in the front of the tent where the other groomsmen and bridesmaids were sitting. "I don't think I want to sit at the table for the wedding party, though."

"I don't, either."

To one side of the bandstand was a small round table shielded from the others by a few strategically placed potted palms. It may have been there for the musicians to use on their breaks, but for now it provided a private place.

Neill led Bianca there and held her chair for her as she sat down. "You look lovely, Bianca," he said.

"Please," she said dismissively, but he laughed.

He leaned forward. "You make even a putrid-pink bridesmaid dress with a butt bow as big as—what did you say it was as big as?"

"Rhode Island," she supplied.

"You make a funny-looking pink dress with a butt bow as big as Rhode Island look like a Paris original."

She groaned. "I know a few Paris designers personally, and they'd all be highly insulted by that comment."

He became more serious. "You must have an exciting life in Paris and Rome," he said.

"Not so exciting anymore," she said. "Not since the baby."

"I'm sorry," he said, and he was. The baby had created problems in her life, and she'd borne them alone.

"I don't mind. Once I would have, but once Tia arrived and she was so wonderful, my life changed. And for the better."

She was so earnest, so direct, and, it seemed to him, so brave, that it brought a lump to his throat.

"I keep thinking of you in Rome, finding out you were going to have my baby. You must have been so angry with me."

They accepted glasses of champagne from a passing waiter, and Bianca took her time answering.

"I suppose I was, Neill, but only at first. And I wasn't only angry with you. I thought I had been very foolish." Her eyes met his, and he realized that she was telling the truth.

"You must know that I didn't think there was a

snowball's chance in hell that you could become pregnant," he said.

"I know. I remember when you didn't come home from Harvard for spring break, and why."

"We both should have been more careful."

She ran a finger around the top of her champagne glass. "I wouldn't change anything, Neill. In a way, I didn't realize how empty my life was before I had Tia. The only thing is that I—" But she stopped talking and looked away.

He reached across the table and clasped her hand. "Don't hold back," he said. "I want to know what you're thinking."

She drew a deep breath. "That I wish I could give her what I didn't have—a stable home life."

Her words stabbed through him like a knife to the heart. "The kind neither of us had?" he said, his voice low.

"Yeah," she said, smiling a sad smile. "Like that."

The band seemed too loud now, too intrusive. Even though he would have liked to leave the tent, taking Bianca with him, and find a quiet place where they could talk without all the extraneous noise and commotion, he didn't want to suggest it for fear that she'd refuse.

"I plan to consolidate the operations of D'Alessandro in one place on this side of the Atlantic and raise Tia in the U.S.," Bianca said. "I'll hire people to supervise the European end of the business. I'll have my career, but travel will be kept to a minimum. I'll find a house somewhere, a good school, everything Tia needs."

"I'll want to visit," he said. "She should know her father."

Bianca looked away. "I suppose so," she said.

"I want to give you financial support, too." He waved away her objection. "I know you don't need it, but I'm her father. She's no longer only your responsibility."

"Does that mean you want to help decide where she goes to school, have a say in the people that I hire to care for her, things like that?"

He met her gaze. "Bianca, I haven't thought these things through. It was only this morning that I realized that I really had a daughter. I don't know all the things I need to consider, I'm only bringing them up as I think of them, and when you look at me like that I can't even think at all."

He thought he detected a slight flush of her cheeks, and he was about to request something of her, something he wasn't sure she would or could do, when Nana lurched by doing her own version of the '60s dance, the Watusi.

"So this is the one," she said conspiratorially to Neill with a wink at Bianca. "Remember what I said—'impress upon her the strength of your ardor.'" She laughed her foghorn laugh and resumed expressing the lightness of her being with some poor schmuck who looked as if he'd been put through a wringer.

"What on earth is Nana talking about?" Bianca demanded.

"I think she wants us to dance together," he said smoothly. "And if you don't, you're going to have to endure dancing with my father." Budge, displaying his trademark cocky grin, was descending upon them from the other side of the dance floor.

"Not on your life," Bianca said, rising quickly and preceding Neill to the dance floor as the band abandoned its foray into the ridiculous and settled back into the sublime.

When Neill took Bianca in his arms, it was as though she fit exactly. He'd been schooled at Miss Anita's Junior Assembly in Lake Forest and knew he was a good dancer, but Bianca was naturally light on her feet and followed him as if it were second nature.

"Have you always been such a good dancer?" he asked.

She smiled up at him. "Maybe you should have asked me to dance in the old days. You would have found out," she said.

Neill wrinkled his forehead. "We were never at a dance together."

"Wrong, Neill. When our parents got married—"

"At our parents' wedding, I was nursing a grudge because I'd been called home from a perfectly wonderful vacation sailing in Maine for what I considered another of Budge's peccadilloes."

She leaned back and stared at him. "You thought my mother was a 'peccadillo?'"

"I didn't think it would last. I was right, wasn't I?"

She sighed and relaxed. "Yes, I suppose so. But back to where we could have danced together before this. I distinctly remember the Stein bar mitzvah when we were holding hands dancing the hora, and the music changed to something for couples and I was devastated because you turned to Jennifer Belknap instead of me."

"Ah, Jennifer Belknap. She had red hair—"

"And a red face."

"And green eyes that lit up when I suggested we take a ride in my new Corvette, which we did. We ended up at her house, where her parents weren't." He laughed.

"I was crushed because you disappeared with an older woman."

"Jennifer was all of eighteen at the time."

"I was sixteen and no competition at all, now that I think about it. I still had braces on my teeth."

"You turned out all right, though," he said, pulling her closer.

"It took you long enough to admit it."

"Too long. And now it's all complicated by other things."

She rested her cheek against his shoulder. She wished he hadn't said that. The things that complicated her life—her work, her child—meant a great deal to her.

She said against his jacket, "For a while, a short space in time, let's not think about any of that. Please?" Her voice trembled.

His arms moved tighter around her. "Okay," was all he said, and she let herself be buoyed up by the music and the solid firm bulk of Neill Bellamy as he guided her around the dance floor. Dancing with him was another part of her dream fulfilled. She'd sat on the sidelines at their parents' wedding, fourteen years old and yearning after a suave nineteen-year-old male who was so full of himself that he didn't even realize she existed, or if he did, he regarded her as a nuisance on the periphery of his splendor. And she'd watched him walk out the door with Jennifer Belknap at the Stein bar mitzvah; Jennifer, who had a voice like fingernails screeching on a chalkboard.

But now she was the one in his arms, she was the one with her hand resting lightly in his, and she was the one he'd been with all last night and even in the morning, and though there probably was no future for them as a couple, he was the father of her child. And he'd made it clear that he wanted to maintain a place in Tia's life. What that meant for the two of them as a couple, she couldn't know yet. Maybe she didn't want to know. Maybe it was enough to enjoy this moment, this closeness. Maybe.

Chapter Twelve

"Let's go," Neill murmured in Bianca's ear.

"Go?" she leaned back and gazed up at him, thinking that never had he been more desirable.

"Yes, go. So I can 'impress upon you the strength of my ardor.' We can go to your room, my cottage, the gazebo—"

"Not the gazebo," Bianca said.

"Then come to my cottage and I'll order champagne and a tray of edibles," he said. "We'll have our own celebration."

"Of what?"

"Of having a daughter," he said.

She looked down at the pink embroidered fabric of the hated bridesmaid dress. "I'd like to go to my room first and change clothes," she said.

"Deal."

Conspiratorially they crept out through a flap in the tent and away through the shadows, away from the reception, into the hotel and up the stairs to Bianca's room. Once inside she turned her back to him and showed him where to unfasten the hooks.

"This," he said, "is fun." He kissed the back of

her neck, but she slipped out of his grasp and slid out of the poufy dress in one fluid motion.

"It's going to get to be a lot more fun," she said with a hint of insouciance. She grabbed slacks and a light summer sweater from the closet. "I'll be back in a minute," she said as she went into the bathroom.

Neill heard her opening and closing the cabinet doors and running water in the basin. While he waited, he went to the window to look out. Out under the tent, the reception was in full swing, and he wondered where his brother Eric was right now. He also wondered what had gotten into Caroline. At least by this time, the helicopters and the airplane had gone away, and from the looks of things in the tent below, Hainsworth was putting on quite a party.

He remembered his promise to order champagne and goodies delivered to Mulberry Cottage and went to the phone beside the bed. He called room service and ordered a bottle of Cristal, his favorite, and then on a whim asked if the dining room could obtain two Burger King Whoppers.

"Whoppers, sir?" said the puzzled clerk.

"Yes. With two orders of fries."

"I suppose we can do that, sir."

"Good. Have them at Mulberry Cottage in forty-five minutes or so."

"Will do, sir. Anything else?"

"No, thanks," Neill said, and as he replaced the phone in its cradle, his eyes fell on the notepad beside it. There were a few doodles scribbled alongside the name "Vittorio."

Vittorio? Who *was* this Vittorio whose name kept turning up?

He turned to greet Bianca as she emerged from the

bathroom. Her eyes were bright, her face glowing. She'd scrubbed off her makeup and looked entirely natural with her lovely hair sweeping her shoulders and simple diamond studs winking from her earlobes.

In his opinion, diamonds were usually given to a woman from a man. And these looked like high-quality diamonds, too.

Still, Bianca was a jewelry designer. She could be wearing any kind of jewelry. And yet, she said she was still considering expanding into gemstones, so certainly she wouldn't have designed these. Besides, they were too simple to have been designed by Bianca, whose well-known trademark was boldness in jewelry design.

Would this Vittorio, whoever he was, have given Bianca diamonds? He felt a pang of jealousy, and he decided that Bianca would look better in emeralds.

"Let's go," she said. "Before something else happens."

He slid his arm around her as they went out the door, but he couldn't help thinking about Vittorio anyway.

"TELL ME ABOUT the mine," Bianca said. They were in his cottage sitting in front of the fireplace, which Neill was determined to light against the chill that he said was in the air. She didn't feel much chill, but she thought a fire would be romantic.

Neill fanned the growing blaze. "When we took it over, it was losing money because of poor management. It's finally turned around, and I'm going to take a less active part in running it from now on. There are some things I really want to do." The logs finally caught, flaring so that the golden light illuminated Neill's face.

"Like climb Mount Everest?"

"That, and learn how to be a good father."

"But that can wait until you climb the mountain, right?" She cut a glance at him out of the corners of her eyes as he came to sit on the floor in front of the couch.

"Bianca, being a good father comes first. But climbing Everest is a chance that happens along only once in a lifetime." His jaw was set in that stubborn way he had, and even though she didn't agree with what he said, she found his stubbornness as appealing as anything else about him. Love, she thought, was dangerous. It made you overlook a person's inadequacies.

"We need to talk about things," she said helplessly. "We might not have another chance."

He picked up her hand and looked at it. She wore a gold-and-silver ring of her own design on the third finger of her right hand, and he twisted it around and looked at it.

"One of the things we need to talk about is Vittorio," he said.

She stared at him blankly. Why in the world, with so many other important things to discuss, would Neill want to know about her manager?

"You told me there isn't a man in your life at present," he said, his eyes burning into her.

"There isn't."

"I want to believe you, Bianca."

"And why shouldn't you?" She was beginning to feel angry.

"I saw the name Vittorio written on the pad beside your phone. It made me think that perhaps you hadn't been truthful."

Bianca yanked her hand away. "He's my manager,

Neill, and we've been calling back and forth to confer.''

He looked at her as if to measure the truth of her words. Then he tipped his head back and laughed. It was full-bodied laughter, long and loud.

''I thought—well, you have to admit that I had reason to doubt you were telling the truth.

''You mean because I didn't tell you about Tia?''

''Of course,'' he said, quieter now.

She stared into the flames. ''I deserved that,'' she said evenly.

''Tell me about Vittorio.''

She drew a deep breath. ''I've finally given him the go-ahead for the gemstone line, and he wants to know all about Viceroy-Bellamy mines and the emeralds. If you don't mind, I'd like to send him the videotape you showed me.''

''Sure. I'll mail it myself before I leave here,'' he said. A knock sounded at the door. ''That's the food I ordered,'' he said, getting up to answer it.

Bianca rallied at the thought of food. She hadn't eaten anything at the reception, and she was feeling shaky. However, the shakiness might be due to nervousness, not hunger, or to everything that had happened at the wedding or to something else that she'd rather not think about.

Neill brought the tray and set it on the low table beside the couch. On it were a bottle of Cristal in a silver ice bucket, two champagne flutes, and—

Two Burger King Whoppers?

She looked at Neill. He looked at her. And they both burst out laughing.

''It's something we both like,'' he said by way of explanation.

"Not just the same old hors d'oeuvres," she agreed.

"Not the same old crudités."

"Or boring onion dip."

He poured the champagne and held his glass up to hers. "To Tia," he said.

"To Tia," she said solemnly, and drank half of it down.

"Do you know, Bianca, I think you're my favorite relation," Neill said when they were lying side by side in front of the fire, their heads propped on pillows.

"We're not related," she said.

"We're something," he reasoned.

"We're parents."

"Do you have pictures of Tia when she was just born?"

"In the delivery room."

"And of the nursery where she sleeps?"

"Both of them—one in Paris and one in Rome."

"I can't wait to see them," he said.

She rolled over on her stomach and looked into his eyes. They were gentle, and she sensed his pain over all the losses he had felt in his life. "Why don't you come to Paris and to Rome after you climb Everest? You'll need somewhere to wind down."

"What do you mean, 'wind down?'" His eyes held a lurking amusement now.

"This," she said, kissing his eyelids playfully. "And this," she added, kissing his lips.

He pulled her on top of him and kissed her thoroughly. He tasted of champagne and of Burger King Whopper and of chances missed, of chances regained.

"I think," he said slowly, cupping her face in his hands, "I'd like to 'wind down' right now."

He kissed her, taking her breath away, and she

melted against him, inhaling his musky male scent, feeling the roughness of his skin against her cheek. She held on to him with all her might, closing her eyes against pestering doubts. For a moment he stopped and gazed at her, in his eyes a complexity of emotions, and then his lips were on her throat, his hands parting buttonholes from buttons, caressing her breasts and belly.

It felt so wonderful to be touched by him. And to be kissed by him on her nipples, darker now than before she had the baby, and to lift her hips so that he could slide her clothes away. Somehow his clothes slipped away, too, and then they were together again, urgently seeking and finding.

Now they were greedy, wanting everything all at once. The fire in the fireplace snapped and cracked, heating their faces and their bodies into a frenzy of desire. She guided him into her softness when she couldn't stand the wanting anymore, and he cried out as she rose to meet him. His arms crushed her to him as she pressed her face into his neck, and then she couldn't see, could only feel, and what she felt was so profound that she felt tears springing into her eyes.

But if he didn't feel the same thing, it was all wasted emotion, leading nowhere.

She held on and reveled in his hot breath on her hair, and she moaned his name and he gasped hers. When they reached their climax, it was together, and it was the best it could possibly be.

Afterward he pulled her into his arms and caressed her hair, saying nothing about the tears still damp on her cheeks. She marveled at the fulfillment she felt and wondered if he felt the same.

They slept briefly, dozing in each others' arms. When Bianca opened her eyes, Neill was wide-awake.

He smiled at her and kissed the tip of her nose, rousing her from a delicious sexual lethargy.

"I've been thinking about something you said," he said after a while.

She angled her head to look at him. He was staring into the fire, his expression thoughtful. Her look was questioning.

"It was when you said that you wished you could give Tia a stable home life, the kind neither of us ever had."

Bianca swallowed. "I remember," she said.

"Well, didn't you ever stop to think that the best way to provide that for Tia was to give her a daddy?"

"I suppose I did, but I didn't think you wanted to be a daddy," she said.

"And now that you know I do?"

"I—I—" Words failed her.

He sat up and looked down at her, his expression serious. "We can give our daughter the kind of home we never had, you know."

She lay frozen, unsure where this was going. "You mean live together? Like you said Mother and Budge should have done?"

He nodded, his gaze never leaving her face. "And more."

"What do you mean?" She felt as if her heart had stopped, as if she couldn't breathe.

"We could marry, Bianca. Do you think it's possible?"

She sat up and pulled the afghan from the couch around her shoulders. He regarded her anxiously.

"Maybe," she allowed.

"We'd have to work out the details. Where we'd live, for instance."

She wrapped the afghan tighter around her. It suddenly seemed too chilly in the cottage, even in front of the fire.

"You're talking about an—an arrangement?" she stammered.

"A marriage," he substituted. A log fell and splintered, distracting him for a moment, and as he prodded the fire with a poker, Bianca's mind raced. A marriage for the sake of raising their child? With homes in Colombia and Rome and Paris and the U.S.? Leading separate lives, their togetherness nothing but a sham? No love, but maybe great sex now and then?

She waited, hardly daring to hope, willing him to say the three words that would make everything fall into place. He only jabbed the logs one more time and carefully replaced the poker where he'd found it.

Out of her innermost soul welled a sorrow so deep that there were no words to express the pain of it. *I love you, I always have,* she wanted him to say. *I love you and I always will.* But he only turned to her, his eyes beseeching but, she thought, empty of the one thing that could have made her say yes.

"Bianca?"

"I can't marry you," she blurted. In that moment, when she turned down the marriage proposal that she'd been waiting all her life to hear, she felt all the desolation that it was possible to feel. She wanted to die, she wanted to run and run as far as she could and never come back, and she wanted Neill Bellamy to fall into a pit as deep as the loss she felt. She stood up and grabbed her clothes, pushing her feet into her shoes, reaching down and yanking one of them on when it fell off.

"Bianca," Neill said. He looked confused. Well, good.

She limped toward the door, still trying to fit her foot into the shoe. She shook her hair out of her eyes and fixed him with a look that would have stopped a tank at twenty paces. "You know what the Bellamy curse is, Neill? It's lack of commitment, and not knowing a good thing when you see it, and being just plain stupid! And yes, you have the Bellamy curse, and I wish I'd never met you, and I don't care if you ever see Tia again as long as you live!"

She flung the door open and hovered for a moment on the doorstep, haughty and looking for all the world as if she could spit nails. Then she slammed the door, hard.

Neill stared blankly at the still-trembling door. He'd proposed marriage to her, which seemed like the best idea he'd had in a long time, and she'd gotten crazy. It's not like he'd ever proposed to anyone before, so he didn't have a lot of experience at it, and he had to admit that maybe he could have approached it differently.

He pulled on his own clothes, determined to go after Bianca and make things right. After he was dressed, he saw that there was one item of clothing left over. He held it up and realized that Bianca had dropped her sweater. And not only that, but she was running around somewhere outside completely naked under that afghan.

ACROSS THE POND, the band was still playing swing tunes. People were laughing and talking; the society non-wedding of the year was in full swing. Bianca, huddled into the afghan, knew that she couldn't go back to the hotel. She'd be spotted in no time.

Where then? She shivered. She knew she'd better put her clothes on, but she didn't want to do it right outside Mulberry Cottage. And she couldn't very well show up at the Ofstetlers' to pick up Tia like this.

She plunged blindly into the shrubbery when she heard footsteps on the path. It was only a couple of hotel guests on their way to their cottage for the night. They stopped a few cottages beyond, let themselves in, and shut the door. Bianca was preparing to emerge from her hiding place when Neill came out of his cottage.

She crouched lower and craned her neck, the better to see. Neill looked determined and headstrong and better-looking than he had a right to be. His jaw was squared in anger, and his eyes were blazing, and despite her anger her knees went weak at the sight of him. At first she thought he was going back to the party, but instead of taking the shortest route along the path to the hotel, he headed toward the Ofstetlers'.

Oh no! Maybe he wanted Tia. All that stuff about wanting to be a good father was one thing, but was he so enraptured with the idea of being a parent that he wanted Tia to himself? Enough to try to get custody? She ran the things he'd said through her mind, trying to figure out if that might be on Neill's agenda. He'd said he wanted to be a better father than Budge. He'd said he wanted to give Tia a home.

What he hadn't said was that he loved Tia. Bianca, in that moment, didn't believe that Neill, Bellamy that he was, knew how to love anyone.

Bianca crashed out of the bushes as soon as Neill was out of sight, and she pulled on her underwear right out in plain sight of anyone who might have happened along. Fortunately no one did. On with the slacks, on with her sweater—but where *was* the sweater?

It was a fine cotton knit, a pretty pale blue, with buttons up the front, and it wasn't there. She flung the afghan around her like a shawl and ran back to Neill's cottage. Her sweater wasn't lying on the ground anywhere, so maybe she'd left it inside. She stood on her tiptoes and peered in through one of the mullioned windows. The draperies were drawn, but there was a tiny chink in the space where the two sides met, and she squinted in an attempt to see better. Her eyelid caught the edge of her contact lens and knocked it sideways, and then her eye started to water.

"Miss?"

She let go of the windowsill and almost dropped the afghan.

It was a uniformed employee of the hotel, the watchman, probably, and he aimed a flashlight full in her face. She blinked, which dislodged the contact lens so that it rolled out of her eye and caught on her lower lashes.

For a moment she considered that this might be the perfect time to let loose with a stream of Italian, something to the effect that she spoke no English. On the other hand, that might convince him to haul her right straight into the hotel security office. In light of that possibility, she opted for the English version.

"I—uh, I was looking for my contact lens. Found it. See?" She snaked a hand out from under the afghan and plucked the lens from her eyelid.

The watchman frowned. "I've seen you around the hotel," he said. "You and your baby."

She smiled, hoping he wouldn't insist that she come

to the hotel office for questioning, that he wouldn't call Hainsworth or any other member of the Knox-Lambert tribe, that she could convince him that she wasn't up to no good.

"Yes, well, I left the wedding—well, you know, what was supposed to be the wedding—and I'm going to get my baby right now. Right this very minute. But my contact was giving me trouble and I had to come over to this window so I could see. Sometimes I can't tell if a lens is in or out. They make them so thin now, you know. And guess what, it's out, but the other one is still in, and I'd better go collect my baby right now." She didn't sound very convincing, even to herself, but as she talked she edged away from the cottage.

"Your name?"

"Bianca D'Alessandro. I'm part of the Bellamy family. More or less." She was desperate enough to grasp at any straw.

It was good enough, however, to convince the watchman. He flicked off his flashlight. "Well, you know," he said by way of apology, "you can't be too careful. Lot of shenanigans going on at Swan's Folly, especially today. Worked for this hotel for the last thirty years, hired on when Mr. Knox was just promoted from bellman to head of the company by way of his marriage to Mrs. Knox, don't you know. Never seen anything like this. Never."

Bianca drew the afghan even more tightly around her, feeling like a fool for standing there talking to a man she didn't even know while wearing only a bra and underpants and slacks and an afghan. She smiled brightly. "I really must go," she said.

"Sorry to have bothered you," he replied, and he

resumed his rounds, swinging the flashlight as he walked.

Well. That was a close call.

She rushed along the path, getting out of breath and thinking that Neill had too much of a head start on her. As she was rounding the curve toward the hotel manager's house, she heard a giant *va-room* and had to jump out of the way as a shiny red vintage motorcycle with a sidecar almost mowed her down. She recognized it as the one stored in the orchard shed.

On it was Neill. The sidecar was empty.

"Get in," he said tersely.

"I'll do no such thing," she said. But on the seat of the sidecar she spied her blue sweater. Not that she could see it all that well, since she still clutched her rapidly dehydrating right contact lens in her right hand.

"We have some talking to do," he told her.

"I don't want to talk." She lunged for her sweater, but she made one crucial mistake: she used the hand that had been holding the afghan together. It fell to the ground and she stood there in her lace bra and slacks.

"I hate to resort to blackmail," Neill said, dangling the sweater in front of her eyes. "But you can have this if you'll go for a ride with me."

"Is this your motorcycle?"

"No. It's Mom's. She said I could ride it."

It was cold standing there without her sweater. Neill held it just beyond her reach. If she tried to snatch it, he'd only yank it away. His eyes gleamed, and she knew it was no use to argue. Anyway, she'd already talked herself out of one tight situation tonight. She could talk herself out of another if necessary. She scooped up the afghan and climbed in the sidecar, which, she noticed distractedly, smelled pleasantly of old leather.

As Neill impatiently gunned the engine, Bianca struggled into her sweater. When she'd buttoned all the buttons all the way to her neck in case he got the idea that she was coming on to him, which she had no intention of doing, he tossed her a pair of goggles and said, "Put these on." He pulled on his own pair of goggles and one of those old-fashioned leather motorcycle helmets that covered his hair and buckled under the chin. "Here," he said, tossing her one. She hesitated only a moment before putting it on and stuffing her hair up under it.

As she buckled it, she said, "Where are we going?"

"Anywhere where we can have a private conversation away from this place," he growled, and then they were bumping along the road, over the bridge and past a group of wedding guests with their mouths hanging open.

"I don't think they recognized us. The helmets and goggles," he shouted. The gates were already open for a departing guest, and they spun through, kicking up a spurt of gravel as Neill skidded past the guest's Mercedes and onto the two-lane road heading away from town.

Bianca, scared out of her wits as they picked up speed, clung to the sides of the sidecar. "Has it occurred to you that there's a speed limit around here?" she yelled.

"So what?" Neill yelled back. Bianca scrunched down low in the seat and closed her eyes. She didn't want to look. Not that she could see much with only one contact lens still in her eye. She didn't know what had happened to the other one.

She opened her eyes for a peek when she inhaled diesel fumes. Ahead of them loomed a Mack truck, a tractor-trailer rig.

"You're not passing it!" she screamed.

"Watch me," Neill said.

He pulled out into the other lane and made a wide arc around the truck. Bianca held on for dear life.

"Where are we going?"

"Away from this nuttiness!"

"We're making our own nuttiness and I don't want to be part of it. You're going to kill us—Tia needs at least one parent and I suggest it should be me!"

"Hang on! We're going to go someplace quiet where nothing is happening!"

"You mean where there are no Bellamys?"

"Exactly."

She slumped back into her seat, contemplating this. As he passed a convertible containing two people sitting very close to each other, she admitted to herself that Neill wasn't driving recklessly, just fast.

This stretch of highway was deserted; they were getting farther and farther away from town. Above, the sky ran silver behind a half-moon, bathing the countryside in a wash of lambent light. She supposed it was what she had always wanted, to ride beside Neill in the moonlight, but in a motorcycle sidecar? It was ludicrous, it was wild. She started to snicker.

Neill glanced down at her. She couldn't see his eyes behind the goggles. "Something wrong?"

She was laughing out loud now. Everything was wrong. And yet something was right. She couldn't explain it, not while they were rushing along at she didn't even know how many miles per hour, running away from the non-wedding of the year and assorted crazy people.

"Bianca?"

She glanced up at him just in time to see the shape of a large boxy truck materialize around the curve ahead. It was moving slowly, too slowly.

"Neill!" she screamed, and he swerved just in time to avoid hitting it. She looked back as the truck slammed on brakes and suddenly angled off the road, jolting noisily down into a shallow ditch and up the bank on the other side. It stopped just short of a tree, and a wiry little man hopped out.

Neill, stunned, nevertheless slowed and turned the motorcycle around, and they went back to the truck. As soon as Neill stopped the cycle within the range of the truck's headlights, Bianca jumped out of the side-car. It seemed to be snowing, an incongruous sight on a midsummer night.

She pulled off her goggles and ran to the little man, who was surveying a blown tire on the truck with an air of resignation. "Are you all right?" she cried.

He looked at her through the falling snowflakes. "More or less," he said, heavy on the irony.

"You!" said Neill, rushing up. "You're the man I hitchhiked back from the lake with last night!"

The man looked at Neill. "Well, well, well," he said. "Neill Bellamy, right?"

The two men shook hands. "Bianca, this is Tully. Tully, this is Bianca."

"I thought you'd be at the wedding," Tully said.

"There wasn't any wedding," Neill said.

An outraged squawking emitted from the back of the truck. Bianca squinted through the snow and saw crates filled with something alive. Chickens! They had almost hit a chicken truck! That explained the snow, which was actually feathers. Neill spit one out of his mouth.

"I'm going to call my son, get him to come out and bring the spare tire. Had to take it out of the truck so I could haul these birds."

"Tully has a day job, but he hauls chickens to market at night. That's how he happened to come along when I was hitchhiking back from the bachelor party," Neill explained.

"Oh," said Bianca. She removed the leather helmet and tossed it into the side car. When Tully went to the cab of the truck to phone his son, she sank down on the low stone wall.

"Well, so much for privacy," Neill said. He rested one leg beside her on the wall. "I hope you don't mind if we wait with him. I might need to ride for help if his son doesn't come."

"Oh, he'll be here," Tully said, sounding more cheerful. "After he watches the late news, he said. You folks hungry?"

"We just ate," Bianca told him.

"Well, I've got a can of spaghetti in my truck. I could build a little fire, heat it up."

"We don't get spaghetti much in Colombia," Neill said with interest.

Bianca sighed. She got plenty of spaghetti in Italy. In fact, she wished she were there at this very moment. She would be in her own bed, sleeping. She wouldn't have to put up with a non-wedding or moonlighting chicken haulers or Neill Bellamy.

Who was looking down at her with eyes that held an expression of tenderness.

Tenderness? Where did that come from?

"You're being a good sport, Bianca," he said.

"I don't feel like a good sport. I feel like I'd rather be somewhere else."

"Maybe this will help." He strode over to the sidecar and pulled out a bottle of champagne that she recognized as the Cristal they had opened at his cottage. "I brought this." He also produced two glasses. As an afterthought, he brought Bianca the afghan and draped it over her shoulders.

Meanwhile, Tully was building a campfire on the other side of the wall.

"Tully," called Neill. "Have you ever had Cristal?"

"Cristal?" said Tully. He frowned at the bottle. "You mean it's a kind of wine?"

"Champagne," said Neill.

Tully shrugged. "I'm a beer kind of a guy, but I'll be glad to try some." He went to the truck and came back with a plastic cup.

They climbed over the wall and sat down around the fire. Tully had arranged a few stones on which he had set an enormous can of spaghetti and meatballs so that the flames licked at the bottom of it. Soon the spaghetti sauce started bubbling merrily, whereupon Tully produced paper plates and plastic forks and dished out plates of spaghetti all around.

"I always carry provisions. You never know when something like this might happen," he said. In the back of the truck, the chickens' squawking had abated considerably.

Bianca, not having much appetite, stared down into her glass. Beside her, Neill ate voraciously, the light from the campfire playing across his strong even features.

"So why wasn't there a wedding?" Tully asked conversationally.

Neill stopped eating so that he and Bianca could exchange glances. "Mostly because we're Bellamys," Neill said.

"Oh, you mean this was that big society wedding? The one with the helicopters and everything?"

"That's the one," Bianca said.

"So you know the Pretzel King?"

"I'm his son."

Tully considered this. "Those are mighty good pretzels. I've been eating them since I was a kid."

"So have I," Neill said with a slight laugh. "And since you like them so much, Tully, I'll tell you what. I'll send you a box of them."

"Great. And you, Bianca. You're the Pretzel King's daughter?"

Bianca didn't want to go into all the gnarls and knobs of the Bellamy family tree and she certainly didn't want to be reminded that she'd ever been a temporary leaf on it. "No, not exactly," she hedged.

Neill dished out more spaghetti. "I asked Bianca to marry me tonight," he said.

Bianca froze. She hadn't expected this. Why would Neill bring this up with some guy they hardly knew? What was he thinking?

Tully regarded her seriously over the rim of his plastic cup. "Did you say yes?"

Bianca set her spaghetti plate down on the ground and said, "No."

"Hmm," Tully replied. He studied Neill for a moment. "Seems like you could do worse, young lady, although I admit it's none of my business. I mean, Neill here seems like a nice enough guy."

"Well," Bianca began.

"Why did you say no?" Tully asked.

Neill shot a cagey look at her out of the corners of his eyes. "Yeah, Bianca, why'd you say no?"

She inspected a chicken feather stuck on the knee of her slacks. "I had reason," she said finally.

"You had reason!" exploded Neill, for once looking as if he were losing his cool. "I'd say you had plenty of reason to say yes, too."

She shot him a look of pure venom.

"Like that baby back at the Ofstetlers'," Neill went on.

"Ahem," said Tully, interrupting. "Exactly what does a baby have to do with this?"

"It's our baby!" Neill shouted. "Ask her!"

Bianca couldn't see him for the tears in her eyes. She blinked them away, wondering if she could figure out how to start a vintage motorcycle. She could make a run for it, leave these two guys to their canned spaghetti and their champagne.

Tully's voice was kind. "Now, little lady, no need to get all upset over this. If you've got a baby, and it's also his baby, it seems like you better talk about this marriage proposal."

"I'm tired of talking. When it comes right down to it, he's just another Bellamy," Bianca said bitterly.

"I guess that's not meant to be complimentary," observed Tully. He tossed a handful of twigs on the fire.

"I can't help being born a Bellamy," Neill said heavily. "I can help acting like one, though. And that's why I want to marry you and give our daughter a decent home. Is that unreasonable?" He turned to Tully as he said it.

"Home, family, those are good things. If I didn't have a son, for instance, who'd be coming to pull me out of this ditch?" Tully laughed and slapped his knee.

"You're denying me the chance to be better than most Bellamys, Bianca. I can't believe you'd do that."

"Well, you might as well," she said.

They sat a while longer, watching the sparks fly up into the moonlight.

Tully said to Bianca, "I hate to think of that baby of yours going through life without a mommy and a daddy. It seems to me that every kid deserves both. Now I'm going to say something, and you can ignore it if you want, being since you're never going to see me again for the rest of your life. On the other hand, if I have the chance to say it and don't, I'm going to regret it. Bianca, I think you need to tell Neill why you turned him down and give him a chance to fix whatever the problem is." This uncharacteristically long speech seemed to wear him out, and he leaned back and extended his legs toward the fire.

"I second that," said Neill. He waited expectantly.

Bianca didn't know why, but the things she couldn't have said directly to Neill seemed easier to say out here in the open with another person present.

"Neill doesn't love me," she said into the silence.

Tully took this in quietly, but Neill leaped to his feet. "I don't love you? Is that what you think?"

She stared up at him. "That's what I think, all right."

"But—"

Bianca appealed directly to Tully. "He says in one breath that he wants to play an active part in our daughter's life, and then in the very next breath he talks about climbing Mount Everest when he could be visiting us in Paris or Rome. He says he wishes he could have been with me in the delivery room and then he starts talking about how I should adjust my life to fit his. He wants a relationship, but I should do all the adjusting. He wants to twist my life around like—like a Bellamy pretzel!''

Neill, fists clenched, went off and stood near the wall, gazing out into the night.

''And what do you have to say about that, Neill?''

''I love her.''

Silence. Then, ''You do?'' said Bianca.

He turned around, and much to her surprise, his eyes were welling with tears.

''I do. I thought you knew.''

''How would I know? You still haven't said it directly to me.''

Tully cleared his throat. ''Seems like those words are real important to women.''

''I've never said those words to any woman. All my life I've watched my father tell one woman after another that he loved her until the words seemed devoid of all meaning. I made up my mind that I wouldn't tell any woman I loved her. I never have and until now I thought I never would.''

Bianca rose slowly to her feet. She stood tentatively, not knowing whether to run to Neill or away from him, not knowing what any of this meant.

Neill's heart was in his eyes as he looked at her across the space between them. ''I love you, Bianca. I think I've loved you for a long, long time. Forever, maybe. I've lost too many people in my life and I can't lose you too. I want us both to have the kind of home we've never had in all our lives—together. I want a chance to be a good father to our daughter. I want to marry you.''

Bianca was no longer aware of Tully sitting on the ground across the campfire from her, or of the chickens' muffled clucking in the truck nearby, or of anything in the world besides Neill Bellamy and the way he was looking at her in that instant. She thought that as long as she lived she would never forget the light in his eyes, or the tears shimmering there, or the expression of abject devotion on his face as he spoke the words that would make her his for the rest of her life.

"I—don't know what to say," she said. Neill's head tilted quizzically, and it wasn't until she realized that he didn't understand what she'd said that she realized she had spoken in Italian.

"I don't know what to say," she repeated, this time in English, and at that Neill walked to where she stood in front of the fire, lifted both her hands in his, and raised them to his lips. He kissed them and said, "Say yes, Bianca. Please."

It seemed as if, in that brief instant between his request and her answer, all of her life beforehand flashed in front of her eyes. She saw herself as an awkward teenager, braces on her teeth, waiting for Neill to speak to her at their parents' wedding reception, and she felt all the disappointment her teenage self had experienced when he'd acted like she didn't exist. She remembered the times he'd come home from college and refused to play tennis with her, going off with some buxom girl of his own age instead. She recalled that night a year ago in the gazebo when she'd given herself to him totally and completely, and how she'd almost picked up the phone so many times to call him and tell him she was pregnant, and then that they had a daughter. But all those disappointments evaporated in the joy of this moment, the moment she'd thought was an impossibility.

"Bianca?"

"Of course I'll marry you," she said. "Of course I will. I love you, Neill. Even though you are a Bellamy." She smiled at him and he gave a whoop of delight and enfolded her in his arms.

"You know," said Tully consideringly from his place in front of the fire, "I think I really like beer better with spaghetti."

One hour later

"What," Neill said, "has gone on in here?"

Bianca, following him into Mulberry Cottage, stared blankly at the confusion within. Clothes were dumped out of drawers, a suitcase stood empty on the couch, and Nana Lambert was perched amid a pile of shoes watching the Viceroy-Bellamy mine video on TV.

She smiled brightly up at them. "I thought you said you mine amethysts," she said to Neill.

"Nana—" he began.

"Well, you *should* mine amethysts. Not these emeralds. I don't like them. I only wear shades of purple, you know. Amethysts give off good vibrations."

"How did you get in?" Bianca said. She leaned up against Neill and he put his arm around her. They had come to the cottage to be alone. Now they weren't, and there was no telling how they would get rid of Nana.

"I walked in. The door was open. Do you know they think I'm a jewel thief?"

"*You* are the jewel thief?" chorused Neill and Bianca.

"Well, they think so. Not that I've found any amethysts worth wearing. Genevieve has hidden hers, and Winnie's are nothing more than bottle glass. I thought I could depend on you, Joe, to produce some nice ones.

And I'm not a thief, for heaven's sake. I buy amethysts. I have a nice collection of them, you know.''

"I'm Neill," Neill said.

"And it looks to me as if you've finally settled things with the woman you adore. Bianca, isn't that your name?'' Nana cocked her head in Bianca's direction and smiled approvingly at both of them.

"Yes," Bianca said.

"Well, I checked out your room, too. You were so kind to leave the door unlocked for me yesterday so I could browse through your things. You've got some nice jewelry, but it's all so modern-looking. I like old-fashioned things, like lavaliers and such. Vittorio said you're going to start a new gemstone line, and I hope you'll include some amethysts in your designs.''

"You talked with Vittorio?" Bianca said, nonplussed.

"Oh, yes, he phoned while I was in your room, and I think I knew him in my past life. He invited me to Rome, you know. I'm going week after next to visit him in his villa.'' Nana, for all the world like a sprightly bird, hopped up from her place on the couch.

"Impress upon her your ardor,'' she said to Neill, wagging her finger roguishly. And then she flitted out the door, trailing scarves and the scent of lavender.

Neill closed the door firmly after her and turned to Bianca. He held out his arms. "Come here. I want to do what Nana says.''

"'Impress upon me the strength of your ardor?''' Bianca allowed herself to be folded close to Neill's chest and to be soothed by his strong steady heartbeat.

"And more," he said. "When do you want to get married?''

"Soon," she said, her voice muffled against his shoulder. *"Vite."*

"And where?"

"Far away from any Bellamys," she said with great conviction.

"Where would that be?"

"On top of Mount Everest?" she said, leaning back to gaze up at him with adoration.

He laughed. "It suits me, but it would be kind of hard on our daughter. I want her there, you know."

"I know," Bianca said.

"Do you think we could just go and do it? On our own? Whenever?"

"I think that's a very good idea. Because," and she smiled up at him, and he joined in so that they repeated together, *"Anything* can happen at a Bellamy wedding."

Epilogue

Eighteen Months After the Non-Wedding of the Century

"Bianca, Vittorio's on the phone," Neill said. He emerged from their joint office on the second floor of their elegant town house in Rome holding Tia in his arms.

Bianca was reclining on a chaise longue in the gallery that linked their office with the other rooms on the second floor, a purple afghan nestled around her feet to ward off the chill of a rainy Roman winter. "I think I'm in labor," she said.

"You are?"

"I'm pretty sure."

Neill set Tia down on the Aubusson carpet and she immediately toddled to Bianca.

"Mommy? Book?"

Bianca kissed Tia and smoothed her silky blond hair. "No, *cara,* I'm afraid I can't read to you this minute. But I'm sure Nana could."

"Nana could what?" Nana appeared from the elevator, an amethyst tiara on her head, a lavender print rain poncho over her clothes.

"Nana! Nana!" cried Tia, running to her with delight.

"Here, Nana, you talk to Vittorio," Neill said, handing the phone to her. Nana immediately launched into a stream of fluent Italian punctuated by bursts of loud laughter, then hung up.

"That Vittorio—what a card. Would you mind if he and I take Tia to get a gelato?" Nana asked hopefully. Tia loved Italian ices, especially strawberry.

"Well, it's certainly all right, Nana, but Bianca thinks she's in labor," Neill told her.

Nana frowned at Bianca. "You do look a bit peaked. I think you should put on that nice leotard I bought you and do some of those dance exercises I showed you, Bianca dear. I danced right up to the moment dear Genevieve was born."

"And we all know how Gen turned out," Neill muttered under his breath as Bianca cast a warning look in his direction.

Nana took Tia's hand. "Come along, Tia. Let's see if Nanny Gabrielle would like to go with us. Uncle Vittorio is coming in his big long car to pick us up. Bianca, I'm quite sure the baby won't come right away. We'll be back before you go to the hospital, tra la, tra la."

"'Bye, Mommy. 'Bye Daddy." Tia waved her little hand as she disappeared into the elevator with Nana. Tia loved Nana, which was not surprising since Nana was so much like a child herself.

Neill sat on the edge of the chaise and took Bianca's hand. He held it to his lips and kissed the fingers one by one, lingering on the one that bore his wedding band and the huge emerald he'd given her as an engagement ring. Of course, he'd placed the wedding ring on her finger first and given her the emerald after she'd had a chance to design a setting for it. Nana had said that was an obvious case of putting the cart before the horse, but then, it wasn't necessary to be conventional, was it? and Bianca had agreed. Neill hadn't cared about conventionality. All he'd wanted was to be married to Bianca and to be a family.

And they were. Nana had struck up a friendship with Vittorio, who had retired again recently and devoted all his time to her. She had bought a new hearing aid so she could hear Vittorio's "sweet somethings," as she'd termed them. For the time being, she chose to live with Neill and Bianca, knitting lots of purple afghans and baby garments while allowing Vittorio to shower her with affection and amethysts in that order. Both Bianca and Neill hoped she would never leave them.

"Are you in pain, darling?" Neill murmured to Bianca.

She shifted slightly. "I'm fine. We don't have to go to the hospital yet."

"I want to get there in time. I don't want to be the one to deliver our child in the back of a Rolls-Royce."

"Of course not." She caught her breath as she felt another contraction.

"Bianca?"

She had to smile because he looked so worried. And so loving. Their marriage, they both agreed, was the best thing that had ever happened to them. Like swans, they considered themselves mated for life. Neill had given up his hands-on work at the mine in Colombia, visiting there only four times a year. Sometimes Bianca and Tia went with him. Often they traveled to Paris for Bianca's business, and after the baby was born they planned to move permanently to New York, where

Bianca's office was enlarging in both scope and function with the help of Kevin, her sales manager, and Storm, who had given up modeling and was a crackerjack public relations person. D'Alessandro's new gemstone line was a huge success, especially after tie-ins with a cable TV shopping channel, which had been Neill's idea. He'd even bought the channel.

"Can I get you anything?" Neill asked.

"You've already given me everything a woman could want," Bianca said, gazing up at her handsome husband. "A beautiful daughter, another baby and more love than any woman could expect in one lifetime."

Neill gathered her in his arms, carefully so he wouldn't hurt her. "I love you, Bianca."

"More now even than at our wedding?" she asked, grinning in spite of the fact that another contraction was following fast upon the heels of the last.

Neill considered this. Their wedding had taken place in Nepal before Neill started out to climb Mount Everest. In attendance had been their daughter, Tia. It was one Bellamy wedding at which nothing unexpected had happened, unless you could count deciding on the spur of the moment to be married by a minister who was making the climb with Neill. Four Sherpa mountain guides had been pressed into service as witnesses. Their honeymoon had waited until Neill had triumphantly ascended the peak and had returned with cold feet that needed warming, not to mention a really bad case of the flu. Bianca had borne all with good humor, and afterward they'd celebrated Neill's ascent of the mountain and their new married state by taking Tia and her nanny to Maui for three weeks. No Bellamys had been invited to any of the festivities.

"I love you even more than on the day I married you," Neill told her. "I didn't know it was possible to love anyone this much."

"Nor did I," Bianca whispered. "And that last contraction hurt."

"You're in pain? Is it awful?" Neill looked so frantic that she had to laugh.

"It's not awful. It's wonderful. It's producing a baby."

"You look so pale. I'm scared to death. What if something happens to you? How could I live without you?

Mirth bubbled in Bianca's throat, and she wanted to laugh. But she didn't want to hurt her husband's feelings because he was so sincere and so earnest.

"Nothing will happen to me, but maybe you'd better tell the driver to bring the car around. And get my small suitcase out of the closet in our room."

"I can't stand to see you in pain. I'm never going to make love to you again if this is what happens. I can't stand it. I don't know why we keep having babies when I'm not supposed to have much of a sperm count."

"There may not be many, but they're definitely potent," Bianca said with great conviction. "And we will make love again. You can count on it, dearest."

"I love you, Bianca. If it hadn't been for what happened in the gazebo that night, I would never have known that I could father children. It changed my life, and for the better. I don't have to be alone any more. I have a real family now."

"Just—get the suitcase," Bianca said, thinking that this was not the best time for Neill to wax eloquent no matter how much she loved him. She reached for the phone to call the driver herself.

With one last harried look into her eyes, Neill rushed off to do her bidding.

Bianca summoned the chauffeur and closed her eyes against the next contraction as it washed over her in a wave. She concentrated on the baby that was coming. She would have a son this time, and he would grow into a tall, strong, charming child with webbed feet exactly like every other Bellamy she'd ever met.

Neill was back and bending over her. "Bianca? Are you okay?"

"I will always be okay as long as you are my husband," she said, reaching her arms up to him.

"And I will always be okay as long as you are my wife." He kissed her on the cheek. "Now let's get the hell to the hospital and get this baby born."

"*Vite*," gasped Bianca in Italian. Which, as Neill knew by now, meant quickly.

Mr. and Mrs. Neill Cameron Bellamy
and their daughter Tia
announce with great joy
the birth of a son and brother,
Neill Cameron Bellamy, Jr.
8 lbs., 5 oz.
December 9, 2001
Rome, Italy

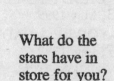

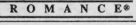

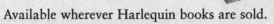

 **HARLEQUIN®**
Makes any time special ™

 WIN A DREAM

In celebration of Harlequin®'s golden anniversary

Enter to win a _dream!_ You could win:

- A luxurious trip for two to _The Renaissance Cottonwoods Resort_ in Scottsdale, Arizona, or

- A bouquet of flowers once a week for a year from **FTD**, or

- A $500 shopping spree, or

- A fabulous bath & body gift basket, including **K-tel's** _Candlelight and Romance_ 5-CD set.

Look for **WIN A DREAM** flash on specially marked Harlequin® titles by Penny Jordan, Dallas Schulze, Anne Stuart and Kristine Rolofson in October 1999*.

 FTD

RENAISSANCE.
COTTONWOODS RESORT
SCOTTSDALE, ARIZONA

 K·TEL

*No purchase necessary—for contest details send a self-addressed envelope to Harlequin Makes Any Time Special Contest, P.O. Box 9069, Buffalo, NY, 14269-9069 (include contest name on self-addressed envelope). Contest ends December 31, 1999. Open to U.S. and Canadian residents who are 18 or over. Void where prohibited.

PHMATS-GR